The Gilt Kid

The Gilt Kid
James Curtis

With an introduction by Paul Willetts

LONDON BOOKS CLASSICS

LONDON BOOKS
PO Box 52849
London SW11 1SE
www.london-books.co.uk

First published 1936 by Jonathan Cape
This edition published by London Books 2007

The publisher wishes to thank
Steve Holland, Paul Duncan and David Collard
for supplying information used in the book's introduction.

A catalogue record for this book
is available from the British Library

ISBN 978-0-9551851-2-0

Printed and bound in Great Britain by
William Clowes Ltd, Beccles, Suffolk

Typeset by Octavo Smith Ltd in Plantin 10.5/13.5

CONTENTS

INTRODUCTION

James Curtis is among the most captivating of the young novelists who illuminated the English literary scene during the 1930s. Unlike such contemporaries as Christopher Isherwood and Graham Greene, though, he shunned publicity, concealing his identity behind a pseudonym. On the dust jacket of one of his books the motive for this is explained. In uncharacteristically flowery language, it is stated that 'he is quite ashamed of his patronymic', yet the source of this deep-seated shame is unclear. So, too, are all but the barest details of his life. If ever there's an author ripe for a *Quest For Corvo*-style investigative biography, it's James Curtis.

Apparently he had a comfortable upbringing, his left-wing politics inspiring him to renounce his background. He then immersed himself in the working-class world in which he encountered the type of low-level criminals and prostitutes who populate his novels. With the outbreak of the 1939–45 war, he was forced to return to the environment he had earlier rejected. When the war ended, he admitted to having 'great difficulty' returning to the world he'd chosen. In the meantime he had married and fathered a daughter. According to an essay by the researcher and Curtis aficionado Paul Duncan, he ended up working as a school caretaker.

The gaping holes in his thumbnail biography encourage rumour and speculation. Thanks to a listing on the normally reliable Internet Movie Database, there's even a theory that he made two uncredited appearances in Hollywood films, one of these as a motorcycle patrolman in *Manhattan Melodrama* (1934), starring Clark Gable and Myrna Loy. Funnily enough, in the grainy photo of him reproduced on the back of the 1947 Penguin edition of *The Gilt Kid*, he has the look of a handsome actor, his high-cheekboned, hawkish profile and piercing eyes evocative of Daniel Day-Lewis.

Despite all the mystery surrounding him, there's one thing about Curits that remains beyond doubt. And that's the enduring power and immediacy of his writing. First published in 1936, *The Gilt Kid* marked his debut as a novelist. It focuses on a convicted burglar and communist sympathiser, freshly released from prison. But Curtis's protagonist, whose youth and blond hair have earned him the nickname of 'the Gilt Kid', isn't the stereotypical ex-con struggling to keep on the straight and narrow. Instead, he wastes little time in plunging back into the London underworld, a milieu that few writers have depicted with such conviction, empathy and sensual clarity. The early chapter describing the Gilt Kid's nocturnal stroll round his old West End haunts sets the matter-of-fact tone, which is never moralistic or sentimental. Nor does it lapse into the absurd, movie-inspired romanticism of so much writing about criminals.

Curtis belongs to a tradition of novelists, Patrick Hamilton among them, whose left-wing politics shaped not only their lives but also their fiction. While Hamilton tended to portray his characters, however vibrant and plausible, as mere embodiments of socio-economic status, Curtis used his plots to highlight the unfairness of society and dearth of opportunity that all too often leads people to break the law.

Politics is one of several areas in which the work of Curtis and Hamilton overlaps. Both men shared a morbid fascination with London lowlife, prostitutes in particular. Both men used the crowded West End pubs as vibrant backdrops to their novels. Both men were capable of writing with impressive narrative verve. What's more, both men wrote books that occupy the hinterland between crime writing and what's now referred to as 'literary fiction'. Were he around today, Curtis would be hailed as a fashionable English counterpart to George Pelecanos, the Greek-American chronicler of the underworld of Washington, DC.

The parallels between the work of Curtis and Hamilton can't hide one fundamental difference between them. For all his brilliance, Hamilton wrote in a slightly archaic manner, rooted in the nineteenth-century novel, a manner that allowed him to pass frequent judgement over his characters and their peccadilloes. Curtis, on the other hand, wrote in a more modern style, based on the desire to portray character through drama rather than exposition. In its lack of either ornamentation or rhetorical flourish, his prose has a lot in common with the kind of writing favoured by John Hampson, Leslie Halward and other 'proletarian school' writers who flourished briefly in the 1930s. Curtis's style is, however, more distinctive and supple, sliding effortlessly into internal monologues peppered with appropriate slang that adds an alluring patina of realism. From the perspective of the twenty-first century, this profusion of slang, this pseudo-American, Cagney-esque tough-guy talk lends *The Gilt Kid* an extra period *frisson*. That said, the book's pre-war trappings aren't always a source of unalloyed pleasure. Modern readers are likely to be uncomfortable with its depiction of the anti-Semitism that tarnished the 1930s, 'Yiddishers' being viewed with distaste by the Gilt Kid.

The latter half of what WH Auden dubbed that 'low, dishonest decade' represented Curtis's heyday as a writer. He followed *The Gilt Kid* with *You're In The Racket, Too* (1937), the tale of a young middle-class paper-pusher who gets blackmailed by a prostitute. After an interval of only a few months, *There Ain't No Justice* (1937), his third novel, was published, its pungent title providing a concise summary of his attitude towards life. The book – which was turned into a much-praised film starring Jimmy Hanley – told the story of an up-and-coming boxer exploited by a devious fight promoter.

By the end of the decade Curtis had also published two polemical studies of the British legal system and a couple more novels. The next of these was *They Drive By Night* (1938), his best-known and most popular book, in which an ex-convict goes on the run after he's wrongly suspected of murdering his girlfriend. Its popularity was fuelled by an atmospheric but inexplicably under-rated film version, featuring Emlyn Williams and the deliciously sinister Ernest Thesiger, brother of the revered travel writer Wilfrid Thesiger. Curtis then rounded off the decade with *What Immortal Hand* (1939), the melodramatic and laboured tale of a poor child's upbringing and gradual descent into criminality. Discouraged, perhaps, by the book's adverse reception, almost two decades would elapse before his next novel appeared in print. The clumsily titled *Look Long Upon A Monkey* (1956), which portrayed post-war society through the eyes of three escaped convicts, turned out to be his last published novel.

From even this bald summary of his writing, Curtis's main themes and preoccupations emerge. Echoing the work of the American social realists Theodore Dreiser and James T Farrell, he produced fiction with an implicit political message. He also created novels that played out similar scenarios with obsessive intensity, their doomed protagonists hurtling towards destruction. In that sense – and in many others – Curtis's work is reminiscent of the contemporaneous fiction of Cornell Woolrich and other American pulp writers. Like them, Curtis wrote about the underside of society, about men and women trapped by circumstance, about a world permeated by an atmosphere of *film noir* dread, a world from which isolated moments of happiness had to be savoured.

While Woolrich and company enjoy a posthumous status that they never achieved when they were alive, Curtis has taken the well-trodden path to obscurity. You won't even find references to him in the standard literary histories and guidebooks. He's one of English literature's missing persons, his work only kept in circulation by a handful of devotees willing to pay inflated prices for his books.

Most established writers take decades to complete this dispiriting trudge from success to failure, but Curtis witnessed his career decline with unusual rapidity. There's a temptation to view his slide into neglect as being the result of some right-wing establishment conspiracy, yet the real reasons for it are probably more prosaic. In all likelihood he was a victim of the inevitable backlash against the politically engaged writing with which the 1930s had been synonymous. His career must also have been undermined by his failure to consolidate his readership by publishing books at regular intervals over a long period. The unremitting pessimism and bleakness of his vision, along with his narrow range of subject matter, must have had an equally corrosive effect on his readership and reputation.

Time is conventionally regarded as an impartial literary filter, separating run-of-the-mill novels from those that possess lasting resonance. In the case of James Curtis, though, the filtration system has let us down. Here's a writer undeserving of the obscurity in which he languishes. His range may be limited and his output may be relatively small, but his best work rivals that of Graham Greene and other more celebrated exponents of lowlife fiction. Reading *The Gilt Kid* for the first time is akin to watching some hitherto undiscovered classic black-and-white British crime movie, replete with memorable performances and tantalising glimpses of a vanished world.

Paul Willetts
January 2007

THE ROOM

Pale grey light filtered through the lace curtains into a dingy furnished room. On the back of a Windsor chair hung a coat; the wash-basin was full of dirty water, and by the bed stood a slop-pail, on the top of which floated a few rapidly disintegrating cigarette butts.

On the bed itself lay a young man. His hands were interlaced behind his head and through his half-shut eyes he was staring up at a patch on the ceiling where the plaster in falling away had left the laths exposed. His body was inert, resting, relaxed. The front of his blue shirt was soiled with fallen cigarette ash and the armpits were dark with patches of sweat.

From outside in the streets came the sounds of the boys calling the evening papers, and the steady tramp of homeward-bound wage-slaves: the light high-heeled taps from the shop-girls' feet mingling with the heavier, tireder tramp of the men. A knot of children were wrangling at the corner.

The sound of a motor-horn drifted in.

The man thought idly: That horn was blown by a green-badged taxi-driver.

There was nothing remarkable about the deduction. He had recognized the pitch of the horn and knew that all London taxi-drivers wore green badges, dangling on their coats. There were a lot of taxis in the quiet streets and squares behind Victoria.

He picked up the book that was lying beside him on the soiled counterpane and began to read.

'By means, therefore, of the value relation expressed in our equation, the bodily form of Commodity B becomes the value form of Commodity A, or the body of Commodity B acts as a mirror to the value of Commodity A. By putting itself in relation with Commodity B, as value in *propria persona*, as the matter of which human labour is made up, the Commodity A converts the value in use, B, into the substance in which to express its, A's, own value. The value of A, thus expressed in the use value of B, has taken the form of relative value.'

He let the book slip out of his fingers on to the strip of carpet which lay beside the bed like an island in the surrounding sea of oilcloth. The dim evening light tried his eyes and it was hard work reading Marx. He wanted to be a good communist but it seemed to him that all this theorizing was rot. He would far prefer to get on with the job. The previous day, while watching an anti-war demonstration in Hyde Park, he had heard the school-children in council dust-carts calling out 'We want milk, not machine-guns!'

Turning to the communist with whom he had been talking, he had said:

'That's just where you're wrong, mate. You'd be far better off with a few machine-guns. Your mob's too milky as it is.'

The incident came back into his mind. He laughed a little and then looked distastefully round the room.

There was no doubt about it. Furnished rooms were hell. If the preachers were right and there was a place of eternal punishment after death, it would not be a scene of leaping flames, nor of dark, enveloping clouds of sulphur, hanging over a withered, blasted countryside. No, damnation would consist in being on your own in a cheap, furnished room in a London back street.

It was funny, he reflected, how excited he had been over taking this room. It had been such a sign of liberty to have paid his rent and to have a front-door key in his possession. The day before his release he had discussed whereabouts with all the boys inside. Some had said the Elephant, but he had turned that down as being too leery: others had suggested Tottenham Court Road, but, wanting a few days' freedom, he had scorned that as being too warm. The boys from Islington had argued the claims of Upper Street and Essex Road, while those from Canning Town, Poplar and Greengate had failed to understand anyone wanting to live very far from the Lifeboat and the Abbey. As a matter of fact he had already made up his mind. All the time he had been in prison he had been picturing himself in a nice little furnished room near Victoria. He had only asked their opinions and talked about districts so as to reassure himself that he really was going to be discharged. It had been nothing more than another manifestation of what the boys called the going-out feeling.

Anyhow, having a room was better than being on the bum. He had spent a few nights in kip-shops from time to time: Tommy Farmer's, Bruce House, the Salvation Army in Old Street, the Wave down in Canning Town, but the worst of rooms was better than the best of kips.

He dropped his cigarette butt into the slop-pail.

And the worst of kips was better than being properly on the ribs. Christ, yes, he thought, I'd rather be back in stir again than have another night on the deck. One of those had been quite enough.

Creeping around the place all night, sitting on the seats in Trafalgar Square and along the Mall until it had been too cold to stay seated any longer; and then walking about to get warm until his feet, blistered from broken boots and sweat-rotten socks, had grown too sore to let him walk any more; sitting down again until it was too cold, and so on until five o'clock when the café opened in St Martin's Lane – that café where they charge three-ha'pence for a cup of tea and let a man sit for two hours or more over it.

Of course, some bums touch lucky, they manage to forget their misery, the cold and their red-rimmed sleepless eyes, by dropping off for a few minutes till a policeman comes along and wakes them up. Crowds of them lie every night on that little triangle of grass behind the Admiralty Arch which they call the Cabbage Patch.

It's funny, though, he thought, about bums. In books, where the hero, who is an impoverished, improvident, but viceless member of the English ruling caste is sitting on an Embankment seat near Cleopatra's Needle – and it's always there that he is sitting – and looking up with hollow mocking laughter at the lights of the Savoy, a sinister figure will sidle up to him in the darkness and, in broken English, will offer him a whole lot of dough. But there will be a string tied to that flock of rent. The hero has to earn it. As a result, the clean-living, straight-limbed, but impecunious Englishman will become enmeshed in the toils of an unscrupulous gang of foreigners, but, with true British grit and bull-dog tenacity, he will win through in the end to wealth and the hand of the heroine, whose charm will have ensnared him far more successfully than did all the machinations of the sallow-skinned, sibilantly-hissing conspirators.

In real life, you could sit for a hundred years by Cleopatra's Needle and nothing would happen except that you felt cold. Yes, there was no doubt about it. It was a bastard being on the bum. He would, he decided, sooner have a lagging or five-stretch than have to do another night out.

Still, he cheered himself up with the thought, there was little question of his being on the floor again for some time to come. He looked affectionately across at his coat, in the inside pocket of which was a nice little roll of notes: twenty-three pounds which he had kept hidden so carefully that the detectives had not been able to touch it when they had arrested him.

Well, he thought, a man who had twenty-three nicker, and lay moping in kip while the boozers were open was a bit of a mug. He certainly was.

With the impetuous energy of a lazy man, he sprang off his bed and began to dress. He just poured some water into the wash-bowl, diluting the dirty stuff that was already there. That was good enough for a sluice.

He got up, spluttering, from the cold greasy water, dried his hands and face on a towel and then shielding a match with the palm of his hand, lit the gas so that he might discover exactly how he stood.

The gas flared up for an instant and, settling down, gave its even, mellow glow.

He stepped across to the dressing-table – the room was so small that he could do it in one stride – and looked at his reflection in the mirror. The collar, cuffs and front of his blue shirt were quite clean – it was only under the arms that it was badly soiled. It would certainly do for that evening. He did up the collar and tied a red tie round his neck. Then, picking up the hairbrushes, he smoothed down his yellow hair, which had earned for him the prison soubriquet of the Gilt Kid. Standing back from the glass and brushing the ash off his shirt, he took another look at himself. He was quite satisfied.

Apart from his prison pallor, he was, he felt, OK. There were, no doubt, just a few unnecessary lines running from the pits of his nostrils to the corners of his mouth, but a man could hardly live in the world for five-and-twenty years without picking up a few wrinkles. He smiled at his own joke. Nobody else would have done and it was a shame to let a joke pass unsmiled at.

He lit another cigarette and began cleaning his shoes. With the cigarette still between his lips he hummed 'If it's a crime then I'm guilty' and then stopped abruptly. It was a grave mistake to hum songs that had gone so completely out of fashion. It as good as told the world that he was a gaol-bird.

His shoes cleaned, he put on his coat, shrugged his

shoulders before the dressing-table mirror and drew great satisfaction from their muscular appearance.

Well, he thought, I guess the Gilt Kid's all set for a night out. From the mantelpiece he picked up his loose silver and the front-door key; from the bed-post he yanked his hat. Everything was fine and dandy.

He went out slamming the door behind him and completely forgetting to turn down the gas.

CURLY

It was after seven o'clock by the time the Gilt Kid had reached Coventry Street and the evening bustle was well under way. He would, he decided, go up into Shaftesbury Avenue and have a drink or so in one of the wallopers there. It was more than likely that he would bump into one of the boys. He walked into Rupert Street, ignoring the blandishments of various prostitutes.

He had nearly reached the corner when a hand fell on his shoulder. Startled, he stopped and looked round. He had grown not to like hands to be dropped on his shoulders.

Behind him was standing a stockily built man of about thirty. Slightly on the side of his head he was wearing a bowler. His nose had been flattened. In his eyes was an amused look.

'Well,' he said, 'if it ain't the Gilt Kid. Don't remember your old pals, eh? Forgotten Curly Simmonds?'

'Christ, Curly, I didn't recognize you.'

Curly laughed. It was a satisfied sound.

'Yes,' he said, looking down on his striped suit with obvious pride, 'this whistle I got on's a bit different from the old grey one they dish you out with back in the queer place.'

'How's the game, Curly?'

'Not so bad. I ain't got a lot of dough, but I'm not what you'd exactly call broke. How's it with you? Working?'

The Gilt Kid laughed.

'Work? What the hell's that? You ought to know me better than to think that sort of thing about me.'

'That's the boy. Only saps work.'

'Too bloody true.'

They stood for a moment, looking at each other irresolutely. The two pairs of shifty eyes did not find it easy to meet. Curly broke the silence.

'Where are you going now?' he asked.

'Well, I *was* going up the Avenue to have a wet.'

'Well, don't let me stop you for Chrissake. I'll come along, too, and give you a hand.'

'OK. But I don't need a lot of help. I'm strong enough to shift it on my own.'

They turned and walked up to Shaftesbury Avenue together. Curly spoke again.

'How long you been out?'

'Only come out last Thursday. You been out a long time though, ain't you?'

'Long enough to've been in Wandsworth and done a carpet.'

'Blimey. What they give you that for?'

'Damnall. I was walking along the Dilly same as you and I might be walking along now and one of the bogies from Vine Street reckernizes me. Up comes the bastard and claims me. Loitering with intent to commit a felony. Next day I'm up at the Marlborough. Bogy says, "The prisoner opened the doors of two cars, your worship." The lying cowson. He ought to know I'm a screwsman and not on the dragging lark.'

It was evident that Curly Simmonds's pride in being a burglar had been sorely assailed by the accusation that he might be stealing from motor cars.

'What the old boy say?'

'Just the usual madam. "The public must be protected. You must go to prison for three months – *with* HARD LABOUR." Down I goes to Wandsworth and does my carpet. And no argument about it neither.'

'What's Wandsworth like? Proper bastard, I suppose.'

'Well, it ain't exactly what you'd call a convalescent

home like the Scrubbs, but it ain't near as bad as they try to make out. First time you get nicked they tell you this ain't so bad, but wait till you get to Wandsworth. When you're there they say wait till you get a lagging and go to the Moor. It's only gee. They just talk that way to make you turn milky.'

'That's right. Here we are.' They had paused outside the entrance to the public house.

'Well, come on, then. Standing about never got you nowhere.'

'Where're we going, upstairs or down? It's nice and quiet upstairs and we can have a bit of a talk.'

'What about? College days? There's a load of janes gets upstairs, ain't there?'

'Sure.'

'Well, let's go up there then.'

They walked up to the lounge. Curly sat down at a table. The Gilt Kid hovered by the bar.

'What are you going to have?'

'Can't get no draught beer up here, can you?'

'No.'

'Well, make it a bottle of Worthington, then.'

The Gilt Kid brought over the drinks and set them on the table.

'Good luck.'

'All the best.'

'Well,' said the Gilt Kid, 'this is a whole lot better than making scrubbing brushes back in the old Monastery Garden.'

'Yes, and saying to yourself, "Roll on cocoa".'

'Where did you graft in Wandsworth?'

'Cleaner.'

'Blimey, that was a bit of fat for you, wasn't it?'

'Yeah, but you couldn't pinch no grub. Those Wandsworth screws got a whole lot of eyes on them.'

They relapsed into silence. Curly took a gulp of his beer and looked moodily about him. Suddenly he leant confidentially across the table.

'You still in the racket?' he asked.

'You mean am I still in the same game?'

'Sure. Use your loaf. What the hell else would I mean?'

'Yes. There's nothing else for it when you've once been inside.'

'That's right, mate. Come-on guy for a con gang, ain't you?'

The Gilt Kid's heart swelled with pride. He must be looking well-dressed if Curly thought that he was the member of a gang of confidence tricksters who picked up the mug. Still, it was better to tell the truth for once in case Curly might have something in line.

'I have done a bit of that,' he admitted, 'but I got nicked for screwing. That's my lark, really.'

Somehow, he felt ashamed at having to admit himself to be just an ordinary burglar, but Curly nodded sympathetically.

'Had it off, since you come out?'

'For God's sake, Curly pal, give us a chance. I've only been out just under a week.'

Curly nodded and took another pull at his beer.

'I had it off last week,' he said with a wink, 'not a big job, just a little snout gaff, but I earned myself a score. And twenty pound's very handy what with things the way they are.'

'It certainly is.'

Curly kept silent for a moment. Then, having emptied his glass, he spoke again.

'Have another?'

'Sure.'

Curly rose, lumbered across to the bar and called for the drinks. The Gilt Kid saw him flash out a pound note to pay for them. It was OK, he thought, Curly had dough on the level and was not just putting on the gee.

'Good luck.'

'All the best.'

They drank to each other. By the way that Curly was moving about in his chair it was quite obvious that he had something on his mind. He opened his mouth undecidedly once or twice. At last he spoke.

'Say, kid,' he said, 'how're you fixed?'

'OK. Why?'

Curly read the reluctance in the other's voice and hurried on.

'It's all right,' he said, 'don't get the wind up. I'm not trying to borry some money. I just wanted to know how you're fixed.'

'I'm OK,' repeated the Gilt Kid a little petulantly. 'I got about twenty-three nicker as a matter of fact, if you want to know.'

Curly sighed.

'Well, if you're fixed like that,' he said heavily, 'I don't suppose you'll be wanting to earn yourself any more dough.'

'Sure, I do. Twenty-three nicker won't last for ever. What's on? Got a gaff?'

'I certainly have.' Curly looked round cautiously. There was nobody within earshot. Nevertheless he lowered his voice to a confidential whisper as he spoke. 'Listen. I got a good gaff. I could do it on my own if I wanted to, but I likes to have a bit of company when I goes on a job. You know what I mean. Gives you a bit of confidence.'

The Gilt Kid, who had lighted a cigarette and was listening intently, nodded reassuringly. Curly caught the nod and went on, hurriedly running his sentences on.

'There's wages for two in it, if you'd like to come in with me. Care to have a go?'

'Let's hear some of the details first.'

'Not bloody likely. Tell you the details and then you'll do

the gaff on your jack and leave me right out or else turn grass and put in the bleeding squeak against me. Not this trip, mate.'

'Use your nut, Curly. How the hell d'you think I'm going to say "yes" until I know something? Just tell me what kind of a gaff it is and what we're likely to get. I don't want to say "OK" and then find out that I've let myself in for screwing the Bank of England or doing a blag on the crown jewels. There's no need to tell me where it is or anything of that sort. You needn't be afraid of me. I never come the copper yet.'

'OK, then,' said Curly, mollified, but still a little dubious. 'It's a private gaff. It'll be dead. It belongs to a jane. She's on the batter – in a big way. There's none of this hawking-her-greens stuff around Lisle Street about her. Matter of fact she's cased up with a bloke.'

'What you mean, she got a ponce?'

Curly made a gesture of irritation.

'No,' he said, 'she ain't got no ponce. What'd she want a Jo Ronce for? She's a right flash brama.'

'Yes, but you said she was cased up with a bloke.'

Curly, who was taking a gulp of beer, nearly choked himself in his annoyance.

'I said as she was cased up with a bloke. I didn't say no one was poncing on her. It's like this. She's got a bloke, a regular customer, get me, who pays the rent of the flat and floats in for a bit of under occasionally, but most of the time she's on the bash round the flash bars trying to see what she can pick up on the side.'

'Oh, I get you. On the make all the time. One of the wide girls.'

'That's right. Well, what with the steamer she's got for regular and the odd ones she picks up she don't do so bad, I should cocoa. Got a bit of stuff hanging around her drum she has. Red stuff, jewellery, furs and the ready. She keeps the dough under the carpet in her bedroom.'

'My God, you got the gaff weighed up good.'

'Not half. A bloke drummed it for me and put me wide. Let her pick him up one night and she lumbered him home. And while he's there he takes a butcher's. We was going to do it together, but he gets nicked for suspect and being on the flypaper, he gets a stretch in the Ville. Care to come on it now you've got the strength of it?'

'Sure. How're we going to get in? Got the key or anything.'

'Blimey. You want jam on it, you do. It's quite easy to get in all the same. It's in a block of flats, see. Top flat. All we got to do is to go up the block and dressed as we are, pretty good, nobody'll rumble us. If they do, we'll have some fanny ready. "Is Miss Robinson at home?" Something of that sort. I'll leave the chat to you, being as how you talk better than what I do. Well, we get up to the top floor, go up half a flight more and there's a door leading out on to a flat roof.

'On the door there's writ, "Not to be opened except in case of fire". Ne'mind about that, push up the old bar, get on to the roof and there's a nice little skylight to the flat. What's easier? Damnall.'

'Sounds all right.'

'It *is* all right.'

'When d'you think of doing it?'

'How'd tomorrow suit you?'

'Sure. Suits me fine. What time?'

'We don't want to leave it too late because of getting up and down them dancers, see. She goes out on the bash round about eight. Tell you what. Meet me about half-past eight tomorrow evening. We can have a couple of drinks and then go up there in our own time.'

'Good enough. But listen, Curly, what about the tools? I lost mine when they done me and I ain't got no new 'uns yet.'

'I'll bring them. Not as we'll need many. Don't need a glim because there's electric light in the gaff. All we want'll be a tin of vaseline and a sheet of brown paper to get that skylight open and a cane to open any drawers or anything. I'll tote all those. Got any turtles?'

The Gilt Kid, having no gloves, answered:

'No, but I'll buy a pair. I'll tell you another thing you'll want too.'

'What's that?'

'A length of rope so that you can let yourself down from the skylight. If you jump you make the hell of a row and wake up everybody in the block when you land.'

'Blimey. Yes, that's right. A tin o' vaseline, a sheet of paper, the old cane and a length of rope. I might as well bring a knife along and all. Comes in useful for slipping back catches and that.'

'Sure. You know how to wear the rope so that nobody'll notice it?'

The Gilt Kid was taking the greatest pleasure in showing Curly, who was really far more experienced in the crooked lark, how to go to work.

'Tie it round your waist, over your shirt, but under your trousers. It's handy to get at then and still don't make no bulge.'

'OK.'

There was silence for a couple of minutes, both men being apparently absorbed in their own thoughts. The Gilt Kid was conscious of the old familiar constriction of the chest and the quickening of the pulses. In spite of the beer that he was drinking, his mouth was dry and sanded. He was finding difficulty in swallowing his drink. It was not fear, he told himself angrily, just pleasant excitement. He set his empty glass down on the table with a bang that startled him and seemed to shatter the silence.

'Have another drink, Curly?'

Curly looked up at the clock and muttered something about having to see a jane.

'Keep her waiting. It'll do her good. Have another drink?'

His voice was almost truculent. Of a sudden he did not want Curly to go. He felt desperately the need of company.

'All right then. I don't mind.'

The Gilt Kid went up to the counter to call for his order.

The cold air of Shaftesbury Avenue made him feel almost drunk. When Curly had gone to keep his appointment, the Gilt Kid had stayed on upstairs. After another bottle of beer, on his own, feeling bored, he had spoken to a woman sitting there. He bought drinks for herself and her friend, and then, not quite seeing the point in standing drinks to all the prostitutes in London, he decided to go some place else.

The four bottles of beer had bitten well.

He stood for a moment on the corner outside the public house. Then, with the illogicality of the half-drunken, came to the conclusion that he needed another drink. Although his purpose was formed he continued standing on the corner wondering just where to go.

'I know,' he said half-aloud, 'I'll go to Jack Bloomfield's.'

He turned down the street, walking rapidly and with long strides. His head was thrown back and he was enjoying the cold wind. The fumes of the beer rising up from his stomach into his head clouded his consciousness; all the self-depreciation which he had felt earlier in the evening was lost. A kind of exultation filled him. He was a crook and he didn't care who knew it. He had money in his pocket and the next day he was going to earn some more. He didn't give a damn for anybody alive or dead. He didn't work and create more . . . more . . . what the hell did the communists call it . . . surplus value, that's right, he didn't create any more surplus value to fill the pockets of the capitalists, not he.

He was walking along Gerrard Street, shaking his head in solemn negation at all the prostitutes, when a man stopped him.

'Hallo, comrade.'

'Blimey, this seems to be my night for meeting people. Who the hell are you, mate?'

He looked at the other closely. He was short, pale and looked scared. Paleface! That was the key-word. Paleface. The man must have met him in prison. Good God, he thought, with a kind of a mock comicality, the place is getting infested with gaol-birds.

The man was talking. The Gilt Kid listened with impatience. He hardly wanted to listen. Talking was more in his line.

'Don't you remember me, comrade? I'm the man what sold you a copy of the *Daily Worker* on the day of the anti-war demo last week.' His voice had a kind of a whine in it as though he were begging.

'That's right.' The Gilt Kid's manner was condescending. 'Come and have a drink.'

'Well,' said the communist, hopefully, 'I haven't any money.'

'I'm not asking you if you've got any money,' he said loftily, 'I'm asking you to have a drink.'

They went to Teddy Bear's at the corner of Gerrard Street.

'What are you going to have?'

'A bitter, please.'

'A bitter, please, and a large Scotch and soda.'

With four fizzy bottles of beer already inside him, the Gilt Kid knew that he could not stomach any more beer. He carried the drinks across to where the communist was sitting.

'Good luck.'

'Good luck.'

They tasted their drinks. The Gilt Kid turned to his guest.

'So you're a communist, are you?'

'Yes.' The monosyllable was defiant.

'Well, I want to talk to you about joining.'

'About joining the CP?'

A smile of joy wreathed the Red's face. He felt that by using such initials as the ECCI and the NUWM, not to mention barbarous composite words like Agitprop and Politburo, he would be certain to tie his opponent up in knots if an argument started. He drank a little more beer and cleared his husky throat.

'It's quite simple, really,' he began. 'You see, we Marxists believe first of all in the materialist conception of history, by which we mean . . .'

This was too much. The Gilt Kid interrupted him.

'Yes I know all about that. I know all about the Materialist Conception of History, and the Class War, *and* the Theory of Surplus Value. And don't for God's sake try to tell me about Economic Determinism.' With a wave of his hand he dismissed all such theories as idle trifles, unworthy the attention of two intelligent men. 'What I want to know is when are you getting on with the job.'

'We are getting on with the job.' The little communist was indignant. 'We are disseminating our propaganda among the masses.'

'Yes, Yes, Yes.' It seemed inevitable that the communist be interrupted. 'That's not what I mean. When's the revolution coming? That's your job.'

'Yes, comrade, but we got to await the revolutionary situation.'

'Why wait for the revolutionary situation? Why in the name of God don't you go out and make one.'

'Yes, comrade, but . . .'

'Don't "yes comrade but" me. Have another drink?'

The poor communist knew that he was on difficult ground. The other was paying for the drinks and, therefore, had the right to direct the conversation.

The Gilt Kid, having come back with the glasses recharged, plunged straight into the argument without any of the toasts or salutations customary among the drinking classes.

'Listen, you hold demonstrations,' he began, 'meetings, hunger-marches and all that bull. What the hell good does it do? Just a few mugs get nicked and a few more have sore heads where the slops have bashed them with their batons. You can't tell me that brings the revolution any nearer.'

'We hold those demonstrations and that for the purpose of spreading our propaganda and keeping the name of the party before the masses. And when the inevitable breakdown of capitalism occurs the workers will turn to the people who have led them in the past.'

'Not likely,' retorted the Gilt Kid. 'When that breakdown of yours happens, the blokes who're coming out on top are the strong-arm guys who can grab all they want for themselves and freeze on to it when they've got it. You can bet on that, china.'

'But you're advocating individualism. The workers are only to be saved by mass action.'

'I'm not advocating nothing. I'm just telling you what's going to happen. Look, here if you want people to follow you you got to give them something. Blokes are going to stick by someone who gets them dough, ain't they?'

'Naturally.'

'Well, then instead of messing about with dopey meetings why don't you give the boys something? Start a riot. Lead a row in Bond Street and loot all the shops. Collect all the bums in London and take them into one of the flash hotels and let them demand to be fed. You hear about hunger-marchers making rows and demanding grub. Where'd they go? To the Ritz, to Lyons' Corner House, even? No! The workhouse. That's just about your mark, kicking up a shine at the spike.'

'Yes, but if we did all that the leaders of the party'd get

pinched and the movement'd be all bust up. Anyhow that's not communism. It's just plain hooliganism.'

'Call it what you like, mate. It's getting something for the bloke on the floor and that's what you reckon to be out for. Communists are all against production for profit, and don't believe in creating more surplus value for the sole benefit of the bosses.'

'Sure.'

'Well, there's only two types of blokes what don't create surplus value. Crooks and bums. Crooks nick the capitalist's dough and bums just don't graft and make any. And now, good-bye, pal, I got to get along.'

The Gilt Kid had grown fed up with arguing the toss, and besides, it had struck him as a good plan to leave the argument as it was, with himself on top.

The door swung to behind him, leaving the communist speechless and with a three-parts empty beer glass in his hand.

The Gilt Kid turned the corner and walked slowly down towards Lisle Street. He was feeling good and lit up. There was no mistake about it, the nick had taken it out of him. He could not stand his wallop as well as he had been able to before he had been arrested.

Where, he wondered, was he going now? If he had another, it would make him have still another and they, altogether, would make him properly drunk. The result would be that he'd get cased up with some old bag and she'd take him for his lot. He pretended to be a wide boy, but what the hell, underneath it all it looked as if he were nothing more than a steamer himself.

Nearby was a little café.

Hallo, he recollected, here's Isabella's. Ribby kind of a gaff, but I might as well go in.

He went inside and sat down at a little marble-topped table. The café swam round him as the fatly bosomed Italian woman came up to take his order.

'Coffee, please.'

Coffee was good. It was reckoned to sober a bloke up.

He looked round the café to see if there were any customers whom he knew. At the top end an Irish girl was sitting with two men, both of whom wore striped suits with wide, padded shoulders. One of them had a north-country accent. All three of them were talking in low vehement tones. They were, apparently, having a row about something or another. Money or women. Very likely the two.

The Gilt Kid ran a disapproving eye over them. He did not like these Grecian cows. They swore like navvies, drank like fishes, and fought like hell among themselves. They always picked up with ponces, usually Yids, and then turned them down for another bloke. That was probably what the barney was about now. Both the men looked as if they might be on the Jo Roncing stakes. Irish janes were good to fellows on the bum and to the boys on the gagging lark, he'd heard somewhere.

He stirred his muddy coffee and looked around to see if there might be anyone else whom he knew or who seemed interesting.

A party of poufs were sitting together. One was eating a salmon roll and another holding up a small pocket mirror and combing his hair. There were no more customers.

What the hell! That was funny; no more customers.

What the hell had happened to all the blokes he used to know who had used Isabella's? All got knocked off or something, he conjectured vaguely. Of course, most of the girls and irons would be out on the bash by now. It must be getting on.

He looked up at the clock which hung behind the counter. Doing so, he noticed a girl come in. She was pretty in a babyish way, but it looked as though all the kittenishness had been knocked out of her. Obviously she had not learned to wear the hard armour of indifference like most of the girls round Lisle Street and Gerrard Street.

Poor kid, he thought, with the ready sentimentality of the half-drunk. It must be kind of fierce when they first go on the bash.

He watched her go up to the counter and speak to Isabella. Try though he did, he could not catch what they were saying. He could not see her face either because she had turned her back to him while she was talking. He could, however, guess by the drooping lines of her figure that she was pleading pretty hard about something. He watched Isabella. A kind of wooden, uncomprehending expression had come over her as it does over all Latins when they're scared of having to give something for nothing. That is, unless maybe there's a chance for them to show off and look big.

The kid moved away from the counter in the direction of the door. Her steps lagged. The Gilt Kid noticed that her cheap, patent leather shoes, which were going over at the heels, had rubbed a hole in the back of both her stockings.

Poor kid. He certainly felt sorry for her. She must have been trying to bum a cup of coffee and Isabella had turned it down. Struck by a sudden impulse he called out to her:

'Here, sister, come over here. I want to talk to you.'

She turned. He noticed that there was a funny expression in her eyes. It was a mixture of hope and suspicion. Her mouth, he saw, had begun to sag at the corners. Maybe she was trying to hold back her tears or else she was getting the tough street-walker mask. He could not make out which. He gave her a friendly smile just to encourage her.

'Come on, kid,' he said, trying to throw a friendly note into his voice, although it was a hard job, since he had not felt kindly disposed to anyone for a long while.

He knew that everyone in the café was looking at him. He knew what was on their minds, too. They were thinking he was going to pretend to give the girl a break and, later, when he had got her flashed up good, start poncing on her.

The hell with it anyway. Let them think what they liked.

34

GIVING THE HAND OUT

She came over to his table and stood looking down at him. He did not get up, or take off his hat, or anything of that sort, since he believed that being too polite to women gave them ideas. Instead, he hooked up one foot on the cross-bar of the chair next to him.

'Hungry?' he asked and could not keep the smile out of his eyes, although he tried to make his mouth look tough as he jerked out the word.

'What's it got to do with you if I am?' She tried to throw a hard shell over her softness.

'Nothing. Not a thing, sister. Only I thought if you *was* hungry maybe you'd like me to hand you a tightener. Come on, sister, sit down. Give it a name. What you going to have?'

As the girl sat down slowly and with reluctance, the Gilt Kid beckoned over Isabella. She came from behind the counter, wiping her hands on her apron.

'Bring over two eggs and chips, a couple of slices and a cup of coffee.' He turned to his guest. 'That do to start with?'

She tried to smile. It made him feel a bit funny to see that her blue eyes were wet with tears. He didn't want to be soft, but damn it, it kind of got a fellow to see a young jane like this kid on the ribs.

'Thank you very much,' she said at last, and as she spoke, he noticed from her accent that she was not a London kiddy. 'I don't know why you should do this for me.' He felt embarrassed.

'Oh, leave that part out,' he said. 'All I ask is that you don't tell me that you're a clergyman's daughter or that you were put in the pudden club by the squire's son.'

An awkward silence of constraint fell between them. The girl started to play with the cruet. The Gilt Kid wondered why Isabella couldn't get a move on with them eggs. Everybody was staring at the pair of them, too, and that made it a whole lot worse.

To fill in the time of waiting he brought out his cigarettes and offered her the packet in silence. She stuck the cigarette between her lips. He became aware of that mouth of hers again. In spite of its turned down corners it was soft and helpless looking. It was quite certain that she was not made for the stakes in which she had entered.

As he held out a lighted match he said: 'You looked about played out, sister.'

She blew out a cloud of smoke and tried to look brave.

'I just came out of Holloway this morning.'

'Out of the Castle, eh? Didn't the DPA give you no dough?'

'They gave me five shillings.' She seemed ashamed to admit the sum.

'Which you spent on having your hair done up good, eh?'

She laughed, but her shyness had not yet properly melted.

'Well a girl's got to look good on this game.'

'Sure, she has, but she's got to have something in her old guts, too, or she won't be able to stand the rack. What did you get done for? Hoisting?'

'Soliciting.'

She tried to make a brave face of it, but it was clear that the admission was distasteful. She hurried on: 'I was taken up to Marlborough Street and the magistrate fined me forty shillings or seven days.' Now that she had started speaking the words came more easily, so much more so, in fact, that they almost tumbled out of her mouth, one on top of the other. 'I hadn't got the money so I had to do the time. The lady missionary wanted me to go into a home or something, but I wouldn't stand for that. It was much better going to

Holloway. I only got done because I didn't know the ropes. I'd only just come to London, you see, but the girls inside put me wide.'

'I only just come out of the Scrubbs myself. I was doing nine moon for screwing. So we're both gaol-birds together.'

They laughed. It was the first natural laugh that they had had together and Isabella came over with the kid's supper. The girl set about it in a way which showed that she certainly was hungry.

The Gilt Kid watching her get stuck into it that way began to feel a bit snackish himself. He had been drinking all that skimish without having had a bite to eat.

'What are you going to have after that, sister?' He asked the question with an attempt at tender solicitude, but it was hard trying to feel tender about a girl who was eating her chuck like a navvy.

'Why, nothing. This will be enough, thanks.'

Her eyes gave the lie to her lips.

'Don't be silly all your life. Two eggs and chips is a lousy tightener when you're good and hungry. Have a plate of spaghetti. These Italians don't half make it good. I'm going to have some too.'

He raised his voice.

'Two platefuls of spaghetti, Isabella.'

He ground out his cigarette in the thick glass tray which had an advertisement fixed some way under the surface.

'What do they call you back home?'

'Molly.'

'I guessed it was going to be Molly; either Molly or Kitty. One of them was a sure bet. They always call you goofy janes one or the other. And now while I'm waiting for the manjary shall I tell you your life-story? If I don't you'll only be telling it to me later on.'

She nodded. He was pleased to see laughter at last in her blue eyes.

'Well, Molly,' he began, 'you came from the country some place. Not the real depths of the country, I know you're not a swede-bashing judy, but some kind of a town not a whole long way off the Smoke.'

'Reading,' she supplemented with her little mouth full of chipped potatoes.

'Sure. You come from Reading. You probably had a couple of jobs there, but they didn't amount to much, so you thought you'd come up to London and chance your arm. You had a hell of a row with your family about it, but you walked right out on them, saying you'd never darken their doors again or some bull of the sort. It was stone ginger, you thought, that you'd get a smashing job up here, a pretty girl like you, who was a fancy dresser and could dance the way that all the boys in Reading was wild about you.

'Any kind of a job would do for a start, you reckoned, crowd work on the films or a mannequin in some right flash kind of a dress gaff until you got your chance and broke out as a stage or film star. Am I right, or am I right?'

'How ever *did* you guess?' There was no irony in Molly's voice as she asked the question.

'How did I guess? I didn't guess, Molly kid. I've been around the place and know my stuff. Shall I go on?'

She nodded, and then, resting her elbows on the table, cupped her chin in her hands. Her chin, he noticed, was weak-looking, and her hands, although grimy and red from stitching, were slender and delicate.

'Well, when you came to London you found that jobs weren't all that easy to get. So, when you'd got to the end of the little dough you'd brought you took a place as a skivvy. And that went along good for a bit until the son of the house started messing you about.

'At first you held him off because you knew what he was after, but a bit later it didn't seem so bad. You had to work pretty hard and you were all done up in the evening and didn't feel like going out and getting a boy of your own and it was nice to have somebody petting you and telling you how pretty you looked. Besides he took you about the place and always bought good seats at the pictures and stood you a box of chocolates and talked kind of posh and polite to you. In the end you came to fall for him.'

Isabella came over and put the two plates of spaghetti before them. The Gilt Kid ignored his plate and went on talking. Molly would have liked to have started feeding, but she felt that he might have got wild if she were to do so before he stopped talking. And it was a pity to let good food get cold and spoiled, too, especially when a girl was hungry.

'Well, after a bit, he got tired of you or something happened. I'm not so certain about this. Maybe his mother found out about it. Anyway, you got the sack and then when all you'd got saved was spent and you hadn't a character you couldn't get a new job. At last you decided to go on the batter and the rest of the yarn you've spun yourself.'

He picked up his fork and started eating. Molly, thankfully, followed his example. She knew that she ought to say something so she spoke between mouthfuls.

'It's wonderful the way you know all that,' she said. 'You must be a mind-reader.'

He looked up quickly.

'Don't try to kid me that way. I'm no mind-reader,' he said brutally, 'but I've heard the hell of a lot of hard-luck stories.'

He went on eating and, with his head bent over his plate, did not observe how she flinched at his plain speaking. A moment later, he looked up again.

'You don't want to think I always get talking this way, Molly,' he said. 'It's only when I've had a couple. And I've had my share of the old skimish tonight.'

'Don't I know?'

The coldness of her tone annoyed him considerably. She

ought to be damn glad he was a bit lit or she wouldn't be getting this tightener. The food he had eaten and the coffee had sobered him. His head was aching. He put his fork down on the empty plate and picked up his cigarettes which he had left lying on the table.

'You don't want to get cross, Molly,' he said, offering her one. 'If you're going to be on this lark you want to learn to take it if anyone speaks a bit nasty. It's all part of the game.'

'Yes,' she said taking a light from the match which he was holding out, 'I know. What do they call you?'

'Well, in stir the boys called me the Gilt Kid, but before I was nicked they used to call me Ken. That's my surname you see. Kennedy.'

'Well, thanks for the supper,' she said. 'I s'pose I'd better be getting back on the job.'

'Siddown,' he retorted waving an imperious hand. 'How do you get that way? You aren't going back on no job tonight.'

She sat down again. Her face hardened with suspicion. She began to think quickly of what she imagined was on his mind. A kind of disgust swept through her. All men were the same, and she had thought he was just being kind in a rough sort of a way. A wave of self-pity possessed her. The Gilt Kid read her thoughts.

'I've never known a girl like you for getting airyated,' he said crossly. 'What the hell's wrong now? Come on, kid, talk sense. I suppose you got no place to sleep tonight.'

She shook her head.

'No, and I don't look like getting one neither, if you don't let me go out and earn some dough. Who was that?'

The Gilt Kid was nodding to a dark, flash-looking man who had just come into the café.

'A fellow I used to know back in the nick,' he said quietly. 'We used to call him Dean Street Dan, because he was in a VD cell on Rotten Row when he first came in. Used to say that he'd been done for kites, but everyone reckoned it was for poncing. This proves it him coming in here.'

Molly's eyes narrowed with contempt.

'So that's what you are, eh? That's what you want out of me?'

Her words stung him to a fury. His head was aching badly and he certainly wanted a drink.

'Shut up, you bloody little fool,' he said savagely, 'before I lose my temper. Can't a fellow do a girl a good turn without her thinking that? I've got a good mind to get up and bash you. I may be a burglar; I may be no damn use; but I've never ponced on no one yet and I'm not going to start now. And – if I was I'd pick a jane who knew a bit more about the game than you do. Why, you haven't got the good sense to provide your own supper, let alone working me one.'

And then seeing the frightened look in the girl's eyes he relented and continued more mildly: 'Let's see, what were we talking about? You've not got your kip tonight; well, I may be a mug, but I'm going to give it to you. I expect when you were lying on your three boards in the Castle you used to promise yourself a nice soft bed in a real comfortable room on your first night out.'

It was with satisfaction that he knew from the look on her face that he had hit the bull's-eye again.

'Well, you don't want to spoil your kip on your first night by having to share it with a fat old steamer. Kip comfortably tonight and kip clean. By yourself, I mean.'

He flipped a pound note out of his pocket at her.

'Take this oncer,' he said. 'You can get into one of those bed and breakfast joints for a dollar. And keep the change. What the hell you do tomorrow I don't mind, but I trust you, kid, to go straight tonight. That a bet?'

'Sure.'

She smiled up at him, incredulously fingering the piece of paper.

'I don't know how to thank you . . .'

'Oh, shut up,' he said wearily as he rose to go. 'Don't thank me; thank Christ I'm a mug and that I got lit up tonight and I'm going to see if I can't grab a drink before they shut. You can do what the hell you like, but I'm trusting you, Molly.'

'Good night and thank you ever so.'

'Aw, shut up.'

He hurled this last command at her as he went out through the door into the street.

RENCONTRE

Out in Lisle Street again, he found himself in an unreasonable temper. Of course, he'd made a fool of himself. Giving away a oncer like that for nothing just because she was a girl, and if a bloke had come up and put the bee on him all the handout would have been nothing more than a lousy tanner, or maybe, a deener. Just because she had a soft body and looked innocent and a bit silly he had let her take him for a quid and he had had nothing in return for it. He ought to have forgotten the reproach in those babyish blue eyes and made her earn it. God, wasn't he as good to kip with as any steamer with a haw-haw voice she might have picked up?

He would have to hurry if he wanted to get that wet. There were still lights in that pub on the corner although they were probably calling last orders. It must be damn nigh eleven.

He dived down the road and pushed open the door of the four-ale bar with his shoulder. He had a bit of a job shoving his way to the bar through the crowd. Most of them were drunk and there was a heavy smell of cheap pipe tobacco about the place. If he was going to get any effect out of the skimish he would have to drink good and quick, and pretty strong, too.

'Gimme two double brandies in one glass. A half-pint beer-glass'll do.'

The barmaid, flustered at the end of the day's rush, looked at him a little strangely. She noticed that there were beer-slops on the bar counter and began to mop them up. Most of the male customers, in the four-ale bar, drank pints of fivepenny ale, all black and frothy in glasses as thick as jam jars; the women usually had stout, or a glass of cheap Lisbon red wine, lizzie they called it. Calling for two large brandies in one glass sounded a bit off, if you asked her.

'You heard what I said.'

He slapped two half-crowns down on the bar.

The barmaid put up her left hand to the tight waves of her hair. The atmosphere of the place was giving her a headache and her feet were sore, standing on them the way she did all day long. She poured out his order, picked up his money, rang up the sum on the cash register and brought him back his change.

'Splash or water?'

With a couple of jerks of her head she indicated the syphon and the water jug, which was advertising matter for some distillery firm. The water had become dusty and discoloured from all the smoking that was going on.

'No thanks, I'll take it straight.'

Her eyebrows went up as she saw him backing away from the bar with the neat spirits in his hand. He must, she thought, be mad, or perhaps his girl had given him the belt. Not a bad-looking fellow he was, neither. Her mind was working mechanically while she drew a pint of ale for another customer.

The Gilt Kid had backed and elbowed his way to a comparatively clear space where he could drink in peace. He had never had such a filthy taste in his mouth before. He drank the brandy as though it were beer. The first gulp went down without him noticing it until he felt it warm his stomach. He tried another gulp, but found that he could not take it. He began to cough.

A shrill electric bell rang and the lights went out. All the staff started shouting 'Last orders, gents, please, your last orders, please!' The landlord's bass boomed out deeper than all the others. The lights came up again.

The Gilt Kid, knowing that he had only five minutes'

drinking time left, took another go at his drink and got it down all right. His stomach felt comfortably warm and he could sense the heat spreading all over his body.

He took a second sip, then a third. He felt really pleasant now. His headache had gone and his heart was beating fast. Contentment stole over him. He felt in his pocket for a cigarette. They were not there.

'Oh Christ, I must have left them on the table at Isabella's.'

To his amazement he heard somebody echoing his remark. No, begob, he was talking out loud. People were looking at him anxiously. A man in a checked cap, who had taken a drink too much, had been sick in the corner and was being led out by his mates.

The Gilt Kid took another sip, a larger one this time and he managed it without the trace of a splutter. He was getting good at this game. He wanted to practise a bit more. Slow beatitude filled him.

Good kid that Molly even if she had taken him for a oncer. She had earned it, too, the way he had chatted her; besides a girl had to live. Not a bad con-man in her own way when he came to weigh it up. She had let him make the running, and suggest the dough himself. Reminded him a little of Maisie, too, with that silly look on her old Jem Mace. She wasn't quite so hot-looking as Maisie, though. That judy certainly had passion. Maisie. Eh? Where in the name of God would she be now?

He took a little more brandy and led off dramatizing himself with an inebriated facility.

Maisie, the only girl he had ever loved! And he had only seen her three times in his life, the third time being arm-in-arm with a Yiddish-looking fellow in Hyde Park. He and Maisie had been made for each other. They both knew it and luck kept them apart.

The first time he had met her had been at a party and he

had taken her home. She and her sister had three rooms out Brixton way. Eileen, or something, that was the sister's monick. Eileen, or whatever her name was, was drunk, proper lit up and had passed out. She did not know what was happening so they put her to bed and he had slept with Maisie. And did the sister create next morning? She did. She slung him out, giving him the gooner proper, not before he had made another date with Maisie, though. But he got tight with some blokes and forgot about it, and although he hung about all the pubs in Brixton and walked around the streets a lot when the boozers were closed, it did not seem as if he could bump into her anyhow. And, since he had forgotten the address, he could not write.

He took a sip.

The next time he had met her had been at an afternoon club in Old Compton Street and they had had one hell of a time. He had done a gaff and was well-heeled with dough, so he toted her around all evening and they spent the night at one of those hotels around Paddington. They both had decided that they were meant for each other and made arrangements to live together, get cased up properly in fact. The Gilt Kid went and saw about the place and was to have met her the next afternoon at the Old Compton Street club, but, while he was walking along Shaftesbury Avenue he got nicked over that Hastings job and had to wait five weeks on remand at Lewes. When he came out, because he got away with it on an alibi which he had previously arranged, paying five pounds for it, he could not find her anywhere.

The third time was when he saw her walking arm-in-arm with a Yid in Hyde Park. He had not spoken to her then, for he had a bit of a hangover and it seemed too much trouble. But Maisie was the only girl he had ever loved! That was straight-up.

He emptied his glass. The lights went out again and there was a great deal of shouting. The staff were calling out:

46

'Time, gents, please, time please! Come along you lords and dukes, time please! Come along please, you gentlemen's sons, time please!'

He walked unsteadily to the door pushing anyone who got in his way. Instead of being content, he was maudlin. The recollections of the Maisie episodes had upset him. Lisle Street reeled up in front of him. He stumbled and fell up against a man. It was Dean Street Dan.

'Hallo, Dan!'

'Why, it's the Gilt Kid again! You're a nice one I must say.'

'Why?'

The Gilt Kid lurched again and steadied himself against the other, catching hold of his arm.

'What do you mean, I'm a nice one?' The sentence came jerkily out of his mouth. A couple of words, a pause, another couple. It was like hot bath-water jutting out of a geyser.

'Well, you ask a girl to have a feed, give her a oncer, and then stroll out without paying for the tightener.'

'Blimey!'

'God's truth. On my life. She had to pester up herself out of the pound you give her.'

'Oh God,' the Gilt Kid began to laugh, 'did I do that? Well, Dan, mate, the joke's on me. I floated because I got fed up and wanted her to turn in thanking me.'

He stood there, rocking with laughter, and belching between laughs. Dean Street Dan looked at him with a twinkle in his eyes.

'They don't want to let boys like you out of stir,' he said. 'You don't know how to take care of yourselves. Got yourself nice and drunk, now, haven't you?'

'Sure. And talking about drink, you know the Wessend . . .' it was too much bother for him to pronounce the 't' '. . . pretty good, don't you?'

'Yes, why?'

'Well, if you know the Wessend pretty good, you'll know where I'll get another drink.'

'Sure, I do, but I won't tell you, Gilt Kid, you've had enough as it is.'

'C'mon, Dean Street, be a pal.'

'Don't call me Dean Street.'

The nickname rankled. People had poured out of the pub and were staring at the pair of them.

'I'll call you what I like. You're only a ponce, anyhow.' He looked at Dean Street Dan with gathering wrath. 'I've got a mind to bash you,' he went on, 'and when I bash a bloke he gets bashed. I'm a bit of a coring mush, myself.'

Dean Street Dan shrugged his shoulders and walked away. He had no particular desire to get tangled up in a street row. And, what's more, what the Gilt Kid had said about being a fighting man was true. He had lost seven days' remission in prison for hitting a cleaner whom he thought to be carving him up over his rations.

'Hi, Dean Street!'

'Your mate's gone, son!'

An old woman with a string bag breathed stout all over him.

'What if he has, ma? I'm going to get a wet. I want a wet and I'm going to get a wet.'

The laughing bystanders raised a ragged cheer.

'That's right, son.'

The Gilt Kid set off down Lisle Street at a fast lurch. He turned down Leicester Street and walked down into Leicester Square. The pavement was crowded with people coming out of the theatres which had just broken. The sky-signs, particularly those which were purple, hurt and dazzled his eyes after the obscurity of tactful Lisle Street. The walk and the cool air had, however, pulled him together a bit and he felt far more sober.

He stood for a moment outside the Empire trying to fight

the drunkenness which kept on rising up with periodic, harmonic waves. He did not want to get arrested for being drunk and he wanted to go into a place with an extension and not have the door-keeper sling him out. He caught sight of the fat-gutted commissionaire outside the Queen's.

Why, he knew that bloke. Tipped him often for grabbing him a taxi.

He went across to him. The commissionaire, who looked as if he could still use them a bit in spite of his big stomach, was arguing with a pair of drunks. The Gilt Kid watched him do his stuff for a minute.

What was the point of asking the commissionaire and showing himself up as a mug? A fellow could get a drink at any place with a supper licence if he had a sandwich. They were allowed to serve wallop up till midnight. There was that Café Something or Another over on the other corner of the square. It was, he knew, a bit aristocratic, but he didn't mind about that. He did not feel choosey; why, he could be a rye mush himself for one night.

He darted across, under the nose of a taxi and hurled an automatic 'Go to hell' as a retort to the driver's curse. A blind man on the corner was playing a violin. The Gilt Kid threw him a shilling for luck. He had a feeling that there was a break coming.

He walked into the restaurant with an air, giving his hat to the cloak-room man. A band was playing. The Gilt Kid tried to work off that vacant smile which he knew was on his face. He sat down at a table with his back against the padded wall. He looked round the room; most of the people were in evening dress; some of them were dancing. Yes, this looked a good place. It would be a good place if he got a drink; any place where a bloke could get a wet was all right.

The band stopped playing. A waiter came across to him and stuck an enormous piece of cardboard into the hands of the Gilt Kid, who stared at it stupidly.

'If I have something to eat can I get a drink?'

'Yes, sir.'

'OK. Bring me a bottle of brandy.'

Brandy seemed a good bet. It sounded real gentlemanly and was strong, too.

'What will you take to eat, sir?'

What! Was that lousy dish-wrestler still arguing the toss?

'Anything. Nothing much.'

'A savoury, sir?'

'Yes. That'd be fine.'

Savoury sounded good. It ought to be nice and tasty.

'Should I suggest a *Croute Diable*, sir?'

'Sure. Go ahead. Suggest what you like. I'm not stopping you. But don't forget the old wallop.'

'Sir?'

'I said "Don't forget the old brandy".'

'Old Brandy. Very good, sir. I will bring some '78.'

The waiter scribbled on his pad and went away. The Gilt Kid, feeling better without him hanging around, stretched out his legs and sighed. It was a great idea, padding the wall. He rested his head lazily and watched the dancing, which had just begun again.

Could you, he wondered, just pick up a jane, any jane here and whirl her around or did they give you the bullet for that? Better not try, he concluded, although there was some real right stuff about the dump.

What seemed like a whole flock of waiters came back and started arranging forks and things. He wished they would float. It made a fellow feel awkward. One of them had brought the damnedest shaped glass he had ever seen in his life. Another was showing him a bottle of brandy.

'Yeh,' he said, 'that ought to do. And, Antonio . . .'

'Yes, sir?'

'Bring me some cigarettes. A large Gold Flake.'

'Yes, sir.'

Where the hell did these mugs get all that sir stuff from? Anyone might think he was a screw back in prison. He splashed a little brandy into the glass. He did not feel like filling it up. The glass looked so damned awkward to manage.

He cut off a bit of the thing that they had brought him to eat and took a taste at it. Not liking it, he pushed it away and had a drink instead. The brandy went down good and packed a real wallop.

Some of the women present, he saw, were wearing goodish rocks. There was one with three groins on her fingers which he would weigh up at about a couple of hundred nicker sold crooked.

A waiter turned up with his cigarettes on a plate. He ripped off the air-tight packing for the Gilt Kid, watched him pull out a cigarette and then held a lighted match. The Gilt Kid blew out a cloud of contented smoke.

Say what you like, he noted mentally, but they had a good line in service here. Would it be worthwhile to grab a fur wrap and make for the door?

He looked towards the way out, figuring out the chances. No, it could hardly be done and, besides, a job of that sort – unless it happened to be a bit extra – was really beneath his dignity. He was a screwsman, not a sneak-thief.

A man and a woman were coming into the restaurant. The woman looked a bit like Maisie. It was Maisie!

He half rose from his seat and found it hard to suppress the 'blimey' that came to his lips. She was all flashed up good and the geezer that was with her was dolled up like a dog's dinner with a white tie and all. It must be kind of hard to tie one of those stranglers without blacking it all up.

He watched them cross the room and sit down over the other side.

Should he, he debated, go across and speak to them? After all it *was* Maisie – the only girl he had ever loved. Still, he did not want to go butting in. She might be playing some old mug and it would be a shame to spoil her racket. She did look good, and still as dopey as ever. A tremendous affection for her came over him.

Maisie, if it was she, gave no sign of recognition. She was darting little glances all over the place and there was a fixed smile on her face as if she were trying to assure everybody that she was having a good time. It was obvious that she was playing little girlishness for all that she was worth.

The Gilt Kid took several drinks out of his glass to fill in the awkward moments. Over and above the kick he was getting out of the liquor he was conscious of Maisie. He had never seen her dressed up as flash before and she seemed to him to be more than ever, the only girl he had ever loved.

It made him feel rather shy to think that he had been to bed with a girl so pretty aristocratic-looking as all that. He would like to crown that bloke she was with, walk over and hit him right on the button. The slimey old steamer.

Of a sudden, Maisie caught sight of him. Her face fell and as it fell, so did his heart sink. She was going to give him the gooner, eh? He clenched his fist until the knuckles showed white.

MAISIE

The Gilt Kid was watching Maisie closely. The effect both of his emotion and of the brandy that he had been drinking was to close up his eyelids. This narrowing of his eyes made Maisie feel just a little frightened. She continued to gawp back at him.

In the meanwhile thoughts beat down on his brain. It was like an Irish navvy wielding a fourteen-pound sled.

The little bitch. So she'd give him the bullet? Was it his fault that the last time he'd seen her, she'd been with a Yiddish-looking gent? Perhaps she had read his name in the *News Of The World* that time he had got his nine months. Well, she knew he was on the crook – he'd been straight with her and had given her the wire right in the beginning. The little cow. He'd a good mind to tear over and spoil her lark with the queer fellow. Serve her right if he swung her up a right-hander into the bargain.

She essayed a weak little smile and said something to her partner. He looked over at the Gilt Kid and raised his eyebrows.

Snotty old cowson.

She spoke to him again. He smiled and patted her quite affectionately on the bare arm. He was rising.

The Gilt Kid began to think fast. He lit a cigarette and tried to look tough.

Perhaps the old bastard was going to call the manager and have him slung out. Well, he'd make a fight for it anyhow. Get them all shown up. There were a hell of a lot of glasses and things to bust and it'd be easy to kick a couple of tables over when the trouble started.

He kept puffing at his cigarette without removing it from his lips. The maxillary muscles in his cheeks stood out and were twitching. The old man was walking across the floor. The Gilt Kid clenched his fists the tighter. The more a fist is clenched the harder a blow feels in a bare-knuckle fight.

If the queer fellow tried to come any acid he would get hit right on the razzo. It was as red as the queen of hearts anyhow. Kick him straight in the guts after that. Old boys never could stand the leather. If he hit him too hard, he'd probably crease him, make the son of a bitch break a blood-vessel or something. He'd get topped for that.

The man was standing near the Gilt Kid's table and was speaking. The Gilt Kid got ready to swing up his right. His eyes measured the distance to the other's chin.

'You're Mr Kennedy, aren't you?'

'So what?' He did not get up or anything. 'What are you going to do about it?'

The old man smiled. He did not understand the way the conversation was running. His voice was affable.

'Miss Gill tells me you're a friend of hers. An old friend whom she has not seen for years.'

What the Gilt Kid wanted to know was who the hell this Miss Gill might be. Oh, that was it. It was the monicker Maisie was travelling under now.

'Yes,' he answered guardedly, perplexed as to what might be coming next. 'That's so.'

'Won't you come over and join us? We should be delighted. My name is Bedborough. Francis Bedborough.'

The Gilt Kid rose. He smiled. He was not quite sure what to do. He knew, however, that he would have to box clever. This might be a trap of some sort and he did not want to show up Maisie by acting the rough-neck. Perhaps he would be able to take the old geezer for a mug and get him to pay the bill for all three of them.

'Thank you,' he said.

That was non-committal enough. It would be a pity to say something out of turn now and show his ignorance. The best bet was to keep the old kisser shut and say as little as possible until he could get Maisie to give him the office.

He took his cigarette out of his mouth. It looked a bit off to be chatting the old boy that way.

'This is my night for meeting people,' he said.

'Indeed?' smiled Mr Bedborough.

'Yes, I've bash – met quite a number of old friends,' replied the Gilt Kid picking his words with care and difficulty.

'Well, come on, my boy. I'm sure that both you and Maisie are eager to meet once more.'

He took the arm of the Gilt Kid whose brain was not too dull to register the fact that Maisie was still using the same Christian name. That was a top worth two.

Mr Bedborough, still arm-in-arm with the Gilt Kid, steered the way round the edge of the dance-floor in front of the orchestra. They arrived at the table where Maisie was sitting. She looked up with a sickly smile. In her eyes horror and excitement were fixed, mingling with one another, but not mixing, like the waters of Lake Geneva.

Mr Bedborough gave an elderly, but kind, tee-hee.

'I've brought you the willing victim,' he said.

The Gilt Kid wished that his feet were not so big; his shoes, however, were clean.

'Hallo, Maisie,' he said. 'How are you?'

'Hallo, Ken,' she said in a refined sort of voice without any – well, hardly any – of her shop-girl whine. 'Won't you sit down?'

The Gilt Kid flopped into a chair. Mr Bedborough sat down between them, carefully lifting up the tails of his coat in a way that made both the others want to giggle. Happily, however, they were avoiding each other's eyes. They were sitting opposite one another.

Maisie spoke. Her pound-noteish voice both annoyed and amused the Gilt Kid. She looked fine, though. Innocent and empty-headed. It was a shame to have her running around with old mugs like this bedbug-fellow. These old boys with the dough always grabbed the best janes – the dirty old cowsons.

'Well, Ken,' she said. 'Still in the valuing business?'

'Yes,' he answered without lifting his eyes. That was a fast one. Valuing. He did not know Maisie had all that eighteen pence. 'Yes, but I had to go out of business for about nine months.'

'Valuing?' Bedborough's eyes were raised in inquiry.

'Yes.' The Gilt Kid was playing up good now. 'You've heard about housebreakers – the firms that demolish buildings? Well, I do the valuing for them. Of course, I value fur coats and jewellery, too.'

'I value a fur coat, if it's a good one.'

Maisie's apt remark gave them an excuse to laugh. For the first time she and the Gilt Kid looked each other straight in the eyes. They began to converse silently, mouthing the words and lip-reading each other.

'Who's the queer fellow?' asked the Gilt Kid.

'Steamer,' answered Maisie.

'Steady?'

She nodded.

'Got a chat of his own?'

She nodded again.

'Worth screwing?'

She frowned and looked away.

Mr Bedborough thought it time that the conversation got started. He turned to the Gilt Kid with a fatherly smile.

'Won't you join us in something to eat? We've just come from the theatre. Been seeing *Yes, Madam*. We had to dine early so we're ravenous, aren't we, my child?'

He looked at Maisie in such a possessive way that it very nearly won him a right hook. Dirty old bastard, thought the

Gilt Kid. It'd serve him right if he had to go without any grub for a few days same as a bloke might get three days' No 1 back in stir.

Maisie nodded.

'Yes, Ken,' she said sweetly, 'won't you have some supper?'

'No thanks,' he said stiffly, 'I just had some.'

He was not going to make an idiot of himself by eating with the wrong knife.

'But you'll have a drink, though. Come now. A glass of champagne?'

Mr Bedborough was very solicitous for his young guest's welfare.

Hell, thought the Gilt Kid, might as well catch the old mug for a few wets. There was all that brandy back on his own table. What was going to happen to that? If the waiter tried to charge for the whole bottle he would find himself getting crowned – and a bit sharpish.

Aloud he said: 'Thank you. Just a glass. I can't be staying long.'

He meant what he said, too. He was he knew pretty nigh drunk and since he was having to keep a good grip on himself in a situation where he needed all his wits about him the sooner he left the better. He did not like leaving Maisie to old Bedbug, but he never had been a bloke to spoil a girl's game. The best bet was just to make a date with her and then slide. How was he to speak to her alone?

Old Bedborough was talking to the waiters, but it was rather chancey.

Casting his thoughts about he looked at Maisie. There was invitation in her wide blue eyes. She was glancing meaningly at the dance-floor.

The Gilt Kid felt a fool. Here was a girl showing him the way and she a tart he had rated dopey. That got a man.

'Shall we dance, Maisie?' he asked.

She turned to Bedborough.

'Do you mind if we dance, Biffs?' she inquired.

'Do, my dear, do,' he beamed.

'What did you call old Bedbug just now?' asked the Gilt Kid as they took the floor.

'Biffs,' she answered. 'He likes me to call him that. It was his monicker at Oxford College or some place.'

'The berk.'

Jealousy and savage contempt blended in the Gilt Kid's tone.

'I won't have you using that bad language.'

'You know what it means all right, so don't get all pound-noteish.'

He took her in his arms. The feeling of her soft warm flesh so close to him filled him with a faint lust. He had thought a lot about her in prison, particularly when he had been lying in his cell reading any book with some description of a love scene in it. Hot words sprang to his lips, but he checked them. She would only get conceited if he started making love to her.

As they danced he felt her breath. A strand of her hair, which she had done in a new way, all smooth on top and fluffy at the back of the head, touched him lightly on the cheek. He was finding it hard to keep those words checked. She was speaking.

'Glad to see me again, darling?'

'Honest, Maisie kid, I'm sorry about that time in Hyde Park,' he stammered, hoping she was not sore about it, 'but I didn't like to butt in on you and that Yid.'

'What *do* you mean?' There was bewilderment in her face.

'Nothing, kid, only it's good to be seeing you again. You know, darling, you're the only girl I ever loved.'

Melodrama filled his voice.

'Mean it?' she smiled up at him, thinking how hard his arms were.

'Sure.'

A look of perfect comprehension passed between them. They were dancing just by the table where Bedborough was sitting and he felt a pang of senile jealousy which he was too well-bred to show. The pair of them were dancing well and Maisie looked even more soft and winning than usual against the young man's sturdy, muscular figure.

'You living with old Bedbug?' asked the Gilt Kid, 'or have you got a chat of your own?'

'I got a place of my own, but the old steamer's pestering.'

'He coming there tonight?'

She nodded in dumb misery as she felt his muscles tense. She looked at his face again. It had gone all hard. Like a film actor's, she thought with awe, loving him with a great pang.

'I got a good mind to give him one on the end of that razzo of his, but I s'pose a girl can't be choosey these days. Is he good to you, kid?'

There was a ferocity in his question.

'He's ever so generous.'

'Does he come any funny business?'

'What you mean?'

'I mean . . .' He paused. 'You know what these old men are supposed to be like. I'd crease him if I thought that, bash him to death slowly, the degenerate old bastard.'

'You know I wouldn't stand for that, Ken darling.'

'You'd better not.' He was gripping her so tightly that her soft body, all supple beneath her dress, was being crushed right into him. 'When am I going to see you again, sugar?'

'Tomorrow afternoon. About three. That suit you?'

'Fine. I'll be there. I got to go on a job tomorrow night, but I'll be there in the afternoon. What address?'

She told him.

'Don't forget to turn up,' she added with a laugh, trying to pass off the intensity of their feeling which was making both of them feel frightened.

The music stopped. The dance was ended. They turned to go back to their table.

'I'll be there whatever happens,' he said. 'If they nick me I'll break gaol.'

It was a white-faced couple that came back to the beaming Bedborough.

'I'm sorry, Mr Kennedy,' he said, as the others sat down, 'I had to order a sandwich for you. They wouldn't let you have a drink otherwise.'

'That's all right so long as it's not ham.' The Gilt Kid was trying to crack a joke. Bedbug would think him a miserable kind of a bloke if he didn't say something bright. 'I'm a four-be-two, you see.'

The joke fell a bit flat.

'It's chicken,' said Bedborough coldly. Ham indeed! Was it likely, he asked himself indignantly, that he, Francis Bedborough, would order anything so plebeian, so reminiscent of a railway refreshment bar, as a ham sandwich?

He poured out three glasses of champagne without speaking. Maisie broke the silence. She did not want to have a good client annoyed.

'Do you think the cabaret will be coming on soon? I do hope so. I *adore* cabaret shows, don't you, Ken? I know *you* do, Biffs darling, so you needn't say you don't.'

She was giving a splendid imitation of a schoolgirl being taken out for the third time in her life. What a merry little thing, so bright. The Gilt Kid gulped down his champagne noisily. It tasted like inferior Eno's salts. He was not going to sit here all night and then see Maisie go off with the queer fellow.

He got up. The legs of his chair scraped along the carpet as he shoved it back with his flat thighs.

'Well, good night all,' he said tonelessly. 'I got to go.'

'But the cabaret! Won't you stay for the cabaret?' cried Maisie in dismay.

'Yes, my dear fellow, do stay,' put in Bedborough.

The slimy bastard, thought the Gilt Kid as he shook his head.

'No, I'm sorry, I can't stop. Got to see a fellow,' he explained with a fine disregard for probabilities.

He nodded curtly and left hurriedly without saying thank you or looking round as he left. When he was outside in Leicester Square and had rammed his hat on to his head he laughed.

That made the second time in one night that he'd left without paying the bill. They would make old Bedbug pay, he supposed. Bloody good job, too. Pity he hadn't given the old cowson one of his wicked rights.

NIGHT

The moment he realized that once more he had left without paying, he knew that he had to move more rapidly, and before an excited waiter came rushing out with a flapping cloth in one hand and a waving bill in the other. He darted down Bear Street, timing his pace just right, not too quickly – that would have made him conspicuous – not too slowly – that would have made it risky.

He caught a glimpse of a bus in Charing Cross Road. It was going to Victoria Station, going his way. Having an excuse he broke into a run and, catching the brass upright, swung himself nimbly up on to the conductor's platform.

While he ran, he thought: Must be the last bus; run very late on this line; a stroke of luck.

He walked up the stairs, timing his body to the swaying of the bus. When he reached the top step, the vehicle had come to a halt. The jerk was sudden. On the left was the shapeless mass of St Martin's Church, on the right was Trafalgar Square with its bench-loads of destitutes.

Just like a boxing match, he thought, as he made his way along the aisle looking for a seat.

The bus was crowded. Every seat was occupied, every window shut. A thick fog of cigarette smoke and the acrid tang of shag made him cough. A party of drunks up in front were passing round quarts of beer and singing. 'Play to me, Gipsy,' they sang.

As the bus started again they changed to 'Knees Up Mother Brown', that inevitable concomitant of Cockney merry-making.

They'll be singing 'Daisy Bell' next, thought the Gilt Kid,

leaning up against the front wall waiting for somebody to get off. Idiots to be drinking all their beer before they got home instead of waiting and having a party.

The bus lurched down Trafalgar Square. A man handed him a bottle.

'Want a wet, chum?'

'Thanks, mate.'

The Gilt Kid took the bottle and drank, first wiping the inside of the neck with his own grimy forefinger. The beer tasted like cheese or diluted blood.

The conductor came up the stairs. A harassed look was on his tired face. The last run was a proper bastard; he would be glad when they got to the garage. He would have a nice cup of tea and go to bed. He caught sight of the Gilt Kid and his anger crystallized.

'Mustn't stand here,' he commanded.

'Shut up.'

The Gilt Kid was too tired to argue. His arms ached, his body was swaying like a sailor's. The drunks backed him up.

'Git aht of it,' they chanted. 'Get aht of it.'

One of them started counting rhythmically and the rest took it up.

'One, Two, Three, Four, Five, Six, Seven, Eight, Nine, Ten! . . . AND THAT MAKES OUT! AHT YOU GO!!'

The conductor changed his tone from command to entreaty. It was not much fun being crowned by a quart bottle.

'Come on, Chummy,' he said, 'you know as well as I do that it's against regulations. I'd get my cards if anybody saw me. Plenty of room downstairs.'

''Ere y'are, mate, 'ave a wet?'

He shook his head at the proffered bottle.

'I got my living to make, same as what you have.' He was addressing the passengers at large.

'Why don't you take off your gawd-forbid? We're passing the Cenotaph.'

> 'It won't be a stylish merridge,
> We can't afford a kerridge . . .'
> 'Dear ol' pal, jolly ol' pal . . .'

The bus stopped. One or two passengers who were crossing Westminster Bridge got down. There was a general re-shuffle, people trying to get the inner seats. The Gilt Kid sat, relaxed, happy. The row was over. He fumbled in his pocket and fished out a penny which he handed to the conductor, who shook his head, eager to be unpleasant.

'Penny ride's up, mate. You got on before Trafalgar Square, didn't you? It's a penny from Tottenham Court Road to Bridge Street, Parliament Street. Want another penny?'

'Ar'ri. Don't keep talking about pennies. I got bags of pennies. Here y'are. Here's one for you.'

He held out another penny between a tired forefinger and thumb. The bell-punch clanged. With the blue ticket in his hand the Gilt Kid dozed down the cavern of Victoria Street, his head nodding on to his chest. He nearly dislocated his neck every time that the bus jerked. The songs, even those coming from the impassioned soloist who insisted on a different tune from all the others, beat against his ear-drums, but did not penetrate to his brain.

At the corner he awakened with a start. Almost guiltily he jumped off the bus and started walking home. His footsteps echoed in the streets, which were empty except for harlots. A tram, all red and white with its lights blazing, came by with a horrid clangour. He was walking in a dream. Not a thought of Bedbug, not a thought of Maisie was in his head. Just sleep. A soft bed, rising up and enveloping the weight of his sinking body. There was grit in his eyes; his nostrils were sore.

A coffee-stall, a red oasis of light and warmth, was before him. It was not such a bad idea. He went up to it and laid a forearm on the greasy counter, resting his left foot on the wheel-spokes as though they were the brass foot-rails of a bar. The man behind the counter had ginger hair. He rose, glad to have a customer to break the monotony.

'What d'you want?'

'Tea please, and . . .' the Gilt Kid's eyes roved the shelves. Cigarettes, matches, tins of salmon, cheesecakes, plum cakes. 'And a piece of plum cake.' He rapped a sixpence on the counter, milled edge downwards.

'Blimey,' Ginger recoiled in horror, 'don't have none of that plum cake, mister, that is if you don't want to go stone-deaf.'

'All right.' The Gilt Kid's grin at the threadbare joke was a weary expanse. 'Give us a ham roll then.'

'Sorry, mister, ain't got no ham rolls.'

'All right, give us a sav and a slice.'

'Cup o' tea, sav and a slice,' intoned Ginger. He poured out the tea into a thick cup, lavishly lacing it with soft sugar from the bowl on the counter, speared the red saveloy out of the urn and laid it on a cracked plate together with a slice of bread and butter. 'Sauce?' He held the bottle poised in his hand.

'No. Yes.' What did it matter anyway?

'You look miserable, mister,' said Ginger taking the six-pence. 'What's a matter? Ain't you had no crumpet?'

'No.' The monosyllable was curt. It was too bloody true that he'd had no crumpet.

'Blimey,' Ginger's back was turned. He was ringing up the sixpence on the cash register. 'Fancy staying up as late as this and not having no crumpet. You must be a bit slow, mister. No wonder you're miserable.'

Another man came up to the stall.

'Cup of tea and hot pie,' he said.

'No,' repeated the Gilt Kid, 'I didn't get no crumpet.'

The other customer looked at him curiously. The Gilt Kid was oblivious. He was being tortured by an idea. He dipped the end of his sausage into the sauce. It burned his mouth. He drank his tea. It scalded his raw palate. Ginger was right. He hadn't had no crumpet. He took off his hat. There were plenty of cows up round Victoria Station.

'No,' he said to Ginger. 'You're right, mate. I didn't have no crumpet. She went off with old Bedbug.'

He drifted up back to Victoria again.

The other customer looked at his retreating back significantly.

'What's the matter with that bloke? Doolally?'

'No,' said Ginger, sympathetically, 'his tart's got the bedbugs so he didn't get no crumpet. Enough to make a bloke a bit miserable staying up all this time and not getting none.'

The Gilt Kid was still bareheaded. His hair hung in streaks across his forehead. He was stuffing all his money except two pounds into the lining of his hat. There was no sense in getting breeched, even if he were following Ginger's advice.

He was in Wilton Road by the time he had his hat on again. A girl stopped him. There was something familiar about her.

'I think you want to talk to me, darling,' she said and then held her hand up to her mouth as if she were trying to push the words back again.

'What are you doing here, Molly?' he asked.

'Things were a bit bad up West so I thought I'd try my luck here.' She tried to brazen it out.

'But I told you to go to kip.'

'Yes, but you left without paying the bill.'

There was no heat in their words. They were not arguing, but simply telling each other facts.

'Yes, but there was plenty of dough for that and for your kip, too.'

'Oh no there wasn't, then. Isabella said you had steak and chips for yourself, sent out for two quarts of beer and treated the others at the top of the café, too. It came to sixteen and a tanner altogether.

'You lying bitch,' he said without rancour and passed on.

When he had got up as far as the New Victoria he paused. Perhaps he was wronging the poor kid. Perhaps she was telling the truth after all. It was quite like Isabella to pull a fast one like that.

He turned round. It was too late. He could see her walking off with a fat man in the opposite direction.

All the women round here, he said to himself, look lousy. None of them are much good. Old Bedbug's got the winner. I got the loser. Bedbug gets Maisie. Molly gets a oncer out of me; Isabella gets sixteen and a sprat out of Molly; and the fat man gets Molly herself. I get nothing but a pain in the neck. Yes, it looks like the Gilt Kid's the steamer, for sure, this time.

MORNING

When he awakened he was alone in a strange room. A weak sunbeam was in his eyes. The bedclothes were crumpled. His own clothes and a woman's were piled on a chair.

He sat up in bed and looked round.

A woman, wearing nothing but step-ins, was sitting by the wash-stand. She had his hat on her knees and all his money in her hands. Suddenly aware that he was looking at her she turned round guiltily.

'My, ain't you fixed well, darling,' she said, trying to brave it out.

'Fixed well be damned,' he said, 'you put that money back, there ought to be eighteen and a half nicker, or I'll get up and break every bone in your body, you lousy old cow.'

'Oh, darling, ain't you mean, only giving me a oncer when you've got all that,' she pouted.

'Come on, hurry up you lousy old mare, unless you want a right hook to that stinking old kisser of yours.'

'Smarty, ain't you,' she mocked. 'Puts all his dough in his hat. The poor kid doesn't know that's the first place a girl looks when she's breeching a fellow.'

She was apostrophizing the wash-stand.

'I won't warn you again.'

'Warn! Hark at him. Why, you poor wet, you couldn't hurt nobody. You're not a man. You're a pouf. A bleeding nigh enuff it's my belief. You couldn't box kippers, you couldn't, talking about right hooks.'

'All right.'

Resignedly he got out of bed. There was a dull ache in his temples and he felt sick, but the muscles rippled on his slim body as he stood there naked on the oilcloth. He clenched his fists.

'I'll show you who's a pouf.'

'Call yourself a man do you this morning, Queenie? Well you wasn't one last night, see. You gets into bed and goes straight off to kip, never touched me you didn't, you great iron.'

'Going to put that dough back?'

His right arm swung up in a semi-circle. She caught the glint of his eye and knew that he meant business.

'You hit me if you dare,' she screamed.

'I dare all right.'

He tensed his arm. The muscles stood out.

'All right, all right, don't be so hasty. I was only kidding. Can't you take a joke? Here's your eighteen and a half oncers.'

She bundled up the money into the hat and dropped it on the floor as though it were something obscene.

'Not that kind of a joke,' he said and vomited into the slop-pail. He lifted his head, feeling rather better. Reaching for his trousers he heard the chink of silver in the pockets.

Ah, she had not gone down his bins then, just looked straight away at his hat, the cunning bitch.

His trousers on, he reached for the pound notes lying in the crown of the upturned hat and stuffed them into his pocket.

'Aren't you going to give me half a crown for my taxi, darling?'

'I'm going to give you a kick in the minge if you don't shut up.'

He sat down again on the edge of the bed.

'Christ, I know I'd had a couple or so drinks last night, but I must have been a bloody sight drunker that I thought to have picked up with an old mare like you.'

'Don't you talk dreadful?' she said.

He pulled his shirt over his shoulders. Lifting his arms made him dizzy again. He flopped on to the bed. Lying there, recumbent and miserable, he asked her questions.

'Well, what happened last night? Where did I pick you up, how did I pick you up, and what's even more important, why did I pick you up?'

'It was up at Victoria, you was blind drunk and half-asleep. That's all, Alfred.'

'Yeah,' he said reflectively. 'That certainly seems to explain everything pretty well. And, you may as well know, my name's George – Pola Negri.'

'And mine's Connie – Frankenstein.'

'King Kongie you mean. And now where the hell are we and what's the time?'

'We're in an hotel just near Wilton Road and it's round about eleven.'

'Christ. Kind of late.'

He tried to struggle up again and found the effort rather exhausting. Suddenly he caught sight of the woman.

'Oh for Christ's sake get me out of here before I set about you. You give me the sick sitting up there.'

'All right, all right, nothing to get excited about.' She crossed her legs. Her thighs were white and shapeless. 'Got a fag, ducks?'

'I've got a wicked right.'

He got off the bed and started fumbling for his shoes. The blood rushing to his head as he stooped down made him feel bad again. He was conscious of having a whole lot to do. He found his shoes and started putting them on.

'What time do they open round here?'

'Ha'past eleven, darling. Watchew going to do – buy us a drink?'

'Yes, of arsenic.'

He walked to the dressing-table and tied his tie.

'Gawd blimey, ain't you dirty?'

'Dirty?' he rounded on her fiercely. 'Dirty? What the hell do you mean, dirty? I'm not a lousy old cow like you.'

'No? But you don't wash yourself in the morning.'

'Wash myself! Christ, I'm going to the barber's and have the whole works. Shave, shampoo, face massage, vibro, friction, and then I'm going to the baths and have a bake-out. I'm going to send my clothes to be fumigated and I'm going into the chemist to have a shot of 606 and even then I expect I'll have got every bloody kind of dose through kipping with you.'

'Yes and a pig in the groin,' she added placidly.

He pulled on his coat and thrust his hat on his head.

'Good-bye. I hope they'll poke you into the Lock Hospital.'

'Soldier's farewell to you.'

He slammed the door behind him. Out in the street he caught sight of a clock. It was just half-past eleven. Good, just right for a livener. He walked into the saloon bar of the nearest pub. He was the first customer and the barmaid was stacking the glasses on the counter.

'Give me a double brandy, please, and a splash.'

She gave his crumpled collar and unshaven face a comprehensive stare, drawing, and drawing correctly, her own conclusions.

'Nice morning,' she said as she poured out his drink.

'Yes? Can't say I've seen much of it.'

She set down the drink on the counter. He looked at it distastefully as though it contained poison.

'Better give me a large Gold Flake,' he said.

Silently she laid the cigarettes before him. He drew a crumpled ten-shilling note from his pocket.

'Sorry it's so dirty,' he apologized.

He felt weak and self-deprecatory. Every movement, every action of his seemed to call for an excuse. He lit a cigarette and watched the bubbles rising in his glass. The barmaid handed him his change. Even then he did not drink. Sitting there, effortless, inert and watching the bubbles rise seemed good enough for him. He did not know whether he was going to enjoy his drink or not, whether, even, he would be able to get it down safely. With a facile acquiescence in his condition he sat looking at his glass. His tongue was dry and swollen.

Suddenly he made an effort. Another customer had just come in and the Gilt Kid did not want to look a fool in front of him. Vanity gave him courage. He lifted the glass, opened his mouth and poured the brandy down his gullet in one draught. Although he had not tasted it the brandy made a warm glow, of which he was immediately conscious, in his stomach. The warmth began to spread.

'Give us another.'

Yes sir, he had needed that drink.

He swallowed his second double brandy and soda rapidly and then, calling for a third, sat over it. There were, he knew, a lot of things to be thought out. He spread, with a characteristic gesture, his long thief's fingers fanwise on the bar in front of him and then, noticing their ingrained grime and the black rims of his nails, hastily hid them from sight.

He lit another cigarette – an action which he knew helped thought. What was the programme for today? Lots of things were on his mind.

Get cleaned up first. A nice three-quarters of an hour in a barber's chair and a clean shirt. And then get drunk again. That seemed to be the best plan, simplest, most obvious, easiest and most comforting, but an awkward notion persisted in the back of his head, a notion that there was something important to be done. Thoughtfully he sipped his drink. A light came into his bleared eyes. He dropped his cigarette on the floor and snapped his fingers.

'Maisie!'

That was right. He had to see Maisie.

A smile formed itself. Gosh, wasn't she the smashing girl, even if she was cased up with old Bedbug. And he was going to spend an afternoon with her. Well, that beat hell. He would have to give up drinking for today. He sipped his drink. The bar was filling up. It was nearly twelve o'clock. Men were shaking hands and buying each other drinks.

There was something else that was damned important. What was it? He shook his head trying to drive the mists out of it.

'Curly.'

He had got to go on a job with Curly Simmonds. He sat up at the bar looking vacantly in front of him for a full minute. All the apprehension, the quick tingling of his pulses which he knew from experience was on him.

This was going to be, he thought, the first job he'd done since he had come out of stir. Had his hand lost its cunning; was he still the screwsman that he used to be? It was one thing to agree overnight to do a gaff. It was something totally different to think about it next morning.

Well, there was Maisie. If he was going to have Maisie, going to get her away from old Bedbug, he had to have money, and there was only one way he knew of getting money. On the twirl. OK. He was going on the job. He was going thieving. He'd get the dough. Maisie was worth it.

'Good morning.'

He finished his drink and walked out into the street. Barber next.

Walking, he passed a chemist's. The thought struck him. He might as well.

He went into the shop. There was a smell of soap, tooth-paste and bath salts. A kind of undercurrent of rubber gloves and disinfectant joined it. A girl was at the counter. He drew back hesitantly.

'Yes, sir.'

'Er. Is the chemist in? The man I mean.'

Damn having tarts in a chemist's gaff, anyway.

'I'll call him.'

Probably she knows what I want, he thought, bitterly. And he was right. She did.

The chemist came out from the interior of the shop. His glasses of rimless pince-nez gave him a disapproving air. He looked at his dishevelled customer.

'Yes, sir, what do you want?'

His manner did not invite confidence.

The Gilt Kid took a step forward and began to stammer in low tones. He felt he was begging a favour rather than making a purchase.

'Look,' he began, 'it's this. I . . . er . . . well, you see . . .'

He glanced round apprehensively at the girl assistant. She was ostentatiously uninterested in him, making little blobs of sealing-wax on white parcels of medicines. He let his words come out with a rush.

'I went with a woman last night, could you give me something, a draught or anything that'll make sure I'm OK.'

'I'll fix you up.' The chemist was not particularly interested. 'Did you have a drink, too?' he asked.

'Why, yes, sure.'

'Well, in that case I'll let you have something to cure your fat head, too, if you like.'

'Thanks.'

Christ, this chemist was a pal.

The Gilt Kid watched him disappear once more into the recesses at the back of the shop. There was an interval of a few minutes while the chemist did things with phials and bottles. All the time he stood shifting awkwardly from one foot to another. It was not so much the fact that the girl was staring at him with disapproval or reproof. She was ignoring him, a fact far more galling to a bloke's pride.

Perhaps it might have been better to have shaved first. Hell!

The chemist came out at last. In either hand he carried a small glass.

'Drink this first,' he commanded, 'then this.'

The Gilt Kid obeyed him without a tremor. He took a glass in either hand and tossed them off – one and the other. His stomach turned over and his mouth became filled with a bitterness the like of which he had not previously known. His teeth were all dried up, his tongue like a piece of tanned leather. He tried to swallow his saliva and found it impossible.

'How much?' he gasped. He was damned if he let a lousy pill-roller know just how bad he felt.

'A shilling, please.'

He paid the coin over in silence and walked out. Never before had he realized that hell was purchasable on such easy terms.

A couple of doors up there was a barber's. He went in. There was still an unbearable taste in his mouth. A chair was vacant. He sat in it.

'Yes, sir?' asked the barber.

'The issue. Hair cut, shave, shampoo, friction, vibro, face massage, head massage and don't talk to me about football or try to sell me any razor blades. Get me?'

'Yes, sir.'

The barber's laugh was sycophantic. He had evidently a client whom it paid to humour. He had given a good order: there would be a good tip. He draped the towel about him.

'And how about a nice manicure?'

The Gilt Kid looked at his hands. Unwashed and grimy they were, with the traces of seven and a half months of making scrubbing brushes and sewing mailbags still on them. He laughed.

'OK. Better let me wash them first.'

When he had sat down in the chair again and the hairdresser was getting ready to take action an idea struck the Gilt Kid. It would save going home anyway.

'Got a lather-boy or anyone spare about the place? Someone who could run a message for me?'

'Why yes, sir.'

The Gilt Kid dived down into his pocket and pulled out a pound note.

'Well, give him this and tell him to go out and get me a new shirt. I want a blue one, Yankee-style, you know the kind with a collar attached and you put it on like a coat. I wear size fifteen and a half. Tell him to pester about seven and six for it.'

The barber transferred these instructions and the money to the lather-boy. The Gilt Kid raised his voice again.

'Oi!'

'Yes, sir?'

'Tell him to get me a bar of chocolate, too. I got the hell of a taste in my mouth.'

'Yes, sir.'

The barber came back.

'Everything fixed up?'

'Yes, sir.'

'Well, shoot.'

The Gilt Kid lay back in the chair with his eyes shut, beatifically ready to suffer in order to be beautiful.

SCALEY

It was a tired-eyed, if comparatively clean, Gilt Kid that walked up Victoria Street. He was not thinking particularly hard of what he ought to do. To eat was the dominating idea. Great omnibuses and vans lumbered and roared past him, taxi-cabs and private cars hooted, bicycle bells shrilled, people thronged the pavements having poured out of offices and shops in search of lunch. We go to work to earn the dough to buy the grub to get the strength to go to work.

All this noise was getting on his nerves. These damned great buses and having to be dodging people, people walking along talking, three abreast, people staring in shop windows, damn great plate glass windows like the Army & Navy Stores. There were some decent furs in that window. Almost worth doing a smash there some day. He had a screwing job to do that night. There was a smell of petrol.

He was crossing the top of Strutton Ground. There was something familiar about the back of the man in front of him. And the way he walked. It looked like – it was – Scaley Waite.

'Hallo Scaley?'

Scaley Waite turned round sharply. He was stocky and dark. One of his eyes had a slight cast. He looked at the other cautiously for about fifteen seconds and then shot his hand out.

'The Gilt Kid,' he said.

'Well, how's the game, Scaley?'

The Gilt Kid's eyes were summing up his acquaintance. He looked fairly prosperous. Decent hat, well-shaved, hair cut loose, clean collar, polished shoes, although, of course, that might be all front.

Scaley pursed up a non-committal mouth.

'Just wages,' he said. 'Mustn't complain I suppose. It might be worse. How you doing?'

'Had a bit of a night out last night and I'm still feeling under the weather.'

Scaley was appraising the Gilt Kid carefully. Then he spoke cautiously.

'Still at it?'

The Gilt Kid nodded. There was no need to speak when signs did equally well.

'Where you going now?'

'Just off to have a tightener some place.'

'Any place in particular?'

'No.'

'There's a boozer round the corner here serves lunches. I've had my grub, but I'll sit and watch you eat and have a couple of drinks if you like. There's something I want to talk to you about.'

'OK. Suits me.'

They turned down a side street. The Gilt Kid felt he must talk. He hated this air of conspiratorial secrecy.

'Seen any of the boys lately?'

'Yes.' Scaley's taciturnity was difficult to break.

'How were they doing?'

'On the ribs most of them and without the guts to take a chance and do themselves a bit of good.'

'Uh-huh.'

They reached the public house which Scaley had indi-cated and entered it, going up the long passage to the saloon bar. The Gilt Kid picked up the menu card and ordered Roast Beef with Yorkshire Pudding, Roast Potatoes and French Beans.

'Aren't you going to have any chuck, Scaley?'

'Didn't I tell you that I'd had it?'

'What'll you have to drink then?'

'Brown ale.'

Yes you would, thought the Gilt Kid. You look just the kind of fellow to drink brown ale. Not wanting to start on the brandy stakes himself he had a half-pint of bitter. He carried the drinks over to a table and sat down, waiting for the waitress to bring the food. Scaley Waite sat down next to him with a deliberation that was somehow offensive.

They both drank in silence and for different reasons. The Gilt Kid was not feeling like opening up a conversation that was going to be rebuffed. Scaley made him feel like a kid, prattling to a not over-attentive uncle. Scaley, for his part, wanted the girl to have brought the order and cleared off before he spoke. What he had to say he wanted to say without being either interrupted or overheard.

When at last the plate had been laid down before the Gilt Kid, Scaley spoke.

'Got any dough, kid?' he asked.

'Yes. A bit.'

The Gilt Kid's answer was purposely evasive and Scaley, who hated lending money himself, could appreciate the motives behind his companion's manner of speaking.

'Could you use some more?'

'Sure,' answered the Gilt Kid, thinking of Maisie and putting a large forkful of meat into his mouth.

'Good. Like to do a gaff with me then?'

The Gilt Kid laid down his knife and fork and looked at Scaley thoughtfully. His eyes narrowed as he considered the other's question. He had never been on a job with Scaley. Yes, he felt, it should be all right. Scaley looked as if he might be a pretty good screwsman. He looked the sort of man who would not leave anything to chance. Probably, thought the Gilt Kid, without malice, there would probably be a carve-up at the end when it came to sharing out the dough. Scaley was certainly the sort of man to stick to more than his fair share.

'I wouldn't trust you, you bastard,' he said to himself, making a resolution to come and see the stuff sold so as to make dead sure that he got his corner all right.

His scrutiny finished, he picked up his knife and fork again.

'What kind of a job?' he asked.

'Screwing. Don't talk so bloody loud.'

'That don't tell me nothing.' The Gilt Kid lowered his voice to the same pitch as Scaley's. 'There's screwing and screwing.'

'Sure there is. But this is a sweet gaff. You can bet on that. I wouldn't be on it if it was a bogy.'

That's true enough, thought the Gilt Kid. Aloud he said: 'Come on, Scaley, come clean. Give me the whole strength of it. I won't let you down.'

'I don't believe you would. Have some more beer.'

'Thanks.' The Gilt Kid emptied his glass. 'I'll take your plate up to the counter, too, if you're through. It'll save the girl coming over here again.'

It was caution, not consideration, that prompted Scaley into this move.

He came back again with the two glasses and sitting down began to talk, if still cautiously, a little more confidently than before.

'Listen, kid,' he began, 'it's a real winner. I'd do it on my jack if I could so as not to have to share the dough, but if you'd like to come in on it with me, we'll split half-way.'

'Of course we bloody well will. I wouldn't come in on it else.'

Scaley ignored the interruption and went on in his even low tones.

'There was another bloke I was letting in on it, but the dopey bastard went and got himself nicked for being in possession of housebreaking implements. The mug was walking about with a cane in his pocket. He wasn't going out on a job or nothing either. Proper soft I call it to take unnecessary risks. And what's more he's under the Act so he'll get a stretch for it at the very least.'

'Blimey, that's tough. But supposing now he's nicked, he comes his guts and puts the squeak in, hoping the bogies will make it easier for him.'

'No fear of that. He don't know the address even. I didn't tell him any more details in case something happened,' answered Scaley grimly.

'Well,' said the Gilt Kid, tolerantly conscious that he was refreshed by food and drink and was going to see his girl that afternoon; facts which would have put him at peace with the whole world, were it not for the fact, less peace-making, that he was going on a job that evening obtruded itself, mitigating his joy. 'Well, come on, let's hear your agony. Make it snappy.'

The cast in Scaley's eye seemed more pronounced than ever as he hesitatingly figured things out.

'OK,' he said at last. 'I'll shoot. Listen. It's in the suburbs. A ready money gaff. There's over £400 there in small notes and snow. It's a rent-collector's office. Feel like it?'

'Sure.'

The Gilt Kid's mind was working fast. Four hundred nicker – that meant at least two-fifty. People on the crook always exaggerated the strength of a gaff. Still, half two-fifty was one-twenty-five. He could certainly use a hundred and twenty-five pounds making a splash with Maisie. No chance of a carve-up either. Scaley could not pretend to have flogged the stuff for less than he had got. He would make him turn out his pockets or break his neck. Sure.

'OK,' he said. 'I'm on. Is it a dead gaff?'

'Sure, there ain't a soul there.'

'Fine. How do we get in?'

'That where the bastard of it comes in.'

'Why? Is it a bogy getting in?'

'No. 'Tain't that. You see it's a bit dangerous. You might break your neck or something if you slip.'

'I get you. It's on the climb then.'

'Kind of.'

'Oh, for God's sake, Scaley, come clean and quit stalling. Give us the whole office.'

Scaley looked round with a caution that was quite unnecessary. There was nobody within earshot.

'Well, don't interrupt. Let me explain in my own way. This dough's in an office on the fourth floor of a building in the main street, see. At the back there's a block of flats which comes up to nearly the same height as the building. This block's got a flat roof. You can get out on to it by the fire-escape door.'

'That's funny.'

'Why?'

'I was hearing about another job that you get at almost the same way. They didn't ought to build those fire-escape doors if they don't want their drums screwed. Ne'mind. Come on. Spill it.'

'Well, when you get out on to the roof of this block of flats, you've got to walk along a girder. It's just the ordinary kind of girder they use in buildings. It's five stories up and roughly fifteen feet long. It goes into the wall in the same block as this here rent-collector's offices are.'

He paused impressively and then went on in what he imagined were dramatic phrases.

'Now, kid, get this and get it good. Just above where that girder goes in is a window. A fellow standing on another bloke's shoulders could open it. It's an ordinary casement window giving on to the staircase. Once you're through the window all you got to do is to get down the stairs and screw the door of that office.'

'I get you. It sounds easy enough. Now what else is in this building?'

'On the ground floor shops, and some more on the first. A draper's. On the floor above there's stock-rooms and the rest's let out in offices.'

'I see. No night-watchmen, caretakers or dogs.'

'Not a one. Didn't I tell you the gaff was dead?'

The Gilt Kid shot out a hand. Scaley took it.

'Right, Scaley, pal, I'm on. I can trust you to have got the details straight and I'm going to trust you to play square with me at the end. No carving-up or else . . .'

He paused significantly. Scaley took the hint and changed the subject hurriedly.

'You don't mind, then, standing on my shoulders on a girder, five storeys up in the air in the dark?'

'Oh, so you want me to do that part then? All right. I'll do it, pal. You can't expect to have a job to do that's all cut and dried with no risk about it.'

'Well, I got the gaff weighed up. I'm entitled to have it a bit more cushy than you,' Scaley apologized.

'That's all right. That's all right,' soothed the Gilt Kid. 'Let's have another drink on it to kind of seal the bargain.'

When he had come back with the recharged glasses and they had toasted each other, the Gilt Kid asked another question.

'When do we go on it?'

'Tonight, of course.'

'Blimey, that's a bit awkward, Scaley mate.'

'What's the matter, turning milky?'

'No, 'tain't that. You see,' he paused, unwilling to let Scaley know that he was going on another job that same night. 'What time do you think of doing it?' he asked suddenly.

Scaley pursed a pair of judicial lips.

'Well, we don't want to be too late. You know what it's like in those suburban districts. Pretty bloody warm if you're out late. We can't have a car either. It would have to be left standing around in the street while we were in the gaff, or else we would have to have another bloke to drive it around and pick us up and that would mean giving him a good drop if not a full corner. How about ten o'clock?'

'No can do.' The Gilt Kid had been working out in his head a rapid time-schedule. 'I tell you what I'll do though. I'll meet you in the West End and you can take me down to the job. We ought to be on it by half ten and you needn't tell me the address if we go down together,' he added slily.

'Right. That'll do then.'

'How about tools?'

'I'll bring them. All you'll need to fetch along is a pair of gloves.'

'Right. Where'll I meet you then?'

'Let's see,' Scaley thought out loud, 'I don't want to meet you outside any place as there's no sense in hanging around in the West End with a cane and Christ knows what else in my sky-rocket. I'll see you in a café some place.'

'OK. Make it Isabella's in Lisle Street.' The Gilt Kid, suddenly remembering the yarn that Molly had told him the night before, thought that he might as well check up on it.

'Yes. I know the place you mean. All right, I'll be there at ten. There's a lot of poufs gets in there, though, ain't there?'

'Sure. What of it? They don't do no harm and sometimes they put you on to a nice little job.'

'Yes. But they talk too much.'

Talking was to Scaley the unforgivable sin. After a couple of minutes he rose.

'Well I got to slide now,' he said, 'got to go over to the Jumbo to see a bloke.'

They went out together into Strutton Ground and shook hands.

'So long, Scaley.'

'Good-bye, kid. See you at Isabella's at ten.'

'Right.'

The Gilt Kid walked along Victoria Street again. He was feeling good, real good. He was going to keep a date with Maisie and soon, with any luck, he would have plenty of money, and would be able to take her away from that snotty old cowson Bedbug. Yes. It certainly did look as though things were going to break good.

He turned into a hosier's to buy a pair of gloves.

MEET THE GIRL FRIEND

At Victoria, for he had walked back in that direction again, he caught a number 16 bus. At first he carried the gloves in his hands, but, thinking that perhaps they made him look a bit too flash and to anyone who knew him certainly gave away the fact that he was still on the knock-off, he put them into his pocket.

Mounting to the top deck the Gilt Kid found he had a nicely padded seat all to himself. So nicely padded was it in fact that he succeeded in making up some of the sleep that he had lost the night before, by dozing all the way up Grosvenor Gardens and Park Lane. It was not until he was well up the Edgware Road that he awakened.

Edgware Road, he thought, as he opened his eyes. Edgware Road, the street that leads to Maida Vale. Funny how many whores live in Maida Vale.

He closed his drowsy, heavy-lidded eyes and fell off to sleep once more, waking up automatically as the bus stopped most conveniently at the corner of the street in which lived Maisie.

He scrambled down the stairs and jumped off on to the pavement before the bus had started again.

He walked down the back street in which Maisie lived. On either side of the road there were blocks of flats. Half-tidy gaffs they looked, too.

He made a resolution to come up this neighbourhood drumming some time and see if he could not pick out a nice little chat to screw. Most of the inhabitants he knew to be either Jews or ladies of easy virtue; both of those types like jewellery and the ladies had a tendency to leave things lying about.

Yes, he thought, if he could get one of these lays weighed up properly there would be an even break of getting a good night's wages.

Then, attempting to change his thoughts abruptly he said to himself: 'Snap out of it, kid, you're going to see your jane. For Christ's sake, can't you feel romantic or something?'

At last he came to Maisie's block. He walked up the stairs, looking to see, from force of habit, whether anybody had been foolish enough to have left open a front door. Eventually he came to Maisie's flat, which he noticed with a laugh to be on the top floor.

Just like the gaff that he and Curly were going to screw that night.

He took off his hat, smoothed his hair with the palm of his hand, straightened his tie and rang the door-bell. For a couple of minutes he waited, then he rang again.

A dark despondency clutched at his heart. It was going to be the same as always. He was going to miss Maisie as usual. He had come on the wrong day, or to the wrong flat, or else she was out. Something was bound to have come unstuck. It was dollars to doughnuts on that.

He was just preparing to touch the bell-push again, this time a little more forcefully to show how annoyed he was – kicking the cat, so to speak – when he heard a rat-tat-tat. That noise could only be made by one thing. By a woman walking in high-heeled shoes over a stone or wooden floor.

He straightened his tie again and stood there waiting, hat in hand.

The door opened. It was Maisie's hand which opened it. There she stood, wearing a *peignoir* and mules. She was welcoming him with a smile.

'Ken!'

'Maisie!'

He took her in his arms. As the intensity of the embrace

increased so did his grip on his hat-brim diminish. At last it dropped from his fingers on to the floor. He released Maisie and stepped back a pace, catching her hands in his. For a moment he looked at her with delectation and then spoke.

'Old Bedbug here?'

'Of course not, darling.'

'Did he kip here last night?'

A nod.

'The bastard. I'd like to break his gaddam bloody neck.'

'Ken! You mustn't talk like that. Come in, too. Don't stand there in the hallway where everybody can see and hear you.'

'Kind of ashamed of me, huh?'

'Don't talk soft. Come on in.'

She pulled him in and kicked the door to behind him so it closed with a slam. He looked around, at the distempered walls, at the oak table with a silver salver, at the hat-stand.

'Blimey,' he said, purposely accentuating the Cockney in his voice. 'Ain't you pound-noteish?'

'Ken,' she pouted, 'don't talk so common.' Then, brightening: 'Come along. Let's go into the drawing-room.'

'Droring-room. Cripes no. Let's go into the bleeding throne-room.'

The Gilt Kid looked round the drawing-room with awe in his eyes. He had seen some caseos in his time but this was just about the flashest. Maisie's choice had been allowed to run riot. There were Louis XV chairs, a satinwood kidney-shaped writing-desk, a heavy leather chesterfield, and an expensive radiogram. The carpet was of thick pile and the curtains of silk. On most of the chairs, and on the mantelpiece, were spindly-legged French dolls; on the chesterfield was an enormous box of chocolates.

'Well, what do you think of it?'

It was quite impossible for Maisie to keep the pride out of her voice as she asked the question. Anyway she did not try.

'Did old Bedbug pay for it?'

Despair in all its keenness was the Gilt Kid's portion. He knew he could not compete with all this, and he could hardly ask Maisie to give it up for his sake.

'Of course.'

'Christ, he must be a generous old bloke. Did he pay my bill at the whatsaname last night?'

'Yes.'

'Good. I've caught him for something then, the old cowson.' The thought gave him the keenest satisfaction.

'Yes. It was very naughty of you.'

'Say, Maisie, kid. Don't talk so bloody grammatical. Naughty? Who the hell ever heard such a word? You don't half come out with some strokes. You'll be slapping my wrist next.'

He put a chocolate in his mouth and sat down on the chesterfield.

'Did he give you these and all?'

'Of course he did.' Maisie took a chocolate and sat down next to him. 'He always brings me chocolates and flowers whenever he calls.'

'Well, if you think I'm going to come that caper you're mistaken.'

'Oh, Ken. Don't you love me enough to do that?'

Maisie put on the expression of a little girl whose stern father has refused her permission to stay up late, an expression which she usually found very effective in arousing the protective spirit in an unwary male.

The Gilt Kid gave her a look of disgust.

'What the hell kind of a steamer do you think I am?' he asked with an unassumed indignation. 'I can get a girl to fall for me without having to dive down in my skies to make her.'

He looked at her so fiercely that she crumpled up. Then, taking her in his arms, he kissed her first with passionate ferocity, an inversion of the way in which Maisie was used to being kissed. Then he released her from his grasp and looked her in the eyes again.

'Can't I, Maisie, kid.'

It was a statement rather than a question. She dropped her eyes in an affirmation which she hardly cared to admit. Pleased at this, he let a bantering tone creep into his voice.

'You're a right person to ask a bloke round to your flat. Haven't you got a drink of any kind around the dump?'

She rose, glad of an opportunity to break the tension.

'Of course.' Her voice – to his annoyance – still aped the lady. 'What would you like? I can offer you whisky, port or gin and vermouth.'

'Make it a scotch and soda.' He spoke impersonally as he would to a barmaid, but his eyes followed her round the room.

For a moment her *peignoir* gaped open, revealing a glimpse of the pink supple flesh beneath. A pulse began to beat in his temples. She mixed the drinks and came back with the glasses. He took his from her without a word. She sat down again beside him on the chesterfield. Her right hand held her glass, her left kept the *peignoir* together. The air seemed electric. She gazed at him over the rim of her glass with her stupid, pretty eyes.

The Gilt Kid swallowed a mouthful of whisky and, putting the glass down on the floor at his feet, fumbled in his pocket for a cigarette. Finding one, he lighted up and then tried to talk normally.

'You happy with old Bedbug, kid?'

She nodded over her glass, her wide eyes till staring.

'Like to give him the belt and come and live with me instead?'

She nodded again. Her whisky was still untasted.

'Well, why the hell don't you then?'

He blew out a puff of smoke with the air of a professor of mathematics dotting the final full stop to a thesis proving the inadmissibility of Vandermonde's Theorem.

That puff did the trick. Its assurance goaded her to speak.

'How can I, Ken, honey?' she asked. 'What are we going to use for money?'

'This.'

He thrust a hand into his pocket and drew out what remained of his wad.

'Look, kid. I got dough. Not much, I know, but a bit. I'll get some more. I never go broke. And when I do it don't last long.' He hurried along to cover up the illogicality of the sentence. 'I'm going on a job tonight and I'll get a big pile out of it. Plenty of the old vodeodo. I'll be well-fixed. You give old man Bedbug the belt and we'll tally up together. How about it?'

She shook her head sadly. As a matter of fact, she was rather annoyed with the Gilt Kid for his periodic reappearances in her life and, unknowingly, resented the disturbing effect that he had on her nerves and flesh.

'Listen, Ken,' she said. 'Why can't we go on as we are? I'll let him go on paying the rent of this place and all that and every minute I can get away from him I'll spend with you. I'll even try to get him to give me more money so that I can work some to you.'

She saw him stiffen.

'Look here, Maisie,' he stormed. 'You can bloody well tie that line of talk up in a bag and throw it into the bleeding Thames. I don't stand for it from you or any other little bitch in the world and the sooner you get that into your nut the better. I may be a thief, but I'm not going to have anyone make a ponce out of me, see? I get my money clean. I take a risk for it. I go on a job and get it. That's me.'

'Why don't you go straight, Ken?' she asked. 'Then you might get a girl to stick to you.'

'What the hell am I going straight on? Selling matches in the Strand?'

'Going on jobs, going on jobs! That's all that boys like you can talk about. It only lands you in prison in the end.'

'What if it does? I've been in stir before and done my time. I can do it again. I'm only just out, come to that.'

'Yes I know.' She waved her glass with a weary gesture. 'Yes I know. That's all you think about. "Oh, I can do my time." What am I going to do when you're in prison?'

He sat bolt upright. There was a spot of red in both his cheeks. His mouth had become a straight line. He was furious.

'Pipe down, Maisie. That's enough of that. You're just like all the other janes of your sort. On the make all the time. You aren't a woman at all. A woman sticks by her man. You just wonder what the hell's going to happen to you while your man's suffering. It's no giggle being in the nick, I can tell you. You ought to be proud that you know a fellow that's fond enough of you to risk his liberty to give you a good time. I know that if I'm going to have you I've got to have money and if I'm going to have money I've got to be on the crook. That's the only way I know of getting it. And I'm going to have you and the sooner you get hold of that the better.'

'Don't shout at me, Ken.'

'Shout at you is it, now? By Christ, I won't be shouting much longer. I'll knock you spark out if you don't pipe down.'

He picked up his glass, emptied it and set it down again on the floor with a bang.

'I notice you don't say anything about marrying me.'

'Marrying you? That's your grief now? How much has old Bedbug said about the splicing stakes?'

She pouted. It was a question difficult to answer. She tried to turn it.

'Oh, that's different.'

'Different, oh, and how may I ask?'

'Mr Bedborough's a gentleman.'

'Oh, so MR BLOODY BEDBOROUGH is a gentleman, eh? Well, he ain't too much of a rye mush to keep a working-class girl as his fancy bit, is he?' He held up his hand. 'Now, don't argue. Just a minute. You call him a gentleman. Well, I don't lay any claim to be that, thank God, but I do claim to be something a bit more'n that. I'm a man and that's more than he can say. And to prove that I'm a man and not afraid, I'll offer to marry you if you like. So there.'

Maisie melted. All this arguing and shouting had been too much for her little brain. The Gilt Kid, by offering to marry her, had completed the task which his assumption of virility had begun. She had not noticed his left-handed compliment. Even while she had been ordering him not to shout at her, she had been capitulating. To the back of her mind she thrust that longing for security.

'Oh, Ken,' she said softly, 'would you do that?'

'Sure, I would, kid. I'd do even that to get you.'

She leant forward and fell into his arms. He kissed her with the air of a conqueror. And then, letting her go, he asked: 'Well, what about another drink?'

'You're a terrible boozer, aren't you?'

With a wry smile she rose and patted him on the cheek.

'Well, a fellow got to celebrate getting married, ain't it?'

She laughed contentedly and went to fetch the decanter and syphon.

'I'd better bring them across and you can help yourself.'

'Sure. That's a good idea. And while you're at it, put the old gramophone on. Let's be a bit lively for Christ's sake.'

He looked around. He was – and he knew it – monarch of all he surveyed. The 'St Louis Blues' began to fill the drawing-room of the Maida Vale flat for which Mr Francis Bedborough paid the rent. All was well.

They had played three records – both sides of each – and now the gramophone was silent. The Gilt Kid, who had been recharging his glass with whisky and squirting a little soda into it every now and again, less each time so that at last it held practically neat spirits, was feeling Nicely thank you. He shifted his position so that Maisie lay not quite so heavily on his chest. Her *peignoir* slipped open again, but this time she did not bother to secure it. After all they were engaged. Absently, he cupped one of her firm little breasts in his hands.

'About this marrying, kid,' he began, 'What do we have to do? I don't know. I never got spliced up before.'

'Go and see a parson. He'll tell you.'

'Yeah, but when he's given me the wire that don't mean we have to get the job done in his church or does it? Tell you the honest truth I rather thought about seeing if we couldn't get married in a registry office. What they call a civil marriage.'

'Oh, let's get married in a church, Ken. Do let's.' She squirmed.

'All right, then. Have it your own way,' he conceded. 'If you're so damn keen on getting married in church, I'll be big-hearted, but I think it's a load of rot.'

'Oh, Ken, how can you say such things? You are awful.'

'Tell you what,' he said thickly. The whisky was doing its work. 'There ain't no God.'

'Shush, Ken. You mustn't,' she remonstrated.

'If there is a God,' he said, histrionically waving his free hand, 'let Him bring down this ceiling on my head.'

'Now, darling, be careful.' She clutched at him frightened.

Magnanimously he waved away her fears. In his position of bridegroom-elect he was prepared to allow such side-issues as the existence of a deity to be counted out. He had got his girl back, found her again after all this time and had cut out old Bedbug. What the hell more could a man want?

As he caught her hand she snuggled up closer to him. He began to laugh.

'What are you laughing at, darling?' she asked reproach-fully, scared that it might be directed at her.

'Nothing, kid, only it struck me it was a bit funny me tearing into a jewellery gaff and buying you a groin. It'd be a bit more in my line to nick one when you come to think of it. It wouldn't half be a cowson if a screwsman broke into your drum and knocked it off.'

'There'll only be one screwsman in my drum, honey.'

'And who'll that be?'

'You.'

Their lips met. After a pause he began to speak again.

'You know, kid,' he said awkwardly, 'I always think a bloke's a bit of a mug to get all soft over a jane, but, blimey, it looks as if I must be just that mug.'

'Why? Do you love me, Ken?'

'Should say I did.'

'Say it then.'

'Why?'

'Because, well, because I'd like to hear you say it.'

'What's the idea? You trying to make me more of a fool than I am or something? I'm not all that lit up yet.'

'If you really loved me you'd say so.'

'Have it your own way then,' he sighed with an exagger-ated resignation. 'I love you.'

Their lips met again. The Gilt Kid's hands began to get just a little bit ambitious. Custom had taught Maisie just the way to thwart ambitions of that sort. She thrust him away firmly.

'Not yet, Ken, darling. Let's wait until we get married.'

'What the hell,' he said, bewildered at this new move. 'You've had a damn big change somewhere, haven't you? Why, gosh, Maisie, we slept together the very first night we met each other.'

'There's no need to throw a girl's past in her face, is there?'

'Now, for God's sake, don't get all airyated. Never known such a girl as you in my life. We're going to get married, so why shouldn't I have what I've had before and what a lot of other men have had in the meantime?'

'Yes, Ken. But this is different. I thought that you loved me for myself alone.'

He fidgeted irritably.

'Oh my good gawd,' he asked. 'Have we got to go over all that madam? "Oh, there's only one thing you want out of me," you'll say like all the other silly little bitches say. Well, you and all the rest of you ought to be goddamn proud we want your skinny little bodies. That's all women are brought into the world for.'

'Don't you put things nasty?'

'Aw, shut up. I'm sick of all these bloody airs you're putting on. Why can't you forget you've been cased up with a rich bloke and act natural? Why when I first knew you you were a real sporty kid, as game as they made them. And now you keep blathering and blandandering about "Oh, it's different". What's the matter with you, mad or something?'

As always when she met a force stronger than herself Maisie surrendered. It seemed to be the simplest thing to do. She crept a little closer to the Gilt Kid, wanting him to pet her.

'Don't be cross with your Maisie,' she pleaded. 'Love her.'

Absent-mindedly, he began to fondle her and then stopped.

'No, Maisie, we got to talk. We got a lot to say.'

She struggled from his grasp.

'Well, you are a nice one I must say. First you want to pet me and then when I let you you don't want to. What's up?'

'Look here, kid,' he answered striving for expression and fighting the drink, which was slowly stealing his ability for expression, 'you're getting this all wrong. Of course I want to pet you as you call it. That goes without saying. And there ain't no "let" about it, neither. I'll do all the petting I want when I want, just get that.'

'Oh, aren't you the strong man,' she mocked. Then, after a pause: 'Well, go on, what are you waiting for now?'

'It's this, baby,' he said patiently. 'When we started arguing it put a whole lot into my head. A whole lot, I mean, of what we got to say. I mean the time's come for a showdown. We got to come clean, I mean.'

'Don't you mean a lot. I wonder how much I mean to you.'

'Stop fooling. This is serious. We got a lot to say.'

'Well? You keep on saying "we got a lot to say" and you never say it.'

'Here's one thing for a start. What are we going to do with old Bedbug? I know you're going to give him the belt, but when? When are you supposed to be seeing him anyway?'

'Tonight.' Defiantly.

'Well, when you see him tonight you got to say "Frankie", or whatever the hell you call him, "you've got to give me back the key you got to my flat. You're not coming here no more."'

'Oh, I couldn't say that to him, Ken. I just couldn't. It's his flat. He pays the rent.'

'Sure. I know he does the pestering. Well this is just where he's going to be unlucky. He's not coming here no more, at least not while you're here.'

'Oh, Ken! He'll have to come here tonight.'

'What? Kip here d'you mean?'

'Well, no. He hardly ever spends the whole night here. But he'll have to spend a few hours like he always does. He's entitled to that much. And you've got no place to take me yet, have you?'

'Oh, I see.' The Gilt Kid's voice was ominously calm. 'I've got to go out screwing tonight, risking my liberty, chancing my arm on getting about twenty-one months or maybe three-stretch while Mr Bloody Bedbug's up here having a good time with my pusher. Not likely. Not this journey, thank you.'

Maisie began to fiddle with a button on his coat. She needed time to think out how she was going to be able to get the best of both worlds. When the Gilt Kid went on speaking, she found his words, although kindly, to be extremely disconcerting.

'I don't want to have a row, kid, because if we do, I know I'll win it and that's no satisfaction to me. I want you to come to me with a good heart. If I was to say "Come on, kid, pack your things, you're going to get the hell out of here and we'll find you a hotel for the night," you'd refuse at first, but after a bit of shouting and maybe a bit of strong-arm stuff on my part you'd come with me all right. And you know it, don't you?'

She nodded in dumb misery.

'But my idea,' he went on, 'is to see if you can't do it the straight way for a change. I'd even go so far as to say "Let's give old Bedbug a break." He pays the rent you say. Well, when's it pestered up till?'

'The end of the month.'

Maisie could hardly keep back those tears. She saw the flat of which she was so proud being given up and she pictured herself going and living in one room with the Gilt Kid round the Elephant and Castle or in Battersea, or somewhere. Oh, if only she could keep on the flat with Frank paying the rent and have Ken as her husband. His next words confirmed her fears.

'Well, we can't have you staying here till then. I'm not going to let anybody have the opportunity of saying I was poncing on you while that old idiot kept you. Now, when are you seeing him?'

'Tonight, I told you.'

She found herself being remorselessly swept along in his tide of words without a chance of acquiescence or denial.

'Yes, but when and where?'

'He's coming round here at about eight and then he's taking me out to dinner.'

'I see. Well, here's your graft for tonight. I'm going to let him down light, you see. When he floats round here tonight you've got to kid him along everything's OK. If he starts to maul you around though, your line is to keep him at arm's length. And keep him there without letting him get wide. You ought to be able to do that. Any girl who uses her loaf ought to be able to do that. When he's had a good dinner and feels kind of happy then's your cue to spring it on him.

'Say to him, "Bedbug" or "Frankie", or whatever the hell you call him, "The time has come. Even the best of friends must part. Even a beautiful friendship like ours must come unstuck. I know you are a noble enough gentleman to let me lead my own life in my own way. You can be godfather to the kid if you like." You know, something a bit pathetic, like Joan Crawford on the pictures.'

'I'll try, Ken,' she promised, sobbing.

'Yeah, and you'd better try pretty hard too. The only thing is you're such a dopey kind of a jane that if he starts to argue you out of it you'll probably fall for it. He's a bit dopey, too, though, so I expect he'll come the better-man-than-you-are kind of touch and everything'll break good. One thing, mind, if when I come round in the morning, and

I'll be around good and early, I find you and Bedbug aren't adrift, I'll get Bedbug and make you eat his tripes. So help me I will.'

'And when'll we get married, Ken darling?'

She was clinging fast to him now, crying quite frankly and unashamedly.

'Just as soon as I see the parson and get it fixed up and I'll go round and see him first thing in the morning. And don't you tell me you're crying tears of joy or I'll crown you, see.'

He kissed her again and again and then, having felt her soft flesh beneath his lips and tasted the salt of her tears, he relented and spoke to her more tenderly.

'It's all right, darling. You've got nothing to worry about. I'll be round tomorrow morning with bags of dough in my pocket and all the dope on the marrying lark. After that we'll be together for good and all without any of these broken dates. It's a wonder I managed to show up today. Outsiders win. I wasn't running true to form.'

She managed a laugh. There was one thing about Ken. He always cracked a joke. Suddenly she became more cheerful. Life hardly looked so black after all. She was going to be married. That was security of a sort. And it was like the pictures, being in love with somebody who was a wicked desperado. Yes, just like a film. She kissed him swiftly.

'Ken, darling, I love you.'

'Do you, darling? Well, let's have a drink to celebrate it and drink good-bye to Mr Francis Bedborough.'

He fumbled on the floor for the glasses. She picked up the decanter and filled them for him.

'No soda, honey.'

He drank the neat spirit. It made him feel comfortable.

'And put the gramophone on.'

She rose, obedient as ever, to do his bidding.

He lit a cigarette and blew out a contented cloud of smoke.

Life was going to be good. Plenty of dough, plenty of wallop, a pretty jane to knock around with, and a gramophone. Could you beat it? You could not.

The disc started whirring. 'The Carioca' filled the room.

> 'You'll dream of that new Carioca
> Whose theme . . .'

'Leave that blasted gramophone and come over here, kid, I want to love you.'

Obediently she came to his outstretched arms.

MILKY?

It was five past seven when the Gilt Kid had left Maisie's flat. Having forgotten all about the time for hours, he had suddenly looked up at the clock.

'Seven! Blimey!' he exclaimed. 'I got to see a bloke in the West End at half seven. I got to float, kid.'

He sprang to his feet, straightened his tie, smoothed his hair with his hands and, picking up his hat, walked to the door. Maisie, with a little cry, had jumped in front of him. Her white arms were around his neck.

'Must you go, Ken, darling?'

'Sure. Got to get the wages, baby. And you got to get all dolled up for Bedbug. Don't let him catch you like that. And, remember that if he has you tonight, it'll be the last woman he ever has.'

Swiftly he had disengaged himself from her arms, kissed her lightly and disappeared through the door. He had not looked back. All the way down in the bus he was alternately exuberant over having got himself cased up with a smashing girl and apprehensive over the night's work. He was tired, too. Making love and drinking such a lot of scotch did not brace a fellow up any.

He held up his hand and squinted along it. It trembled slightly.

Jumping off the bus at Piccadilly Circus, he had hurried up Shaftesbury Avenue. It would be too bad if he were late and Curly had gone.

He had pushed open the doors of the public house and leapt up the stairs, two at a time. Curly was sitting there at a table, his flat boxer's face expressionless, over a glass of beer.

'Hallo, Curly.' He was so breathless he could scarcely speak.

'Hallo, Gilt Kid. Siddown. Watchew going to have? Begun to wonder if you was going to show up.'

'Sorry I'm late, pal.' The Gilt Kid sank into a chair. 'I'd better have an angostura and soda.'

Noticing Curly's raised eyebrows he explained.

'Been knocking it about a bit this afternoon. Up at the jane's I been.'

'Oh,' Curly leered. 'Nice little bride was she? Well I'll get you your drink. What do you call it again, for Christ's sake.'

The Gilt Kid told him once more, and Curly went up to the bar to fetch it. When he came back the Gilt Kid looked round the practically deserted lounge, noticed nobody was within hearing and said: 'It's OK, Curly. Nobody can hear us. Let's get down to cases. We've got a whole lot to say.'

'Right.' Curly began to speak ponderously. 'I brought along the tools. Stick, flash, gimlet, vaseline, brown paper, knife and this.'

He flashed a diamond ring on his right forefinger.

'Comes in very handy if you got to open a window and it comes in handier still if you got to bash a bloke,' he explained. 'Got your gloves?'

'Sure. They're in the old sky-rocket.'

They both were breathing heavily. There was a short silence. The Gilt Kid broke it.

'Come on, Curly,' he said with a show of impatience, 'put me out of my agony. Give me the strength of it. You know I'm on now.'

'I give you the strength of it yesterday.'

'Sure you did, but you never told me where the gaff was.'

'Up in Maida Vale.'

'You sure of that? Up in Maida Vale, you say?'

'Sure. Of course I'm bleeding sure. Why wouldn't I be? What's the matter with you, gone mad or something?'

The Gilt Kid leaned forward. His breathing was even heavier.

'I only wondered. You say it's a tart's drum on the batter and it's on the top floor of a block, eh?'

'Yes, why?' Something in the Gilt Kid's manner disturbed the phlegmatic Curly. 'What's a matter? What the hell you looking that way for?'

'Nothing. Just tell me one thing. What's the address.'

Curly told him. The Gilt Kid fell back in his chair. His mouth drooped open. He felt as if someone had hit him in the wind.

At last he managed to speak.

'Sorry, Curly, I can't come on that job with you.'

Curly looked at the Gilt Kid for quite a minute, trying to understand what was happening. When he spoke, it was with narrowed eyes and a jutting jaw.

'What's a matter, turning milky?' he sneered.

'No. Curly, it's not that. Honest to Christ it's not that.'

'Then what is it?' A sudden light dawned on him. It was with a snarl, not a sneer, that he spoke this time. 'I know. You're a grass. You've let me tell you the job and you won't come in on it. Oh no, you're going round to Vine Street to shop me. Well, you're not coming the copper against me, you bastard.'

He jumped to his feet, knocking over his chair as he did so. The Gilt Kid was on his feet, too. If there was going to be a bundle, he was not going to be bashed sitting down.

Curly was snorting down his nostrils.

'Come on and fight, you bastard,' he called, oblivious of the attendants who had rushed in to try to separate them.

The Gilt Kid waved them away.

'I'll manage him,' he said. 'Listen, Curly. Sit down and I'll explain everything.'

He had command of the situation. By force of habit, Curly obeyed. Strong in the body, his will was weak. He sat down, glowering. The Gilt Kid looked round impatiently at the people who were hovering about near them. How could he give Curly the wire with them snooping around the gaff?

'Float, for Christ's sake,' he said. 'Show's over. There ain't going to be no fight. You're unlucky tonight. Float.'

Seeing that what he said was apparently true, the crowd withdrew. The Gilt Kid leant forward and touched Curly on the hand.

'Listen, Curly,' he said. 'You've got two ideas to get out of your head. I'm not going to shop you and I'm not turning milky. I'm not going on that job, and what's more, you ain't. And that's flat.'

'Yes, but,' Curly's head was as full of wrinkles as Clapham Junction is of railway lines. 'What the hell's all this about anyway. Who says I'm not going on that job? Blimey. I'll bash . . .'

'All right, all right, just a minute,' the Gilt Kid soothed him as he watched him going up in the air again. 'Just keep quiet and listen. The address you've just told me is my judy's gaff. I was round there myself all this afternoon. We can't go screwing that place. She's leaving that steamer and she's coming to me tomorrow. Now do you see?'

'Yes, I get you.' Curly nodded portentously. 'It would be a bit off. Still, it's a pity to have to let it go. It was a nice little job.' He sighed. 'Well, they say she's a smashing bride. You're lucky.'

'Yeah, I'm lucky all right.'

The Gilt Kid lit a cigarette and smoked reflectively in silence for a bit. Gradually his expression changed.

'Look here, Curly,' he said eventually, 'perhaps I'm making a mistake.'

'Watchew mean? Perhaps you're making a mistake? You mean maybe she don't live there at all, maybe it's another jane's gaff?'

'No. There's no chance of that. It's her gaff all right. What I mean is perhaps it ought to be screwed.'

'I don't get you, Gilt Kid.' Curly scratched a puzzled head.

'Don't you see. All the stuff in that flat's been paid for by old Bedbug – by the steamer that's keeping my tart, that is. Well, if you go and screw it, she can't take none of it away when she comes to me.'

'I'm there.' Curly almost shouted with excitement. It was a rarity for an idea to penetrate his head so quickly. 'If I screw the place and she comes to you with oxo nobody can call you a ponce.'

'That's it, Curly.'

'OK. I'm on. I'll always do a pal a good turn, so help me Christ I will. Kind of funny though this. Like what they call a coincidence. Marvellous, ain't it?'

'Too bloody true it's marvellous. Now listen, Curly, mate. The steamer's getting up there at eight to take her to dinner. So if you're up there at half eight, you'll find the gaff dead. Now that's what I call good drumming if you like.'

'Yes, you can't hardly drum a place better than if you know the people what's living there.'

'Have another drink?'

'Sure. I need one. Make it a Worthington.'

The Gilt Kid fetched him the requested drink and then said: 'I don't think I can tell you anything about the gaff, Curly, that you don't know already. All I can tell you is that they'll be out at about eight-thirty and I don't suppose they'll be back before ten. You've got an hour and a half to work in, I should say. You ought to be able to sweep the joint clean in that time.'

'Ought to,' agreed Curly. 'But I wish you was coming along, too. I don't like working on my jack.'

'Well, you know how it is. I can't come along with you the way I'm fixed.'

'That's right, mate, I'll do it on my own. Have to, I suppose. Watchew going to do tonight?'

'Oh, I'll go along and see some of the boys. Maybe they've got something on.'

The Gilt Kid did not want Curly to know that Scaley and he had a job in hand in case the boxer thought that the Maida Vale job was being ditched purposely.

'I want to get to graft as soon as I can,' he hurried on, for he had learnt that the best way of managing Curly was that of not allowing him time to think. 'I haven't done anything since I've come out of the nick and the old rent's running a bit low.'

'Yes. You want a nice little gaff to put you on your feet again like.'

They sat there opposite one another talking trivialities until the Gilt Kid could stand it no longer. After the emotional uprising that had existed between them, silence was an impossibility. There was nothing important that remained to be discussed. Small talk was an art which neither of them possessed. The Gilt Kid was wise when he rose.

He clapped Curly on his muscular shoulder.

'Good-bye, china,' he said, 'and good luck. I must be pushing along now. Let me know some time how you get on tonight. I'm always round about in the West End. You're bound to bump into me some time.'

'Good-bye, mate. All the best.'

They shook hands.

The Gilt Kid began to walk rapidly down Shaftesbury Avenue in the direction of Piccadilly Circus. He had not the vaguest idea of what he intended to do. There were two hours to fill in. He could go to the pictures if he wanted to; he could go and have a few drinks; he could go and pick up a girl. All London was before him.

Outside the Trocadero a tall man with square shoulders and a brown moustache hailed him.

'Hello, Kennedy. Where you off to?'

The Gilt Kid's face became an expressionless mask. He did not recognize the man, but there were unmistakable traces of his profession about him. The use of the name Kennedy was a good enough tip.

'Oh, nowhere much. Just having a stroll round.'

He tried to throw a hint of casualness into his voice. Anyway they had got nothing on him. He had gone straight so far since coming out of prison.

'Come and have a drink?'

The big man seemed to be the soul of easy affability, but the Gilt Kid was not falling into the trap. He shook his head.

'No thanks. I don't drink.'

'Since when?' laughed his interlocutor.

'Oh, given it up, you know. Mugs' game drinking.'

'Yes? Well, there are a lot of mug's games, eh, Kennedy?'

'Sure. Well, I've given them all up. See?' He ended on a truculent note.

'I see.' The man's lips were twitching. 'Working?'

'Give us a chance.'

The Gilt Kid was anxious to make a getaway. Supposing Curly was to come along and see him chatting a bogy? The very idea sent cold shivers down his back. The detective, however, seemed keen on holding him in conversation.

'Oh, yes, of course. You've just come out. Seen many of your old chinas?'

'No. Ain't seen none of them.'

'No?'

'No. Well, look here. Sorry and all that, but I'm afraid I must blow now.'

'Oh, I thought you said you were just having a stroll round.'

'Sure. I said that.' The Gilt Kid was thoroughly exasperated. 'I know damn well who you are and I don't like people seeing me standing here chatting you. They might get wrong ideas.'

'I see. You're scared of being contaminated. That it?'

'Don't be a berk. You know what I mean. I might have been a screwsman, but I've never yet been a grass, nor likely to, so there.'

He started to move rapidly away.

'Don't forget about giving up the mugs' games,' called the detective, after his hurriedly retreating figure.

He went down into the Piccadilly subway and then, realizing that if he were seen it was dollars to doughnuts that he would be arrested for 'loitering with intent to commit a felony, to wit by picking pockets in the Piccadilly Circus Underground Station', he left by another exit, not bothering to look which.

On coming up into the night again he found himself at the top of the Haymarket. He lit a cigarette in order to give himself an excuse to stand still for a couple of minutes and collect his thoughts.

If he hung about the West End streets for two hours he would be mad. It was asking for trouble. If he wanted to get nicked there was nothing simpler than to walk over to Vine Street and give himself up. Anyhow, what with his escapades of the previous night and excitements of the afternoon, he was feeling tired. The best plan would be to go into a caff somewhere, have something to eat and rest up so that he would be in good trim for going out on that job with Scaley.

Which caff though? Isabella's? Two hours in Isabella's would be too much of a good thing. There used to be plenty of caffs around Panton Street. These damn caffs changed so. A bloke stayed out of the West End a few months and everything was different. Still, there was no harm in trying. It would give him something to do if nothing else.

He threw away his cigarette and walked to Panton Street, cutting down the back way through Oxendon Street as a result of a horror for the brightly lighted clattering main thoroughfares. The café was still there and looked much the same.

A crowd of painted boys – it was just a little too early for them to be going out on the batter yet – were standing round a pin-table gambling for pennies. A down and out slouched in a corner over a cup of tea. There were no other customers.

The Gilt Kid went up to the counter and spoke to the Italian woman behind it.

'Watchew got to eat?'

'Eggs an' chips, steak an' chips, sausages an' chips, col' 'am, col' beef, salmon, eggs and bacon, liver and bacon, spaghetti.' She reeled off the unvarying bill of fare like a Catholic priest saying the Mass.

'OK. Give me a steak and chips, not too well done, two slices and a cup of tea.'

'Steak and chips, not too well done,' she bawled down the lift.

He sat at a table and took up a newspaper which he soon

threw down again. Most of the sheets were missing. Only the financial and women's pages were there. He propped up his head in his hands. He was feeling all done up.

There was, too, an unpleasant feeling at the back of his mind. He did not know quite what it was and yet he could not get rid of it.

What the hell was the matter? Was it because he had promised Scaley to go on a job with him? Was he turning milky? Something was wrong. It was a bit off having bumped into that bogy in Shaftesbury Avenue. He hoped, and hoping cursed himself for his silly superstition, that it was not a bad omen.

He tried to focus his mind on a more congenial subject. He tried to conjure up a mental picture of Maisie. Thinking of her, however, only irritated him all the more. Silly little bitch. He hoped Curly would give her flat a good turning over, strip the bloody place bare. That would teach her to go running about the place with old steamers like Bedbug.

What the hell though. Something was wrong.

He had a presentiment that he was going to touch unlucky. For a moment he toyed with the idea of carrying a lump of coal in his pocket like some of the old-time screws-men did when they went to graft. Might bring him luck, but it would make him look a dead mug if he were to fall. Just imagine getting a rub-down at the copper-house and the bogies dragging a lump of coal out of his sky. They would certainly hand him a big laugh for that caper.

Fall? Who the hell was talking about falling?

He tried to tuck the idea into a watertight compartment from which it could not seep through into the rest of his mind.

The Italian woman brought him over his supper. Uninterestedly he ate it. Maisie was running through his head again.

Thought he was going to marry her, huh? Fancy him

getting tied up with any judy. He should worry. Maisie would have to wake up and come to earth. She would have given Bedbug the belt, come home and found her flat done and have to turn to him.

That was exactly where he would have to box a bit clever. He would spin her a fanny about the marriage laws, tie the poor kid up. It ought to be money for old rope. She was a smashing piece, too, if only she could remember to forget that 'you'd do it if you really loved me' line.

He pushed away his empty plate and lit a cigarette. It was not nine o'clock yet. The time was dragging worse than in prison.

One of the boys detached himself from the group round the pin-table and swayed gracefully across the room to the Gilt Kid.

'Isn't your name Kennedy?' he asked. Beneath the feminine pitch of his voice there was the flat tone of some Midland accent.

'What if it is?' The Gilt Kid was not particularly anxious to make friends with all the irons in London. They talked too much for a start.

'They used to call you the Gilt Kid back in the Scrubbs, didn't they?' The pouf was not easily put off. His nightly promenade had accustomed him to rebuffs.

'Well?'

'Don't you remember me?'

'Can't say I do.' The Gilt Kid stared at the smoke he had just blown out of his mouth.

'Used to be in the Monastery Garden the same time as you. While you was on the pitch pots, I was making naval scrubbers. Doing half I was.'

'What for? The other?'

'Yes,' the pansy simpered. He seemed to be making an impression. 'Mind if I sit down?'

'Well, I'm not stopping you, am I?'

The pansy hooked out a chair with his foot and sat down. He put his elbows on the table and, cupping his chin in his hands, smiled across at the Gilt Kid.

'Give us a cigarette, ducks,' he said.

The Gilt Kid pushed the packet across at him. His gesture was surly. It wouldn't look so good if anyone were to come in and see them.

'Well, what is it?'

'What's what, loov?' The Midlander in him broke out more strongly from time to time.

'What the hell do you want out of me?'

'What have you got to give me, ducks?'

'Damnall. If you think I'm going to take you to live with me you're bloody well mistaken. I knew a geezer once who took pity on one of you who was on the ribs. Well, he takes this iron back to his room and the bastard goes and shops him. The bloke gets nicked. He gets a stretch for screwing and another stretch on top of that for the other. Two-bloody-stretch for trying to do a cowson a good turn.'

'What a bitch! I wouldn't do that to you, darling,' the pouf said. 'Listen, I nearly got ninety pounds the other day.'

'How?'

The Gilt Kid was mildly interested. The mention of easy money was always enough to awaken his attention.

'I was on the Dilly the other night and a steamer come along. In evening dress he was, all done up like the dog's dinner and proper drunk.' He pursed up his lips in feminine reprobation of insobriety. 'I watches him, but I can't go up to him on the Dilly, because there's a copper there, see. So I follows him when he turns up Park Lane, but the copper tails me up, too, see. And then another bitch goes up and speaks to him and gets away with him in a taxi.'

'Well?'

'Well, ducks, he nicks the steamer's wallet in the taxi and there were ninety pounds in there, there were.' In his excitement his voice became less and less feminine and more and more dialect.

'He didn't give me a light of it. Just went away, the rotten whore. The other girls are going to give him a bad time when he comes back on the Dilly.'

'What are they going to do? Slap his wrist or pull his hair? Go on. You make me sick. The other bloke had got more guts than you. He went on and chatted the steamer. You were too milky because there was a slop there. You don't deserve none of that money.'

'Well, he was my man.' Queenie was looking prim.

'Shut up. You and your man. I'll kick you where it'll put you on the dole for a few weeks. Don't you know any job worth doing? Proper jobs I mean. Not nicking skins from blokes what are lit up.'

'I shan't tell you. Not if you're not nice to me.'

'What you mean, nice to me. If you mean going to kip with you you're out of luck, brother. That's all.'

'There's a sauce.' The Midlander tossed his head indignantly. 'I wouldn't go with you, not if you was to give me five pound. So there.'

'You silly little bastard. All I'm likely to give you is a couple of right hooks to the jaw.'

'Don't you talk rough?'

'Yes, and I'll act bloody rough, too, if you don't sling your hook.'

The Gilt Kid got up, paid his bill and went out. He was sick of that café with its unnatural habitués.

'Not that I'm not sorry for the poor bastards, and all that,' he soliloquized as he walked along, 'but still they get on my nerves. I'm not one of those blokes who want to sling them up a right-hander as soon as I look at them, but I don't like the cowsons, that's all.'

He had walked into Trafalgar Square. For a few moments he stood still, resting on the parapet and looking at the unfortunates sitting huddled on the benches. Vaguely he remembered someone in prison telling him that it was essential to get a seat before eight if you were to get any sleep in at all. Why, he could not remember. Across on the corner of Northumberland Avenue the lurid sky-signs stuttering across the building front mocked the outcasts. A chill wind was blowing up past King Charles I's statue from Whitehall. It was twenty past nine.

The Gilt Kid began to feel depressed. Bums always made him feel unhappy. For some reason he felt a sort of responsibility for them. At the same time he knew that he was of their kin. He had sat penniless on those benches. It was not unlikely that he would have to do it again some day.

He moved away in the direction of the Strand with his hands deep in his trousers pockets. He walked down King William Street and then eastwards along the Strand. Suddenly, he felt an awful sense of loneliness.

The pavements were crowded, girls hung on men's arms, laughed up in their faces. A sound of laughter, a buzz of conversation, a busy rattle of glasses issued out from all the public houses. He was companionless. He could, naturally, if he wanted to do so, go into a bar and help to increase its hum; he could, if he wanted to do so, pick up a girl, even a straight-cut, and have her walk arm-in-arm with him. What was the use? He would have only purchased companionship in the bar by virtue of the money in his pocket, he would only have a girl hanging on his arm because he was a man and she craved male society in order to show off in front of her friends. In cold truth, nobody in the world cared a damn about him. He was as lonely here, at liberty in the streets of London, as ever he had been, sitting on the floor of his locked cell in prison sewing mailbags. It was a hell of a life.

Once more he tried to thrust the gloomy thoughts out of his mind; once more he succeeded; once more the heavy sense of oppression lingered behind.

At the corner of Wellington Street he stood still watching the traffic go past him. There was no point in going on. Beyond lay the city where, if he were to be pulled up and questioned, he had no excuse for being. Walking about aimlessly only made a man tired, and a burglar to be successful must be fresh. The only thing to do was to have a drink.

He went into the four-ale bar of a pub and called for a pint of bitter. He stood at the counter drinking it slowly. The beer, he thought, looked the colour of diluted blood. It was just the same colour as the water in the tooth-glass of a man whose gums have bled as he was brushing his teeth. It gave him acidity in the stomach. He had not digested too well the heavy grease of the fried potatoes which he had eaten.

A street-hawker came into the bar. He kept his goods – razor blades, cards of studs, boot-laces, safety-pins and ties – in a cheap suitcase made of paper grained to look like leather. The management here, as in most other public houses, would allow him only to go into the public bar.

Public bar customers were only working men and having, for the most part, less money than the harlots and *petit bourgeois* in the saloon, were entitled to be worried by the importunities of hawkers and street musicians.

Most of them stared the hawker blankly in the face when he held his open suitcase in front of them; some turned their heads away as if they did not care to look upon the unholy sight of a poor man earning his bed for the night – they were of the stamp who, rather than see a man starve, would shut their eyes; others, the kindliest of them, shook their heads, shook them sympathetically, but none the less firmly.

The Gilt Kid watched them. A nausea rose in his throat. He felt inclined to rush in among them shouting: 'Do you know a homeless man's trying to earn the price of a night's kip?' The feeling vanished as quickly as it had risen. Poor bastards, none of them was far above the poverty line himself. Some of them, maybe, would have to go hungry as a result of having drunk a couple of pints of fivepenny ale.

When the man came up to him, the Gilt Kid picked up a penny razor blade and gave sixpence for it. Six copper pennies so that the hawker would realize the intention at once and would not have to suffer the humiliation of being told to keep the change. Almost angrily the Gilt Kid told himself that he was not doing it out of charity, but because he wanted to talk to a human being, that he was simply exploiting the man's defenceless poverty.

'Thirsty work, ain't it, coming round the boozers?' he asked. 'What you going to have?'

The hawker's eyes lit up with expectant gratitude in a way which made the Gilt Kid feel ashamed of himself.

'I'll have a glass of ale, thank you, sir.'

'Cut out the "sir",' retorted the Gilt Kid as he paid the twopence-ha'penny for the order. 'I'm not a bloody baronet or prison warder. Not in this lifetime, anyhow.'

He handed his guest the glass.

'Best respects.' The hawker drank it down at one gulp.

'How's the game?' The Gilt Kid wanted to hear him talk.

'Very bad. Nobody don't seem to have no money. Can't take hardly a penny. Well, thank you. G'night, mate.'

The Gilt Kid watched him hurry out of the bar.

Anxious to catch another mug, he thought bitterly. Well, the poor bloke's got his living to earn. Can't expect to buy a man body and soul for a tanner and half a pint of ale.

He glanced at the clock. The hands indicated that it was three minutes to ten. Allowing for it to be ten minutes fast as public-house clocks always are, there was just nice time for him to walk back to Isabella's and meet Scaley.

As he walked along the Strand again he tried to forget the crowds by forcing ideas into his head.

He was not, he told himself, lonely. He was not useless. On the contrary, he was performing a useful function in society by removing from the rich some of the surplus value which his half-hearted study of economics had taught him that it was wrong for them to possess.

Anyhow, he decided cheerfully as he was passing the Irving statue, there's no sense in worrying. A screwsman has to keep his wits about him. Yes, a screwsman had to keep his wits about him. That was an undeniable fact.

It was after ten when he walked into Isabella's. Scaley was sitting drumming his fingers angrily on a table. He was wearing a bowler hat and a light tweed overcoat. Propped up against the table was a silver-mounted umbrella. Probably he thought it gave him an unburglar-like look. His face became momentarily less stern when he caught sight of the Gilt Kid, but, almost immediately it resumed its harshness. He was relieved that his partner in crime had turned up, but he was not going to sing a mammy song about it.

The Gilt Kid paused at the counter to give an order to Isabella.

'Cup of coffee, please.'

'Oh, you vair bad boy,' Isabella shook a reproving fat finger at him. She could afford to be facetious since she thought that there was a chance of getting money. 'You go out last night wissout paying. You owe me – let me t'ink . . .'

She stopped for a minute trying to consider just how large a bill the Gilt Kid would stand for. To her surprise he broke in on her computation.

'You can forget that caper, Isabella, sister,' he interrupted. 'I bashed into that judy myself later on last night and she told me that you'd made her pester up not only for me and her but, what's more, for all the other mugs that were here. So you can't catch me for it. That racket won't work tonight.'

Isabella began to stammer a hasty apology, but again the Gilt Kid cut in.

'You can forget that, too,' he said. 'All's fair in love and war, and it's both when you're around the place.'

'Oh, you vair bad boy,' repeated Isabella, trying to hide her chagrin at losing the easy money and her relief at the Gilt Kid's taking it well by badinage.

'Strikes me you vair bad girl,' he said. 'Anyhow, hurry that coffee along and, mark you, I'm paying for it now.'

He took the cup, paid, and went over to where Scaley was sitting.

'Hallo, Scaley. Sorry I'm late.' He sat down.

'Yes?' questioned Scaley. 'Well, hurry up and drink that coffee and we'll beat it. I want to get on the job, not sit here wasting time.'

The Gilt Kid looked up with quick surprise at the acid edge which there was to Scaley's words.

What was the matter with him?

Probably he was a bit jumpy just before going on a job and, as a result, inclined to snap. A lot of people were like that. It needed a man of iron to be able to go on a job without getting any kind of a thrill out of it. But Scaley was pretty tough. Nobody would have thought him likely to get an attack of nerves.

The Gilt Kid looked at him a little more closely. There was no sign of nervousness in his face. His pale eyes were as pitilessly unwavering as ever. Perhaps his jaw-line was a little tenser, but, if that was so, it was all.

Christ, thought the Gilt Kid stirring his coffee. Scaley must be the hell of a man to get up against. He would kill a bloke as soon as look at him.

Scaley's voice interrupted his thoughts. It was pitched low, but carried an authoritative bark.

'C'm on,' he was saying. 'Snap into getting that coffee down you. What d'you want to sit there staring at me for? I'm not a bloody oil-painting. You ought to know my map by now.'

'All right, Scaley, all right. Don't get airyated. Who the hell d'you think you are, anyway? You sound like you were a sergeant-major in the Guards or some goddamn thing like that.'

The Gilt Kid knew that if he allowed himself to be ordered about so easily, Scaley would soon establish an invincible ascendancy.

'That's all very well, but we don't want to make a tumble out of this by getting down there too late. I don't want to fall, even if you do.'

'Don't be silly, we're not going to fall, neither of us. Did you bring the tools along?'

'Of course. What d'you think? That I'd be berk enough to forget them? Did you bring your gloves?'

'Sure. They're in my sky. What, did you think that I'd be berk enough to forget them?' There was a mocking cheerfulness in the Gilt Kid's voice. The argument had driven away all the fears that had been worrying him.

He had finished his coffee. He got up.

'Come along. I'm ready,' he said. 'Which way do we go?'

'We can get a bus at the Circus.' Scaley was still unwilling to divulge the destination.

'Let's go.'

In silence they walked along to catch the bus. None of the people in the crowded streets so much as looked at them. The Gilt Kid prayed inwardly that they would not run into the same detective again. It might, he knew, lead to cross-questioning and, if there was a search, the fact that Scaley had house-breaking implements in his possession was a practically certain passport to six months' imprisonment apiece.

He was thankful when they had boarded the bus. They mounted to the upper deck. Since the theatres, picture palaces and pubs had not yet closed, the stream of passengers outwards from the West End was slight. The conveyance was almost empty and they easily managed to secure inside seats, one behind the other, on the left – and more comfortable – side of the bus.

Scaley took the tickets and smoked on in silence. The Gilt Kid, sitting behind his companion's broad and uncompromising shoulders, let his mind wander.

ROLLING DOWN

The bus lumbered carefully but thrustingly along the uneven hills and dales of Piccadilly. Whores and clubmen, penniless outcasts and provincials, criminals and wage-slaves were walking along its pavements. Undoubtedly there was a detective or two among them: undoubtedly he would have been delighted to have been able to capture the two prospective burglars who were sitting smugly like respectable citizens in the bus.

It's a strange world, thought the Gilt Kid. Curly would have screwed Maisie's place by now. Probably – certainly, if he had any sense – he would be selling the goods by now. Maybe he was in a little shop in South London, or perhaps in a café in Aldgate, waiting while a man fingered and valued the jewellery and furs which Bedbug had given Maisie. He would be there, waiting eagerly for the money, knowing that he was to be caught and given less for it than he deserved, while hoping that he would not be caught too badly, and all the time Maisie would be standing in the flat, not really believing that it had been broken into. That sort of thing, she was almost undoubtedly thinking, happens to other people. And old Bedbug himself. What would he be doing? Bitterly bemoaning the fate which had deprived him of the pleasure of keeping a girl as pretty as Maisie and wondering whether the next piece of female flesh he would buy would be as nice.

The bus had finished with Piccadilly now and was careering and curveting down Knightsbridge. On the right the Park was a patch of darkness, lighted only by the transient headlights of passing cars. At the two coffee stalls shone the red coats of Guardsmen.

Was Maisie insured, wondered the Gilt Kid. That would be damned unlikely, unless Bedbug had made her do it.

Suddenly a thought, ludicrous and comical, came into his head.

Supposing Bedbug was a bit tight with his dough. Supposing he had demanded of Maisie that she return him all the presents he had given her. There would be a nice turn out then.

His vividly visual imagination pictured the scene.

Bedbug would have come back to the flat for the last time. His face, in his anger, would be paler than ever. There would be something very haughty about the way in which he stood about. Maisie would have opened all the drawers and cupboards. There would be nothing there. Dismay would be on her stupid, pretty face. Bedbug's anger would have turned at first to unbelief and then to anger again. He would believe that it was a put-up. That Maisie had had the place screwed on purpose so that she would not have to give him back anything. She would try, without the slightest chance of success, to convince him that it was not so. Bedbug would be haughtier than before and ever so bitter.

'This,' he would say, 'is the result of associating with a common prostitute, a veritable whore whom I picked up out of the gutter.'

And then Maisie would fly into a temper because there was nothing which a girl like that hated more than having a spade called a spade.

Yes, it certainly would be damned funny if that happened.

The bus was now running smoothly along the empty, if aristocratic, stretches of the Kensington Road. Scaley pitched a cigarette end out of the window on to the well-bred pavement. For the first time he turned round.

'Now we shan't be long,' he said tritely. 'Feeling all right?'

'Sure. Why wouldn't I?' answered the Gilt Kid. Bloody

neck that on Scaley's part. What, did he think everyone, bar himself, was milky or something?

'That's the boy. Cigarette?'

He held out a packet of cigarettes. The Gilt Kid helped himself and lit up, wondering all the while what had suddenly come over Scaley. Friendly actions of this sort were by no means in keeping with his general attitude.

The bus slid by the top of Earl's Court Road. This part of London was almost dead, only a few odd people walking about the streets. Funny place the Smoke, thought the Gilt Kid, puffing at the cigarette which Scaley had so kindly given him.

Scaley turned round again.

'When we get off at Hammersmith,' he said, 'we can have a cup of tea at a coffee stall.'

'Yeh. That'd be a good idea.'

Getting off at Hammersmith, were they? Well, that was handy to know, anyway. Scaley looked as though he might be going to open up any minute.

Olympia. Cadby Hall.

Scaley swivelled round once again. There was a curious expression on his face. A kind of furtive shame. Something was impelling him to talk, while he knew that tough guys always kept silent tongues in their heads.

'Pity the pubs shut so early down here, or we'd be able to have a drink before doing the job. Well, ne'mind, if we have it off we'll have plenty of dough tomorrow for drinking. P'raps it's just as well. When you've had a couple o' wets you start taking chances. A lot of blokes can't go out to work unless they are about three sheets in the wind for a start. I'm not like that, thank Christ. Are you?'

'No. I'm all right. Always open to have a go.'

It was manifest that Scaley was talking just for the sake of talking. The Gilt Kid was with him there. Nothing like having your mind taken off things.

Hammersmith Road. The bus travelled on, a mechanical thing driven by a mechanical man. When the bell rang once, the driver stopped the vehicle; when it rang twice, he started it again. When the lights were against him, he stopped; when they were with him he went on. There was no need to think. He just did his job. When he had finished his day's work, when he had punched the time clock, he would have become a man again. Until then he was just another unit in the industrial system.

Hammersmith Broadway.

Life, movement and vitality once more. Above and beyond all a smell of fried fish and chips. One of London's focal centres.

Scaley heaved himself, not without reluctance, out of his seat.

'Get off here, mate,' he said.

The Gilt Kid followed him down the steps. He was feeling exalted. The first job he had done since he had come out of prison. Well, he had never been caught on the job yet, been chased out of the gaff times without number, but never been caught there. He hoped his luck was going to be good.

Scaley was standing on the pavement when the Gilt Kid alighted. Impatience was portrayed in his expression and in every line of his figure.

'Come on, mate,' he was saying in his habitually guarded tone. 'Put a jerk into it. It's none too healthy standing here, not with all I've got on me.'

'Which way now?'

'You'll be all right if you follow me.'

He led the way across the Broadway, diving through the traffic hurriedly under the noses of the buses and cars. Drivers cursed him. His preoccupation did not permit him to retaliate.

By Hammersmith station stood a coffee stall.

'This'll do us,' he said.

Leaning on the counter he called for two cups of tea. The Gilt Kid watched him with suppressed amusement. Scaley, the great, tough, cautious Scaley, Scaley, the man who always had everything weighed up proper, was as shaky as a cat with kittens. There was a laugh for anyone who felt that way.

He stirred his tea.

'I thought you said it was in the suburbs,' he said.

'Well, what the hell you call this, Leicester Square?'

'Yes, but I thought you meant Streatham or Hendon or some place.'

'No, it's near here. Know this district?'

'No, can't say I do.'

'Well, I lead the way then. Ready? Come on, let's go.'

He walked off at a great pace. The Gilt Kid felt like a nephew trotting along beside an uncle. Scaley turned round several corners, apparently he was going back on his tracks. All this caution exasperated the Gilt Kid.

'Hey, what lark are you on now, dodging around like this? Think we're playing follow me leader or something?' he asked indignantly.

'If anyone's spotted us and they're tailing us up, we'll soon throw them off this way. Might as well be on the safe side. Are you superstitious?'

'Can't say I am,' replied the Gilt Kid untruthfully.

'Nor me, not usually that is, but I kind of got an idea tonight we're going to be in a spot, touch unlucky somehow. Christ knows why. We ought to be all right. Still you never know, not in this game.'

The Gilt Kid heard his companion's remark with a curious feeling. At first he was amused at this sudden manifestation of humanity in Scaley, not that it had not already been clear that something was in the wind. Then, with a sudden rush, all the doubts and fears, all the curious forebodings which had been oppressing him, returned to his mind. Terror seized him.

Christ, he thought wildly, supposing Scaley's right. Supposing something bad is going to happen.

He tried to speak, but could not find any words. Only listening with a part of his mind, he heard Scaley's next words.

'You know what we've got to do? You've got to climb on to my shoulders on that girder. You'll be all right, won't you? You're sure of that, aren't you?'

Scaley was almost begging. The Gilt Kid had the idea that his pal would be relieved were he to say 'No'. He tried to drive the thoughts from him.

'Sure. I'll be all right.'

'You're a daring bastard, all right,' grudged Scaley.

The Gilt Kid was not listening. He was too interested in what was going on so turbidly in his own mind.

Blast Scaley, he was thinking. What the hell does he want to get this way for? Bloody idiot. He's getting me in the same state. Why can't he be a bit cheerful? This won't be a tumble. It seems as if it should be a snip. Perhaps he's right. We may be going to come unstuck. What the hell if we do? They can't do any worse than poke us inside again. I've been there before. I've done my time once. I can do it again.

Resignation filled him. He was quite calm. Everything, the deserted street, the little patches of light from the lamp standards, suddenly became much clearer and more vivid.

If it happens, he decided mentally, it does and that's all there is to it. Aloud he said:

'There's not a porter, is there?'

'Didn't I tell you the gaff was dead,' snarled Scaley, glad to have an opportunity of expending his irritation on something tangible.

'I don't mean at the offices, I mean for the flats, dopey.'

'Hell, I don't know.'

Scaley stopped dead. He was absolutely dejected.

'You're a right one to send drumming. I thought you was

the fellow to get everything weighed up proper. Why a kid going to school'd know better than that!'

'What'll we do then? Give it the go by until I find out?'

This most unusual irresolution on the part of Scaley annoyed the Gilt Kid. His temper flared up.

'Well, we can't stand around here spare. We'll get knocked off for a dead cert if we do. I don't want to get a carpet just because you haven't the eighteenpence to make your mind up. Come on.'

He went on walking. Scaley caught him up.

'What are we going to do?' he asked, almost piteously.

'Go on the job, of course. What's a matter with you? Gone yellow or something? Hell, I thought you were more of a man than that. You haven't the guts to go on the job and you're trying to squirm out of it the easy way. Come clean, that's so, isn't it?'

'No, honest, it ain't. On my life. Only there don't seem to be much point in getting claimed when you needn't be.'

'Well, I'm not coming all this way to go home empty-handed. We're down here now. We'd better have a go. That's all. If we do fall, it'll be your fault and I hope that's going to be on your mind every day while you're doing your time. Come on, let's stop hanging around and get on the job. How much further is it?'

'See that block of flats down the end of the street there?'

'Yes. That it?'

'Yes.'

'Good.' The Gilt Kid looked around him. 'Well, there ain't nobody in sight. We look like being in luck. Snap out of it, Scaley, there's no sense in being scared.'

Now that he had pushed himself more or less in command he felt no fear or faltering. His sensation was merely one of resignation to the existing circumstances and to the outcome whatever it might be. There was also a pleasurable tinge of excitement.

Scaley was swallowing the spittle that had welled up in his throat. 'Yes, I guess you're right, kid. There's no sense in losing your guts. Look. There's a stroke of luck.'

A black cat, with his rigid tail held up like a cavalryman's sword at the carry, stalked past them.

'Blimey, yes. Bring us luck, puss,' he called out after the cat, who moved on without looking round and as dignified as a butler.

'Hell,' said Scaley, 'there's a lot of lights burning in them flats.'

He half-checked his stride. The Gilt Kid realized that he would still be relieved at an excuse for going home.

'Ne'mind. That's all to the good. If there's people up and moving about they won't think there's anything queer in us floating up the stairs. Carry on. Go straight ahead. If you stand hanging about now you'll make a dead tumble out of it.'

'Best put your gloves on now. You don't want to leave any dabs on the stairs.'

'Suppose so. Still, banisters in a block of flats always get a hell of a lot of fingerprints on them. Ours would get all blurred up.'

'Sure, but you might as well be on the safe side.'

The Gilt Kid laughed.

'Still the same old Scaley,' he bantered.

Nevertheless he drew out his gloves and put them on. It felt like old times to be wearing gloves and going to graft. A wild happiness came over him. His heart began to pound madly. It felt as if it weighed about a ton, thumping there in his chest.

THE GAFF

The block of flats was built of red brick and the inner walls of the staircase were made of those white glazed tiles with which public lavatories and police-court cells are built. Their feet sounded hollowly on the stone steps. There was a nasty iron handrail. The flats were obviously for the lower middle class. It was unlikely that any of them contained anything worthy of a burglar's time or attention.

On each landing there were three doors, with brightly shining brass knockers and letter-boxes. In one flat a man and a woman were having an argument, the woman's voice high-pitched, shrill and more frequent, the man's an occasional bass rumble like a lorry running through an empty street. From another flat came the sound of either a gramophone or a radio playing dance music.

The Gilt Kid was noticing every little detail with an observation that was meticulous in its accuracy.

It's funny, he was thinking. Every one of these gaffs holds a family. Each family is cut off from the others. Nobody has the foggiest what is going on anywhere else. They read the crime news in the papers and get a thrill out of seeing a film about crooks, yet if they were to know that a couple of burglars were walking up their main staircase they would fall down dead with fright.

They had reached the top landing now. Scaley held a gloved finger to his lips.

'Don't let anyone hear us going up any higher,' he breathed in the Gilt Kid's ear, 'or they might rumble that something's up.'

The Gilt Kid nodded. This was no time for unnecessary words. A sign would serve the purpose as well.

Cautiously letting the weight fall on to the ball of his foot before he shifted it, Scaley went up the half-flight of stairs to the roof; equally cautiously the Gilt Kid followed him. Their passage was as soundless as possible. At the fire escape door they halted. Scaley nodded significantly towards it. The Gilt Kid pushed up the iron bar and released the catch. His careful work seemed to him to be taking an age. Even so, there was a slight click. They both stood still. They were statues frozen in the positions they had held the half-second before the click sounded. Scaley was leaning forward; both the Gilt Kid's hands raised a half-inch above the bar. There was no sound except the beating of their hearts and the breath of their nostrils. Both of them had their lips tightly compressed. Every muscle in their bodies was tensed.

Thirty seconds went by. There was no sign of anyone having heard the noise. No one was coming up the stairs. It was quite all right.

With telepathic consent they nodded simultaneously. A tremendous relief was in their hearts. They stepped over the sill of the door on to the roof. The darkness distorted the shapes of everything. High in the sky a three-quarter moon was riding in a ragged bank of clouds.

The Gilt Kid was experiencing a sense of infinite and awe-striking solitude. He was alone on a roof, high above the sleeping or heedless flat-dwellers, with a man whom he hardly knew, with a man with whom he was working for mere expediency's sake. Either of them would cheat the other of their division of the spoils if half a chance presented itself; that was an understood fact. His hand was against every man and every man's hand was against him. He was lonely, and he knew it.

He took a step and he was close beside Scaley. He could

hear the beating of his heart, feel the warmth of his body, smell his sweat.

'Better give me the tools,' he whispered. 'I got to get the old window open and we might overbalance if you try to work 'em to me on the girder.'

Scaley nodded.

'I'll keep the torch,' he said. 'I'll have to go first along the girder.'

Out of his pocket he drew a case-opener, one end of which was curved, a tin of vaseline, a sheet of brown paper and a broad-bladed putty knife.

'Try to use the chiv to force back the catch,' he whispered, doing his best not to let his voice rise or quaver. 'Won't make any noise that way.'

'Right.' The Gilt Kid stowed the house-breaking tools about his body. A wild feeling of exultation came over him at the touch of them. Many a time he had boasted to his prison pals: 'Just let me have the tools when I'm out and you'll never find me starving.'

'Which way now?'

Scaley pointed with his head at a corner of the roof, and flashed on his torch, guarding the beam of light downwards with the palm of his left hand. His neatly rolled, silver mounted umbrella hung by its crook over his left arm. He set off in the direction which he had indicated, the Gilt Kid following closely behind him. At the corner he halted, unhooked his umbrella and propped it against the parapet, hoping to pick it up again on his return.

The Gilt Kid stepped up beside him. His eyes followed the beam of Scaley's flashlight. Opposite lay another block of buildings, their outline formless in the surrounding gloom. A couple of feet lower than the roof on which they were standing a girder ran six inches from the wall of the connecting parapet, to the other building. In the darkness he could not judge the length of the girder.

'Got the idea?' Scaley's breath was hot and faintly repulsive in his ear.

He nodded affirmatively.

Scaley stepped down hesitantly on to the girder. He tried to walk along it, putting one foot in front of the other. The Gilt Kid watched him with a fascinated fearfulness. Scaley had only taken a couple of steps when he began to sway a little. It was quite clear that he would slip to destruction were he to take another. He steadied himself with one hand on the parapet and sank to his knees. He dropped his left leg over the girder and tried to do the same with his right. He found it impossible owing to the nearness of the wall. Neither could he rise to his feet again. He was too frightened to try.

The Gilt Kid watched all this manœuvring. The fascination which he had felt while Scaley was stepping down on the girder left him. He was watching him now with a detached interest. His own plan for the crossing was already made out clearly in his mind.

Scaley hesitated there, about two and a half feet along the girder, for half a minute, and then drew his left leg back. He was now kneeling on both knees. His left hand still clutched the parapet. He made his way along in that manner. He looked, the Gilt Kid thought, like a pilgrim at some sacred shrine. Well, that's what he was. A pilgrim at the sacred shrine of dough.

Scaley knelt his way across, painfully conscious of the Gilt Kid's eyes on the small of his back, pitifully frightened of being afraid, pathetically proud of his craftsmanship as a burglar, and anxious to do nothing that might detract from his claim to be a pastmaster of his peculiar trade. The Gilt Kid read all this with scorn rather than with sympathy. Scorn was an emotion so much more easily aroused and maintained with so much more superiority.

Scaley arrived at last, on his sore knees, at the point where the girder ran into the wall of the offices. Laboriously and not without fear he pulled himself up, catching the coping this time with both hands. Dangerously he swivelled round on the coping, better to be able to help the Gilt Kid's mounting, and stood with his back to the wall. He flashed his light along the girder.

It was the Gilt Kid's turn now. He dare not hang back. He knew that if he was going to keep that power he must move, or else, in losing it, lose his nerve also.

He took a deep breath, a breath so deep that his pounding lungs hurt. With both hands he caught a grip on the edge of the parapet as he leant forward and lowered his feet on to the girder. He stood there with his face to the parapet while he expended all the breath which had accumulated in his lungs. The parapet, he noticed, was constructed of crumbling stucco, the wall which it surmounted, of red brick. He turned his head to the left and looked behind him. The black emptiness seemed to be extending for ever, going down to an unbelievable, unplumbable depth. Hastily he turned his face to the parapet again and caught more firmly on to the crumbling stucco. The moon had burst from its ragged cloudbank. The light it gave was bright, revealing and shadowless. Scaley, true to his nature, took his finger off the button of his torch. It was pointless to waste electricity while Nature was doing the job.

The Gilt Kid began to move to the left. He stretched out his left leg to its uttermost extent and then brought his right foot up to it. Moving thus, he made a rapid progress.

The quicker the crossing, he thought, the less time to get windy.

Once his heel slipped on the iron girder. He felt his whole body lurch backwards. Sweat broke out on his brow. He hung on to the coping the tighter. His gloved fingers ached with the grip. Rescuing his foot, he began to move more speedily to avoid feeling fear for his narrow escape.

Christ, he thought, when's this bloody girder going to end?

He moved along, pace after pace, until a stride took him into something softer than the empty air. It was Scaley's body. He had arrived.

'Hallo, brother,' he said. 'You all right?'

What he meant was 'Hallo brother, I'm all right.' Scaley's body was, he realized, trembling. He swivelled himself round. They were facing each other. Scaley had his right hand, the Gilt Kid his left, on the parapet. The pair of them were panting.

'Can you get up on my shoulders all right?'

'Sure. I'll hoist myself on to the parapet and then step on to them. Keep still and steady me with your hands.'

'Right. Don't show yourself too much though. Don't forget there's the street the other side of the parapet.'

'Christ, yes. I mustn't let anyone see me. How're the flats?'

'There's some lights in the windows facing us, but all the blinds are drawn.'

'We're in the shadows here, ain't we?'

'Yes.'

'Well, it ought to be OK then. Stoop down and shove me up with your hands. I'll hang on to the parapet like hell. Be careful when you get up or you'll pitch me off. This is a bit of a cowson.'

'It's a bloody sight worse than I thought it was going to be. Ready? Come on then.'

Scaley stooped down. The Gilt Kid gripped the parapet with both hands and then put one foot on Scaley's linked fingers. The hand felt soft and boneless beneath his tread.

'Ready, hoist away.'

Scaley began to lift. He was not steadying himself at all now, since both his hands were engaged. A slip on his part meant death for them both. Each of them knew it: a fact which did not add to their joint security. Slowly he raised himself to his normal height. As Scaley rose, the Gilt Kid transferred himself from the aching hands to the quivering shoulders. By the time that Scaley had resumed his full stature, he was able, too, to catch hold of the parapet. When his hands had reached a resting place his body ceased its swaying.

'I'm all right. Are you?'

'Sure.'

'Good. Let go of the parapet with one hand and catch hold on my legs till I get a hold on to the window sill, will you?'

They were no longer giving commands to each other. The time had come for requests, not orders. Later, when they began to split up the takings, there would be another opening for hot words.

When he felt one of Scaley's arms encircling and making secure his legs, the Gilt Kid let go of the parapet, and reaching up, caught hold of the window sill. It was on a level with his eyes. For a moment he stayed as he was. Then, still gripping with his left hand, he reached up his right arm. The tips of his fingers extended just about to the dividing line of the two panes.

'All right?' queried Scaley. The weight on his shoulders was becoming intolerable.

'Guess so. I can just about reach the sash. Hang on like hell. I'm liable to jerk about a bit feeling for the catch.'

Scaley's grip tightened. The Gilt Kid felt in his pocket and brought out the broad-bladed putty knife. Again he reached up. There was a little fumbling and he had worked the blade in between the sashes. He moved the knife to the right. There was a faint chink of metal. His heart leapt up into his mouth.

'Got the catch,' he whispered exultantly, 'now to push it back.'

Scaley's steadying arm was trembling. He also, then, was

feeling the thrill. The Gilt Kid pushed the blade a little more, manipulating the catch. There was another faint chink of metal on metal. He had pushed the catch back.

'Got it,' he said. And there was pride in his whisper.

'Got it?' echoed Scaley. 'That's the boy.'

'I'll have to get on the sill now. Stand by.'

He dragged himself up on to the four-inch-wide window ledge. He found just a bare foothold for him there.

Scaley felt a great relief when there was no longer a man's weight cutting into his collarbone. He took another grip on to the parapet and turned around so that he might watch what was happening.

The Gilt Kid was crouching on the window sill, pulling down the top half of the sash-window. It seemed to be stuck, as he was tugging hard with straining muscles. At last he got it to move. It came with a jerk. The sashcords creaked like the sheets of a sailing ship in a high wind. If he had not steadied it with both hands, precariously leaving go of the sill, the window would have come down with a crash, probably shattering all the glass, awakening everybody in the vicinity and discovering the two burglars.

The pane was down. The Gilt Kid transferred his hands to the top of it and swung himself over. His feet touched first the inner sill, and then, noiselessly, the ground. It was too dark for him to see where he was. He knew, of course, that he was on some kind of landing. The further details would have to wait until Scaley arrived with his glim.

Pushing the sashes about with as little noise as he could contrive, he arranged the window so that the lower half was open. Then he leant out over the sills and extended both his arms.

'It's OK, Scaley,' he said. 'Catch on to my hands and I'll pull you up.'

He felt Scaley's firm grip on his hands and hauled with all his strength. Scaley was helping by getting a foothold on the wall below the sill. Gradually the Gilt Kid felt the tugging relax. Before his arms had been completely pulled out of their sockets, Scaley was kneeling on the sill. He leapt lightly on to the floor.

'Well,' he said, pushing forward the button on his torch, 'we're in. I'll say this much for you, Gilt Kid, you got guts.'

The Gilt Kid felt his chest swell with pardonable pride.

'Of course I have,' he said, 'wouldn't be much use at this game if I hadn't. Got to take a risk if you want to earn any wages.' Then the Englishman's habitual dismay at the appearance of any emotion other than anger came over him. 'Come on, don't let's stand here all night arguing the bloody toss. Let's get on with the job. Go on ahead. You know more about the gaff than I do.'

Scaley put his left hand once more over the torch and shone it down a short stairway to another landing. Stepping slowly, with his feet straddled to either edge of the stair-boards to avoid creaking, he led the way. The Gilt Kid watched him and then, seeing him on the level flooring, swung himself on to the banisters and slid down them. That was, in his opinion, the best way of descending the stairs silently.

When they were both on the landing, Scaley tip-toed over to a door. It had a name, indistinguishable in the dark, painted on it and a letter-box. Scaley's light was shining on the Yale lock.

'Better let me have the cane,' he said.

The Gilt Kid shook his head. If Scaley took the jemmy and did all the opening up himself, he would probably be able to work some of the money by sleight of hand into his pocket and it was stone ginger that none of that money would come out into the general split-up. The Gilt Kid was not going to stand for any of that nonsense. He had had some already.

'No, I'll screw it,' he said. 'Just keep your old glim steady a bit.'

He pulled the case-opener from his inside pocket. All of

it except the bent end had been wrapped in brown paper. As ever, Scaley had been taking no chances on leaving any fingerprints.

Holding the jemmy in his right hand the Gilt Kid felt the door. First he pushed it right up at the top. There was nothing holding it there. It bent back quite easily. Still shoving against the door his hand travelled downwards. There was a centre of resistance just around the lock. That was all. At the top and bottom, there was nothing else holding the door. It was merely a flimsy piece of quite ordinary wood.

'There's nothing special about it,' said the Gilt Kid. 'It don't need any wedges or starting at the top or any of that caper. Here goes.'

Putting his left hand on the door again about three inches above the lock he leant with all his force. The door bent back slightly. Rapidly and without relaxing his pressure one whit he slipped the bent edge of the case-opener into the tiny opening he had created. Then he caught hold of the end of it with both hands and began to exert all the leverage of which he was capable.

The door creaked and groaned. It was only the metal flange of the lock, stuck like a tongue into the surrounding woodwork, that held it at all, and with the force that was being brought to bear upon it, it could hardly resist very much longer. There was a louder creak than before and then a sound, which to their straining ears and tensed nerves, seemed as loud as a pistol shot. The door gave way beneath the Gilt Kid's pressure and swung open. He had screwed it successfully. They had surmounted the last obstacle between the money they sought and themselves.

In spite of the fact that the door was now open and there was nothing to resist their entrance into the office, the pair of them stood still. They were listening to hear whether the final cracking of the door had aroused any undesired attention on the part of some honest citizen. Apparently it had not. All was still.

They stepped into the office. It was pitch black except in one part where the window glowed squarely like a framed portrait of dusk.

'Where does that window give on to?'

'The street.'

'Well, shine your glim round the room so as we can see where things are, but for the love of God keep it low. We don't want it shining out of the window and giving us away.'

'All right, all right. I know my job even if you think I don't,' snarled Scaley. He was getting annoyed at the way in which the Gilt Kid was running things. Now that he was safely in the office which he had set out to burgle his confidence had returned to him. The old burglar's adage that you're much safer in the gaff than on the street had recurred to him. Nevertheless he shone the torch round the office, carefully keeping his back to the window as he did so.

The uncertain pallid light given by the torch, partially obscured as it was by Scaley's thick fingers, revealed a very ordinary office. In the centre was a pedestal desk and a padded swivel chair. Up against the desk stood a waste-paper basket. Beside the empty fireplace was a filing cabinet, and on the mantelpiece were four or five books. In one corner of the room was a black leather armchair. Over underneath the window were another table with a typewriter on it and an ordinary Windsor chair. The floor was covered with linoleum. On the distempered walls hung a cardboard-mounted omnibus map of London and a calendar, obviously a gift from a stationery firm. There was no safe.

'There ain't no peter.'

'No.'

'Where's the dough kept then?'

'In one of the drawers of the writing desk. It's in a cash-box.'

'Know which drawer?'

'No.'

'Well, let's open them all then.'

They moved across to the desk. On top of it lay a pen tray, a blotter, a box of paper clips and a tin of cigarettes. This last the Gilt Kid promptly put into his pocket. It seemed the most sensible thing to do.

He pulled open the middle drawer of the desk. As it opened so easily he guessed there was nothing in it of any value. His guess was right. All it contained was sheets of blotting paper and a ruler. He tried to pull out the top left drawer. It was locked. With fingers trembling with excitement, for here maybe was the object of their raid, he forced it open. Inside was a sheaf of letters which he threw all over the floor in disgust.

Serve them right, he thought petulantly. Who the hell ever heard of anyone locking up letters like they were dough?

The remaining drawers on that side held nothing but stationery and books.

He tugged at the top drawer of the right hand side. That too was locked. Once more he thrust in his case-opener, this time rather irritably. The floor round the desk was now strewn with letters, stationery and account books which lay open as they had fallen.

The lock of the drawer burst. Without removing the case-opener, the Gilt Kid jerked the drawer open. When he saw what was inside his pupils dilated and his heart became like a steam-hammer once more. Scaley made a dive for the two cash-boxes.

'Keep your mauleys off,' growled the Gilt Kid. 'This is my job. Holding the glim's your end of the business.'

In spite of the fact that he was only whispering, there was enough in his tone to show Scaley that he meant what he said. And so Scaley remained silent, not eager to precipitate a quarrel at that important moment.

The Gilt Kid laid his case-opener down on the top of the desk, and lifted out the two cash-boxes. He nearly dropped one of them, for his hands were shaking. It was a moment of tremendous excitement, because here in front of them lay what they had been risking their lives and their liberty to earn.

One cash-box had two lids which opened up from a central hinge. There was no lock on it. All it held was a sheet of postage stamps and a load of silver coins.

'We'd better divvy up here,' said Scaley, 'so as we don't have to carry these bloody cash-boxes around.'

'Sure we'll divvy up here. What's up with you? Think I'm going to carve you up? You can have the stamps if you like, but count up that snow while I go through the other drawers.'

The other drawers had nothing of interest to him. He flung their contents down to add to the mess which was already on the floor, and got to work on the other cash-box. Before Scaley had finished stacking up his silver into neat piles of one pound each, the second box was open.

'How much have you got there, Scaley?'

'About fifteen nicker, near as makes no matter. Watchew got?'

'Paper. Halves and oncers. Ain't half a hell of a lot.'

He lifted up the top tray and turned it so that a cascade of notes fell on to the desk. In the lower compartment were more, neatly done-up-with-elastic bundles of twenty pounds. They were all old notes. There was not a snowball's chance that the numbers had been taken.

Scaley left the silver. His eyes were jutting out of his head at the sight of all that money. It certainly looked good.

'Get on with counting out that snow. I'll tend to this.' The Gilt Kid snapped out another command. Through his mind were running pleasant thoughts of what a splash he would be able to make with Maisie.

He'd show her what spending meant. She hadn't learnt nothing yet – not with old Bedbug. Jesus!

His hands flipped over the bundles of notes. His mouth was quite dry in his excitement and, although his head was throbbing violently, he was only half-aware of the fact. He divided the bundles into two heaps.

'What's that snow worth?'

'Fifteen pun' seventeen and six.'

'I got exactly two hundred nicker here in these bundles. Let's count up those loose notes.'

They fell to work stacking up the loose notes. In all, there was forty-three pound ten.

'Two hundred and forty-three ten, and fifteen seventeen and a sprat. Let's see. Forty-three and fifteen makes fifty-eight. We got two hundred and fifty-nine quid seven and a tanner. Split that even, one hundred and – er twenty-four pound odd. Tell you what, Scaley, I'll take a hundred and twenty-four and let you have the odd twenty-seven and a sprazer. After all, you put me on to the job. That odd bit of cash might come in handy for you sometime, Scaley. They charge twenty-two and six for a dock brief, don't they?'

In his exultation the Gilt Kid had permitted his voice to grow recklessly loud. Scaley snarled at him

'Nark it for God's sake,' he whispered angrily. 'You'll get us done, yelling around the gaff like that. Use a bit of common.'

With an effort the Gilt Kid brought himself under control once more. The next time he spoke it was in a subdued tone. He was filling his pockets with money while he talked.

'Well, I'm going to leave all these tools here,' he said. 'There's no use dragging them back. Bloody ridiculous to get done for having a cane in your sky when there ain't no need. You've wiped them clear of dabs, eh?'

'Sure. They're OK. Sling them. I'm going to keep the old

glim though to light us out. Remember we've got to get across that lousy girder again.'

'Oh blimey yes. Cowson. Well, come on. We needn't stay here all the bloody night arguing the toss. Light us out.'

Happy, and with their pockets full of stolen money, they crept out of the rifled office.

Scaley looked out of the open window on the staircase. He turned round sharply to the Gilt Kid, dropping in his excitement the torch which went with a clatter on to the girder and then, bouncing off, ricocheted down the well between the two buildings.

'You berk. You gone and dropped the bloody glim.'

'Damn the glim. Take a butcher's out o' the cinder.'

Obedient to the urgency in his companion's voice, the Gilt Kid looked out of the window. The moon was now freed from the lowering clouds and shining brightly. The awesome girder glistened. Beyond it lay the shadow-wreathed roof of the flat block. He could see nothing special.

'Well?' he asked.

'See anything?' Scaley almost pleaded as he put the question. A strong negative would have made him the most relieved man in the metropolitan area.

'Nothing to shout about. Why?'

This was not a definite enough denial for Scaley.

'Sure you can't see nothing? Take another look. I reckoned that there's someone moving about on the roof.'

The Gilt Kid peered again. He threw every ounce of energy that he possessed into his eyesight. The opposite roof was shadowy.

He struggled to pierce the shadows. He succeeded. With a heavy heart, but a flippant manner, he spoke.

'Yeh, there's someone on that roof all right. Two some-ones. So what?'

'You sure?'

'Course I'm sure. Didn't you see the bastards yourself?'

'Well, what the hell we going to do? Oh Christ, I thought this job was going to be a tumble.'

'Well, why in God's name did you bring me on it? Stop squealing now or I'll bash you. Let's get it thought out. Some lousy berk must have been snooping around the place and found that rory open.'

'You mean the door at the top? The fire escape door?'

'What other door d'you think, you daft bastard? Well, what's happened's this, the way I weigh it up. Bloke finds the door open. Hallo, he says, something queer's on. He calls someone else to give him a hand and they go out on the roof. Well, they got us by the cobblers.'

'How d'you figure that out?'

'Simple. Nothing's wrong in the flats. There must be something wrong over here then. That sticks out a mile. They look over this way and see the old glim: then they go and drop the blasted thing. That caps it. They got our number all right. All they got to do now is to shut that bloody door and drop the bar. You can't screw that, not with the bar down. We can't get out that way. If we go down the dancers here . . .'

'Sure, yes.' Scaley gripped the Gilt Kid's arm. 'Let's go downstairs here and out into the street.'

'Use your nut, Scaley mate. Ain't you got no eighteen-pence at all? They'll get on the blower and have this place surrounded by slops. There's only one thing for it.'

'And what's that?'

'Let's have a go for it, and stop chewing the fat. We might as well get nicked over that side as here. Let's dive across there and try to bash our way clear. If we get free, we're lucky. If we don't, we go to stir. And remember, it's every man for himself. If you make your getaway, well, good luck to you. Blimey, I wish I got that cane. It'd be handy in a barney. Come on, let's go.'

He swung one leg over the window ledge and started

feeling for the girder. The tip of his toe touched it. Gingerly he let himself down. When both his feet were on the girder he let go his hold on the sill and, taking a grip on the parapet once more, began his climb, this time with the knowledge that on the other side was waiting a man anxious to deprive him of his liberty if not, indeed, of his life. His pockets, filled as they were with stolen coins, weighed him down.

Raising his voice, he shouted to Scaley.

'Come on, china,' he called, carefully remembering to name no names in case that might lead to the calamity of subsequent identification. 'Come on! Try to get across at the same time as me so the bastards won't be able to take us singly. Safety in numbers.'

To his satisfaction he saw Scaley drop over the window ledge on to the girder.

The Gilt Kid moved quickly. His passage back was much more rapid than that across had been. There was no time to feel scared. If he fell over the side, he fell and that was all that there was to it. Perhaps the fellow waiting for him the other side had a gun and would kill him anyhow. Come to that he might as well be good and dead outside as half-dead in prison for three years. At least a lagging it would be if he fell this time. It would make his third con, counting that time he had been bound over. Only been out the matter of a week too. That would make things a hell of a sight worse. Old Bailey it looked like this stop. There hardly seemed much chance of it being a Sessions job. And the Inky Smudge would have quite a few kind words to say. Give him a proper caning he would.

He could hear Scaley panting beside him.

'Hurry up, kid. Let's get the agony over.'

'OK.'

He tried to move his hands and feet faster. There were only a couple more steps to take. He jerked his head to the right trying to see what was in store for him. As far as he could make out there were a couple of men kneeling on the roof just where the girder ran into the world. It was going to be hell trying to get up there. Suddenly the moon broke out of the clouds and lighted up everything clearly.

Yes, there were two men. One of them was hollering out.

'Got you, my beauties,' he yelled.

'Half a minute, pal. Come and get us.'

The Gilt Kid had reached the end of the girder now. His shoulders were up against the edge of the roof. He stared his two prospective captors in the face. It was stalemate.

The two men knelt there staring at the Gilt Kid. He gave them back stare for stare. Scaley was alongside him now. One of the kneeling men had red hair. His face was pale and there were freckles on his high cheekbones. The Gilt Kid smiled at him.

'Hallo, Ginger,' he said.

'Ginger yourself.' Redhead's voice was indignant.

'Not yet, mate. 'Spect I will soon, though.'

'What the hell you talking about?'

'Nothing. Everything I say will be taken down and used as evidence against me at my trial.'

'What's up with you for Christ's sake, kid? Come doolally tap?'

Scaley was getting worried. Here he was in a real bad spot and his pal seemed to have gone mad just when he ought to be using his head.

'That's all right, buddy, just stalling for time,' breathed back the Gilt Kid, who was thinking hard and fast while he talked rot. He stared at Ginger again.

'You blokes cops?' he asked.

'No. But we've 'phoned for them though.'

'Have you, by Christ? Well, we'd better give ourselves up.' There was no point in stalling any longer. If the police had been telephoned, it was clear that the sooner that

Scaley and he made their getaway the better. He moved his hands from the parapet to the edge of the roof, preparatory to heaving himself up. With dispassionate hatred Ginger put his foot on the Gilt Kid's knuckles. The bones squelched.

'Hey, don't do that, you bloody idiot. You'll make me fall. I'm going to give myself up. Give us a hand.'

Ginger knelt there undecided. The other man caught the Gilt Kid by the wrists and hauled him on to the roof. He stood there for a moment with his hands loosely holding his captive's wrists. With his heart beating even faster than ever the Gilt Kid stood waiting while he watched Ginger helping Scaley. This needed careful timing, he knew. If he struck too soon he would spoil everything.

Be careful now, kid, be careful. Use your loaf, he said to himself.

Pretending to be getting into a more comfortable position, with clever care he shifted his left foot forward so that the toe of his boot was against the other's instep. Still keeping his eye on Ginger and Scaley he flexed his knee, groping blindly for the man's shinbone. He felt his kneecap touch something solid. That was it. Triumph sang through his veins. He was going to win through against impossible odds.

The kneeling Ginger had just pulled Scaley on to the roof. Both were off their balance and temporarily out of action. Scaley was safely on the roof. Now was the time.

Now.

'Bash him, Scaley,' he called out, 'and then duck for it. Make it snappy. The slops are on the way.'

As he spoke he jerked his knee to the left, at the same time swinging his arms upwards and outwards. His wrists broke free from the other's encircling fingers. As the Gilt Kid's knee shot against his shinbone the man fell towards his right. A right hook to his left ear helped his fall. He hit the roof with a crack. He gave one convulsive gasp, cocked up his legs and arched his trunk. All the breath came springing out of his nostrils and open mouth in a groan. His body slackened and then sagged; he was spark out.

Without another thought for his vanquished adversary, the Gilt Kid sprang across to help Scaley. They would have to be working fast if they were to make their getaway before the police came.

The light of the moon showed them up plainly. They were locked on the roof. Both had fallen from their kneeling positions. Scaley had his arms round the other, pinning his hands to his side. Ginger was threshing wildly with his legs, trying to roll over so that he would be on top.

'Bring your knee up in his guts, Scaley. Christ, we ain't got the time to fight clean.'

Scaley tried to obey, but Ginger's floundering feet caught him on the kneecap. He grunted. The other man was coming round now. He had struggled up, but the effort was too much for him. He was on his hands and knees. In ten seconds he would be up and fighting again. Speed was imperative.

'Hold him still while I jump on his face. That'll put him out.'

Putting forth all his strength Scaley managed to hold his adversary still. His muscles were standing out and the veins in his forehead and hands bulged until they were nearly tearing themselves clean of the flesh. The Gilt Kid jumped into the air, expecting to feel his feet sink into the soft flesh of Ginger's face, crushing the nasal bone flat and breaking into his cheeks.

He landed on the roof.

With a terrific effort, in his terror Ginger had jerked himself and Scaley clear of the Gilt Kid. They had rolled to the edge of the roof. One of his hands had come free. He punched Scaley in the face. Scaley's head fell back.

The sudden movement had jerked him completely off his balance. He nearly rolled off the roof. With eager strength he clutched the harder at Ginger, dragging him, too. Ginger struck again.

This time he had done it.

Scaley fell off the roof. Wildly he had clung to Ginger and dragged him too. They disappeared from the Gilt Kid's scared sight into the inky blackness of the well. There was not a sound, not even a curse or a prayer, except the dull thud as their joint bodies hit the ground five stories down. There was not a chance for them. Dead they were. It was stone ginger.

The Gilt Kid peered with horrified eyes, trying to listen to any sound which might let him know what had happened. Nothing broke the silence.

The Gilt Kid turned away.

If they'd been creased, he reasoned, they were creased. He could do precisely nothing about it. The only thing for him was to get away while he could. He started for the fire escape door. It was very quiet and still. Everyone seemed to be killed, not only Scaley and Ginger.

In the meanwhile, the other man had come round completely. He was standing, panting heavily, with his clenched fists hanging loosely by his sides. There was a big swelling on the back of his head as he waited there, blocking the Gilt Kid's exit.

The Gilt Kid sprang at him with concentrated fury. Not only was he a savage fighting for his life and liberty, he was also venting his exasperation at the way in which everything had gone wrong. He swung a vicious right hook at the man's jaw, missed, and caught him on the ear again. At the same time he brought up his knee in his opponent's crutch. It was all out now: no holds barred.

The man, already weakened by the fall he had suffered, could not withstand this new onslaught. He collapsed to the ground limply, and lay there groaning and clutching with his hands at the injured part of his body.

The Gilt Kid, with the red mist of battle still in front of his eyes, shot a single glance at him. For a half-second he debated whether he should finish him off as he lay there on the roof. Dead men, he knew, told no tales. Then, a recollection of his need for hurried flight came over him.

He darted for the door.

Once more the stone steps sounded hollow beneath his flying feet. He spun round the corners of the stairway, steadying himself with one hand on the floor. Some of the flat doors were open, the bewildered tenants staring at his fleeting figure. The radio still blared forth its tune. A curious thought dashed into the mind of the speeding Gilt Kid: Radio's going. Can't be midnight yet.

One tenant, a man more intrepid than the rest, leapt across the landing to cut off his retreat. The Gilt Kid cannoned into his body. His impetus was now such that it was almost impossible to check his career. He barged his shoulder against his interceptor who fell heavily to the ground and rolled over. He, himself, staggered, recovered and went on.

The last flight of steps did not feel the touch of his scurrying feet. He jumped clean down them, almost pitching forward on to his face when he reached the ground. He had completely lost his breath and was gasping when the cold street air hit him in the face. Long strings of slime were streaming from his nostrils. He dashed out into the street.

A car, shapeless and indistinguishable in the night, was zooming up the street in the same direction Scaley had led him.

That'd be the slops, he figured out. Blast Scaley and his damned secretiveness. I don't know where the hell I am now.

He knew that it was out of the question to stand there thinking. Like a rabbit, he sped off in the opposite direction from the approaching police.

As he ran his brain worked fast. The officers were over there to the right. There must be a main road somewhere then. Somewhere near. The radio had still been playing. Buses ought to be running in that case. If he could find the main drag and jump a bus before the bogies got him, he should be able to make a clean getaway. There was no chance of fingerprints, and very little chance of identification.

The road bent round to the left.

When he had borne round the curve the Gilt Kid saw with a sign of thankfulness in his heart that there was a blaze of light at the end. A main road then. He looked like making that old getaway. He tried to increase his pace. His lungs were bursting.

Behind him he heard running feet. Not one pair, but two.

Hell. They were tailing him up then. Could he make it?

His legs were made of lead. They would not answer his command. His calf muscles had turned into blocks of iron. In spite of the speed at which he was undeniably moving, he felt as though he were making no progress.

His mouth was dry and had a dirty taste of salt in it.

The running footsteps were gaining on him. That much was clear. He was beaten.

Running, he noticed that a house door stood ajar. Probably one of the occupiers had gone out for six-penn'orth of fish and chips. Here was his chance of safety.

He careered through the tiny suburban garden and into the house, pulling the door to behind him to cut off his pursuers. The narrow hall in which he found himself smelt musty and was lighted by a flamingly naked gas jet. He stood still for a moment, steadying himself with one hand on a bamboo hat-stand as he fought to recapture his breath. His chest was heaving in spasmodic shudders. It felt as if there were a blazing furnace within it.

Whoever was in the house, if anybody were there at all, must think that the inmate who had left open the front door had returned since no notice was being taken of his presence.

As his breathing became more normal, he heard his pursuers rushing up the garden path. He could wait no longer. He must get out of the whole district soon. Directly they knew that murder had been committed there would be a cordon out to cut off the fugitive's escape.

Murder. That was the hell of a word.

At the end of the narrow hallway there was a small kitchen. He fled into that as he heard the police thundering on the front door. As he unlocked the back door a window opened in the front of the house and the sound of a questioning voice came to his ears.

The back garden was cluttered up with dustbins and tin buckets. It was just the sort of backyard that is seen in thousands by anyone entering London by train. A clothes-line hung with flapping white linen impeded his progress. His foot stumbled against a brick that was lying about for no clear reason. At the end of the garden was a low board fence surmounted by a trellis work.

He scrambled over this and dropped into the garden of another house. A dog barked at him, rattling his chain as he strained to get out of his kennel to attack the intruder. Again a window was thrown open and an indignant head was poked out.

With relief the Gilt Kid noticed that the house was semi-detached. He rushed for the open side, hurling up an insult at the expostulating householder.

The side gate was locked. He scaled it, clambering up by means of a rainwater butt. He fell on his hands and knees when he jumped down on the other side. Getting up, he dusted himself as best he could. He walked slowly down the front garden and let himself out of the front gate, not wanting to make himself look suspicious if there might be a policeman on beat outside.

He glanced up to the left: the road looked clear. He glanced down to the right: there was nobody in sight that way, and, there, about twenty yards down, lay the main road.

He broke into a run. It was even money that his pursuers were hot on his trail again by now. There was a bus in the main road. He swung himself on it, grasping the brass upright rail and running alongside the vehicle for about three steps.

As he hurried up the steps he noticed that the number of the bus was 27. That route ran, he knew, to Paddington. Well, Paddington would do as well as any other place. Throw them off the scent it ought to. A man bound for Victoria was unlikely to be going to Paddington. He subsided, panting, into a seat. The conductor came up to take his fare.

'Out of breath, ain't you, chum?'

'Yes. Been running,' replied the Gilt Kid between gasps. 'I didn't want to miss the bus. Last one, ain't it?'

'Nah, chum. There's plenty more.'

'Well, Paddington Station, please.'

He handed the conductor the fare. The conductor punched the ticket, with a satisfied if automatic 'cling'. He thought no more about the incident, not even when he read the paper next morning. Passengers to him, even when they were out of breath, were nothing more than slips of cardboard representing their destination.

The omnibus travelled along up past Hammersmith and towards Kensington. On this journey the Gilt Kid was taking no notice of the route. He slumped in his seat, his chin resting on his chest and his hands dangling over the back of the seat in front of him. At first, on realizing that he had, temporarily at any rate, escaped, he became the prey of a wild fear. His face, underneath the dirt and sweat which it had accumulated during his flight, grew quite pale; his teeth, which for some reason were as hard and dry as if he had taken quinine, chattered so that he had difficulty in stilling them. He wanted to look round to see whether anyone were standing with an outstretched accusing finger. Then, lassitude overcame him. He had been through an overcrowded twenty-four hours. His heavy eyelids closed. His head, still lolling forward, nodded to the irregular rhythm of the bus. He fell asleep.

Suddenly, he awakened with a start.

He looked out of the blurred, steamy window to find out where he was. It was Notting Hill Gate.

Hell. He was sick of this bus anyway.

He got off.

JIMMY

At Notting Hill Gate the Gilt Kid caught another bus and dozed his way to Trafalgar Square. Why he wanted to go there was quite incomprehensible even to himself. Still, he might just as well go there as anywhere else.

At Trafalgar Square he got off. There was a nip in the night air. He shivered, wishing that he were wearing an overcoat. He had no overcoat to wear. It had been summer when he had been arrested and so, naturally, he had gone to the court without one. All his belongings prior to his arrest had been lost.

Who had them God alone knew. Probably it would be the bogies at the Yard, he reflected bitterly.

He had money now to buy plenty of overcoats. That is if they did not do him on this murder rap. It was a hell of a lot of money he had. How much was it exactly?

He thought for a moment.

A hundred and twenty-four nicker apart from what was in his pocket before. That was OK. Pity, though, that they had divvied up. If only he had Scaley's share, too, in his pocket, that would not have been wasted when he got his.

Scaley.

Poor old Scaley. That certainly had been a nasty end for the poor mug. Yes, and all the time he had not really wanted to go on the job. Something had been telling him to lay off. Let anyone say what he liked, there must be something in that sort of warning. Time after time they seemed to come round. It was kind of funny. Poor old Scaley, though. Even with all his caution he had come unstuck at the end. Well,

Scaley had got his and that was the end of it. Everybody had to die some time.

He shivered again.

Die. That was the hell of a note. Damn nigh as miserable as murder. How did a bloke stand over this murder business anyway? Was he in it as deep as Scaley? After all it was Scaley who had killed Ginger. Perhaps there was a chance of getting away with it. Bloody slim chance. Take robbery with violence f'r instance. All the blokes on the job were in that as deep as each other. The fellow driving the car caught a bashing with the cat just as much as the fellow who carried the cosh. It looked like if a guy went on the crook with another they were both responsible for each other's actions and had to take the rap. Well, if anybody had recognized him and could pick out his dial in the Rogues' Gallery up at the Yard, it was going to be too bad at nine o'clock one morning in the Ville.

'Hallo, Gilt Kid!'

The Gilt Kid, while ruminating, had walked right across Trafalgar Square from the corner of Duncannon Street to Spring Gardens. Hearing someone call his name in this fashion he nearly died of fright. He looked round guardedly, ready to fight or run as the case might warrant. Perhaps they had tailed him up or maybe sent out a radio with his description to all the Squad patrol cars.

'You don't half look scared, son.'

To his relief the Gilt Kid saw that the speaker was an old tramp. Somehow his face and voice were familiar.

'You don't remember me, do you, mate?' The tramp's voice was a curious mixture of humility and truculence.

The Gilt Kid looked a little more closely. The light of recognition dawned in his eyes. He knew the face beneath the grime and the weatherburn won through days and nights in the open.

'Blimey, yes. It's Jimmy,' he said. 'Old Jimmy Nunn who

used to be in "C" Hall in the Scrubs. How you getting along, Jimmy boy?'

'On the ribs, mate, on the ribs. Nothing ain't gone right, not since I come out of stir. Got another packet I did. Fourteen days in Pentonville.'

'What did they give you that for?'

'Begging they reckoned. A bloke came up and he arsts me the way. It was in the Strand it was. Well, I shows him and he slips me a tanner. Blimey if a copper don't come up and nick me. "You was begging from that gentleman," he says. "What, me?" I says. "Yes you," he says. Just like that. He takes me along to Bow Street and next day I gets fourteen days. Bomp.'

'What's it like in the Ville?'

'Bastard.'

Jimmy Nunn spat to show his comment on His Majesty's prisons in general and Pentonville Gaol in particular.

'How you fixed, Jimmy? Stuck for the price of a kip, eh?'

'"Stuck for the price of a kip?"' Jimmy repeated the Gilt Kid's phrase with a bitter contempt. '"Stuck for the price of a kip." Blimey, son, I ain't had me bleeding clothes off without a word of a lie not since I come out of Pentonville. They gives me a couple of bob they does, the DPA, and by the time I has a bit of grub, why I'm on the deck again.'

'Well, here's your kip for tonight, anyhow. I don't like seeing one of my old pals on the floor.' The Gilt Kid produced half a crown from his pocket. As he spoke he was thinking hard and fast. 'Go to Bruce House I would if I were you. It's one and a penny, but God, it's worth paying the extra fivepence. I've had one night in Tommy Brown's. Never no more.'

'Thanks, mate. You're a toff.'

'How'd a fiver look to you?'

'A fiver? Say it again.' Jimmy was frankly incredulous. Youth and its optimism were over for him. He never expected to own more than ten shillings at a time in his life again. And that would be in three years – if he lived so long and was able to qualify for the Old Age Pension.

'A fiver. Five pounds, five nicker, five quid, five oncers, pangy bar. That clear?' The Gilt Kid laughed.

'You're asking me how five pound'd look to me?'

'Yes.'

'You wouldn't kid me, would you?'

'No.'

'Well, I'll tell you straight. It would look like heaven, it would.'

'OK then, Jimmy boy. It's yours if you want it. Provided you do something for me.'

'I'd do anything for a quid, let alone five of the bastards, I would, so help me Christ.'

'Even tell a lie?' The Gilt Kid was now laughing outright.

'Even telling a thousand bloody lies. What's on your mind?'

'Listen, Jimmy, I'll come clean. I done a job. I got a bit of dough, but there's a decent chance of me being recognized. S'posing I give you a fiver, will you swear blind I been with you all night?'

'Sure I will, son. You picked me up on the Embankment at seven o'clock . . .'

'Make it eleven. I'm fixed all right till then.'

'Have it your own way. You picks me up on the Embankment at eleven o'clock. Takes me into a coffee shop and stands me a bite of supper . . .'

'All right, Jim,' laughed the Gilt Kid. 'I'll do that, too.'

'Stands me a bite of supper, you does. We sits talking in the caff till about half pas' twelve and you goes home having given me the price of a kip. How about that? I'll swear that black, blue and green before all the juries and judges in England, Lord Hewart and Sir Percival Clarke included.'

'That'll do fine, Jimmy. Come along. We'll go and grab

that supper right now. But, listen, if you try to come any funny stuff, putting the old black on me or any of that madam, well, one fine day they'll find you floating the Thames and nobody'll worry two damns about how an old lag like you come to fall into the Drink. Get that into your old filbert.'

'Blimey. I wouldn't come none of that acid. I wouldn't never. I plays straight with my pals. That's me.'

'I'm not so bloody certain about that, Jim. Still here's your fiver. And remember.'

Jimmy Nunn took the five flimsy pieces of paper with fingers which trembled as much from unbelief as from cold and old age. He stowed them carefully away somewhere between the layers of clothing that wrapped his malodorous body. When next he brought them out they would smell of sweaty flesh.

'Where am I going to buy you that grub, Jim?'

'Well, there's a caff in King William Street. That's about the nearest place.'

'Right. Let's go there then.'

They walked across Trafalgar Square together and in silence. Each was thinking his own thoughts. Jimmy was wondering what to do with the five pounds. It would be quite ridiculous to buy any new clothes. The tousled rags that covered his itching body were quite good enough for an old man. The most sensible thing would be to pay for a cubicle at Bruce House for a fortnight and then sling the rest of the money away as he felt. Beer. That was what he wanted. To hell with food. Tea and bread and margarine. A man could keep alive on that, particularly if he dived into a fish shop every now and then and came out with a tanner's worth of rock salmon and taters. Yet it'd be all right, though, to have one decent tightener in a cawfee shop. Just a bit of the old-style chuck he had been used to eat in the old days when he had swung a pick and sled as well as any man. A great lump of steak, he would have, none of your imported muck, but a real good lump of English steak about three-quarters of a pound in weight. And with the steak he would have tomatoes and cabbage and potatoes, boiled potatoes they would be, none of your bloody chips, and the cabbage would be a great heavy green square of squelching vegetable. After he had eaten the meat he would have currant duff and custard. Sure, yes, that would be a real meal. After that, he would be content with tea, bread and margarine for the rest of the few years that were left to him. But the most of the fiver would go in the old pig's ear. Fivepenny pints of ale, all black and with plenty of froth on the top, drunk in public bars where a bloke could swear and spit on the deck if he felt that way. Yes, and maybe have a couple of nice games of darts before he got too much skimish into his guts. Finally, forgetting everything, that he was condemned for the rest of his existence to a life which looked upon a cheap bed in a kip house as the greatest of luxuries, he would go out and vomit in the gutter, spewing up all the pints that would have settled so uneasily in his worn-out empty stomach.

The Gilt Kid's mind was occupied, too, with old Jimmy.

Had he, he asked himself, been a bit stingy with the poor old bum? A fiver was little enough to have to pay for an alibi. A tenner could have easily been afforded. But the old chap seemed as pleased as punch at getting the fiver. It was to be hoped that he would play straight. Still, as he had said, a carve-up could be settled very easily. Nobody misses an old man when he's on the ribs.

They arrived at the café. It was a little bar built into the wall. Jimmy climbed on to a stool and leant his forearms on the counter.

The man at the bar looked at him askance. He was not, as a matter of fact, particularly fond of having down and outs in his place. For a start, they sat about too long over one cup of tea. Spending twopence they seemed to think they had bought the right to remain for a couple of hours.

What was more, the sight of them often frightened away more lucrative customers who did not want to have the bee put on them. And the other fellow who had come in was a bit rough-looking, too. He was dressed good enough, to be sure, but his face was all grimy except where rivulets of sweat had cut channels in the dirt. Probably he was drunk. Well, if he started any nonsense, out he would go on his neck – and no questions asked.

He began viciously to swab up the tea stains on the bar just to show his disapproval.

It was Jimmy Nunn who broke the silence. When he came into a place he liked to talk. He had been a homeless wanderer, with silence enforced on him, for long enough to comprehend the pleasures of conversation.

'Well, mate, what you got to eat?'

'Hot pies, pork pies, cakes, cheesecakes, ham rolls, cheese rolls, boiled eggs.'

Jimmy rubbed his hands.

'Well, give us a nice hot pie and a cup o' tea. There ain't nothing like a nice cup of tea to keep the cold out on a night like this. Fair perished them poor blokes in the Square must be.'

'Yes?' The man was not particularly interested in the fate or sufferings of them poor blokes in the Square. His own troubles were quite enough for him. 'What's your order?' he inquired almost fiercely of the Gilt Kid.

'Make it the same as the other bloke.'

The man went to get the pies from the hot plate. The Gilt Kid turned to Jimmy.

'You must know the down-and-out lark pretty good by now, don't you, Jimmy mate?'

'Know it pretty good. So help me, I knows it inside out, upside down and a couple of other ways as well.'

'Perhaps you can tell me something about it then, what I've always wanted to know?'

'Tell you anything you want to know about it, I can.'

'Well, what the hell are those little bundles you always see bums carrying about. They're always lashed up with little parcels of Christ alone knows what.'

'They carries their stuff about with them. A spare shirt and a couple o' tins in case they want to have a shackle up.'

'But you can't drum up in London.'

'Who said they was going to drum in London? Some of them blokes is dossers what has just hit the Smoke. Then there's a lot as carries a load of newspapers and brown papers around with 'em. They say it keeps out the cold when they're skippering. What's more there's some what reckons brown paper next the skin keeps off the rheumatism.'

'I see.'

Their hot pies and cups of tea were handed to them. Jimmy cut open his pie and liberally dosed it with sauce. He stirred his tea, then drank a little of it, holding the spoon tightly against the edge of the cup.

'That ain't all,' he said, when the tea, creating a grateful warmth in his stomach, had stimulated his desire for conversation. 'There's some what carries a lot of old tots around. In the mornings they go knocking at the doors of houses.

'"Beg your pardon, lady," they says. "I ain't had no breakfast. Could you spare me a few old rags what I could sell." They nearly always touches lucky and cops. When they've got about a hundredweight of tots – and mind you that takes some doing – they takes them to a shop over Southwark and flogs them. There ain't a hell of a lot in that lark, but they do get a bit of money on the side like. Enough to pay for their kip for a week p'raps.'

'They don't spend none on grub and snout then?' said the Gilt Kid with a mouth full of pie that he was not enjoying very much.

'Grub and snout?' There was a tremendous scorn in

Jimmy's echo. 'Gawd, who'd want to buy snout? There's plenty of dog-ends lying on the pavements, ain't there?'

He delved beneath his coat and brought out a flat tin box. He opened it.

'Look at that now,' he said with the calm pride of a man who knows that he really has achieved something.

The box was filled with cigarette ends of all kinds; long, short, broken, some flattened with the impress of a careless heel, some idly thrown away with only a puff or two drawn out of them. The Gilt Kid made a vow never again to tread on an unwanted cigarette end.

'What do you do with them?' he asked. 'Smoke them as they are?'

'Smoke them as they are! Blimey no. I rolls them up with a bit of fag paper. There's some smokes them in a pipe and there's others what flogs them round the spikes at three nooks an ounce. I don't go to no spikes, though. They can keep their lousy spikes.'

'And grub, what do you do about that?'

'It's easy enough to bum a bit of chuck. There's a lady and gentleman comes into the Square every night and all the boys on the ribs queues up and gets a thick cheese sandwich apiece. Then there's a convent down Victoria way where they hands out two slices of bread and marge and a lump of bread pudden at twelve o'clock every day. Then, there's another place up Theobald's Road where they dishes you out with a couple of slices of bread and marge at three in the afternoon. If you get about a bit you don't go hungry.'

'Yes, but that's not hardly what you'd call substantial. It's damn near the same as doing No 1 in the nick.'

'But that ain't all. There's a lady comes into the Square once or twice a week. Tuesdays and Fridays she comes as a rule. The Silver Lady they calls her. She comes there dishing out tanners to all the boys. And there's Charrington's in the Mile End Road, Sundays.'

'Charrington's? You mean the brewers? For God's sake don't tell me that they dish you out with free beer. I'll come on that lark, too.'

'Free beer? You ain't half got a hope, ain't you? You'd get a lot of free beer going there. No, there was a bloke name of Charrington what used to be connected with the brewery. He give the dough for free teas on Sunday. Turned a bit religious he did and you have to sing a few hymns and then you has tea and bread and butter and a lump o' cake. Good tea it is and all. And as you go out they give you a bit of tobacco and a card letting you come again next week. That's what I call a good charity.'

'Good charity? It certainly is. Singing hymns is a bit off though, ain't it?' The Gilt Kid yawned. He was getting sleepy.

'Well, you can't expect to get your tea for nothing. You got to put up with something. There's another place like that down Walthamstow way, but I've never got there yet. It's a bit far and I likes to keep hanging around the Square.'

'Strikes me then,' said the Gilt Kid between his yawns, 'the only thing a bloke's stuck for is his kip. How d'you manage about that?'

'Sitting around the Square until the parks open and then having a bit of a lie down there.'

'You can get a bit of a kip in during the day then while it's warmer?'

'In the day? I should say not. You're too busy in the day dashing around queueing up for your bit of chuck. Mustn't miss that you know. Got to keep well-nourished on this caper.'

The Gilt Kid suppressed a laugh at Jimmy's idea of keeping well-nourished.

'Well, there's tricks in every trade,' he said banally and with a sigh.

'Yes, that's true. Too bloody true, mate. Look. You call yourself a real wide boy. You reckon there ain't many dodges you aren't up to. What I say is, get on the ribs for a bit. You'd need an old bloke like me to show you how to get along cushty.'

'Yes, but I'm enough of a wide boy not to be on the ribs.'

'That's true.'

Jimmy sucked a reflective tooth. The Gilt Kid heaved himself off his chair.

'Well, good night, Jimmy,' he said extending his hand. 'I got to be going now.'

'Good night, mate.'

'And remember, Jimmy, what I told you.'

'That's all right, son. You can count on me.'

HOME

The Gilt Kid paid his bill and left. There were no buses running and he had to walk down Whitehall. The wind blew piercingly up from the river. The dullness, added to his weariness, made him feel depressed. Poor old Jimmy. Glad enough now to perjure himself for a fiver.

That's what happened to all blokes on the crook. They got too old for the game and had to end their lives sitting about in Trafalgar Square and on the Embankment. That was, unless they touched real unlucky and went down for a long time. Five years' penal servitude and seven years' preventive detention. Some copped that. They died in Camp Hill instead of coughing their lungs up under Hungerford Bridge. It was a bastard whichever way you looked at it.

Some got topped, too.

His neck shivered and he walked a little more quickly as if he wanted to leave the thought behind him.

At Parliament Square he found a cruising taxi.

'Victoria Station,' he said as he got in. In the first place, he could not remember his own address. Such a lot seemed to have happened since he last had left home. Secondly, he did not care to give it to a taxi-driver, even if he knew it: there might be a tumble that way if he should have been recognized.

Once inside the taxi he leant his head back against the black leather cushions and, without a thought of its previous occupants – lovers maybe using a fast-moving vehicle as their only insulation against peering London, mourners hurrying to a station to catch a train to a deathbed, and even crooks escaping the pursuing police – fell asleep.

When the taxi stopped at Victoria the driver, disgruntled at the thought that possibly he had for a fare a drunk who had no money, had to shake him violently into wakefulness.

The Gilt Kid rose reluctantly, paid off the fare and started walking home. There was nothing in his mind but a terrible lassitude that seemed to come up and hit him in a regular monotone of waves. When he reached his own street, it was with an effort that he remembered the number of the house.

He stood on the steps leading up to the front door, leaning against one of the pillars of the portico while he fumbled in his pocket for his key. He was yawning in a way that nearly dislocated his jaw. At last his fingers closed over the key. It had been in one of the pockets of his waistcoat.

He thought, as he inserted it in the lock and turned it noiselessly from force of habit, that it would have been damned ironical if he had lost the key and had to break into his own lodgings.

The narrow hall of the house was pitch dark and smelt with that mustiness usual in country vicarages. He walked up the stairs, successfully preventing them from creaking beneath his ascending footsteps.

His own room was, naturally enough, dark also. He lighted a match to guide himself across the room. It burnt itself out before he had arrived at the gas jet. He swore softly, and put his scorched forefinger and thumb to the lobe of his ear in the hope that he might, thereby, kill the pain.

He struck another match and held the flame close to the gas jet, at the same time fingering the tap.

Queer, he thought, the gas is on. Oh hell, it must have been left on ever since – when was it? – yesterday, and burnt itself out.

He went out on to the landing once more and slid a penny into the meter. The gas, for he had not yet snapped it off, rushed out of the jet with a roar. He had to turn the tap off again before he finally had the flame ignited.

The light leapt up in its glass globe, illuminating the narrow room which wore that curiously impersonal look which rooms always wear while they are still tidy after having been 'done'.

The Gilt Kid undressed himself swiftly, slinging his clothes around the room recklessly. He was too tired to be bothered to hang them up neatly on stretchers and, anyhow, he had enough money to buy himself a new suit now if he felt that way. The money he heaped on the dressing-table. It reminded him of pictures in boys' papers of pirates' hoards.

Something would have to be done about that money. It would have to be sent to a place where it would be, at the same time, easily accessible to himself and completely inaccessible to the inquisitive eyes of the police.

Well, that was simple and could be taken care of on the next day. Sleep was, for the present, the most important thing. Only once, in the rapid process of his undressing, had he paused. That was to debate the suitability of wearing pyjamas. Eventually he decided against them. Pyjamas were effeminate things for a man to wear, and it was far simpler to sleep in a shirt.

He lighted a cigarette from the gas, damaging the mantle a little more by doing so. The gas was now spurting out on one side. The flame was yellow, tinged with blue. The Gilt Kid picked up the book that lay on the mantelpiece and got into bed.

At first it seemed to be Paradise to be lying there. Never had there been softer pillows or a more comfortable mattress. He stretched his legs further down the bed, enjoying the icy touch of the sheets against his naked legs. He distended his tired muscles. It was an orgasm of pleasure to be merely in bed. He blew great clouds of cigarette smoke luxuriously down his nostrils.

Then he turned over the book that lay in his hands. It was, for this was his only book, *Capital*, once more.

He opened it at random. Any page was just as likely to be incomprehensible as any other.

'The surplus-value,' he read, 'generated in the process of production by C, the capital advanced, or in other words, the self-expansion of the value of the capital C, presents itself for our consideration, in the first place as a surplus, as the amount by which the value of the product exceeds the value of its constituent elements.'

Well, that was simple enough.

'The capital C,' he read on, 'is made up of two components, one, the sum of money c laid out upon the means of production, and the other, the sum of money v expended upon the labour-power; c represents the portion that has become constant Capital, and v the portion that has become variable capital. At first then, C = c+v; for example, if £500 is the capital advanced, its components may be such that £500 = £410 const. + £90 var.'

His attention was beginning to wander. This struck him rather as gilding the lily. Nevertheless he struggled onwards.

'When the process of production is finished, we get a commodity whose value = (c+v)+s, where s is the surplus value; or taking our former figures, the value of this commodity may be (£400 const. + £90 var.) + £90 surpl. The original capital has now changed from C to C/, from £500 to £590. The difference is s or surplus value of £90.'

He threw the book on to the floor. It tumbled over and lay sprawling and open face downwards.

There was not, he had come to the conclusion, a lot of action in it. Old man Marx seemed to be flogging a dead horse. Now, the sort of red bible that ought to be written . . .

He closed his eyes.

In a moment he would have been asleep.

He opened his eyes again and stared up at the over-familiar ceiling. He was lacking in the requisite energy to get out of bed and turn off the gas. Bitterly he upbraided gas-lighting. With electricity now, it was possible to tie a piece of string to the switch and just flick the light out whenever convenient. A candle could be moved about the room to the most suitable spot, but gas, well, a man with gas had to get out of bed and put it out. Even in prison a warder came round and turned off the lights, but then a prisoner's life had many pleasurable simplicities which a free man's lacked. A prisoner need only shave once a week if he felt that way and spit on the floor whenever he wanted. Come to that, a prisoner always seemed to be spitting. On the exercise ground, in the workshops, lining up to go to work, there would always be at least one greycoated prisoner letting a white dollop of spittle fall from his lips on to the ground. Perhaps it was because they did not have enough to eat. Some book once had something in it about the way saliva abounded in a starving man's mouth.

Hell, if he did not put the gas out soon he would be lying there thinking until morning came. Funny how a fellow's mind ran on from lights to spittle.

He caught hold of the edges of the bed and pushed himself into a sitting position. For a moment he remained like that, his shoulders uncovered from the blankets' recent warmth, shivering a little. Then, with a sudden movement he jumped from his bed and put off the gas. He leapt in again even more rapidly than he had leapt out, for the oilcloth struck cold against the soles of his naked pattering feet.

In bed once more, he snuggled down under the sheets, his head denting into the pillow. It was really rather nice being in kip. He closed his eyes. Great grey walls came before them; a blanket which had somehow worked itself clear of the sheet below it, scratched against the flesh of his face. It was a pleasant sort of caress. He liked it. His breathing became deeper and more regular.

There was a lot of stuff to be done next day. All that dough would have to be planted and some sort of fanny would have to be worked up so that he might explain to Maisie just why he couldn't marry her. He would have to buy a paper, too, so that he might find out exactly what had happened down at Hammersmith. Poor old Scaley.

Still it was an awful lot of dough. Quite enough to show off with in front of Maisie. Maybe there would be other nice little jobs waiting to be pulled in the future. He would show Maisie what spending meant. There was a good time coming.

He had fallen asleep.

The room, no longer permeated by his conscious presence, became impersonal again. The window, with its undrawn blinds, was a grey patch of sordid light. The walls stood mute guardians of one hundred and fifty-six pounds of sleeping flesh and bone.

AWAKENING

The Gilt Kid awakened suddenly. He sat up with a start, as though he were expecting an attack from some quarter. There was in his mind a dull feeling of apprehension which he could not quite properly place.

Scaley. Hammersmith.

The two words came into his consciousness and dull apprehension was replaced by a vivid, actual fear. The previous evening he had been half-cut and unable to see things in their real perspective; the excitement of the fight on the roof and the chase over the garden walls had been an emotion strong enough to banish any others. His relief at a temporary escape had been great enough to grant him the illusion that the escape was permanent.

Now, he knew exactly what that illusion was worth. This was going to be a real big job. The Yard would be called in, the bogies would be at work now, picking up clues. Already the vast machinery of Criminal Investigation had been set in motion against him. What weapons had he with which to fight against it? Only his own wit and an alibi which he had bought for five pounds from a down and out.

If this were to be classed as a murder rap the noose was as good as placed around his neck. Even if they did not rate it so high it would be robbery with violence.

His back muscles began to shudder beneath the blows of an imagined cat o' nine tails.

He looked around the room for a cigarette. It was quite impossible to think things out coherently without a smoke. The stolen tin lay, together with the matches, on top of the dressing-table.

He got up out of bed to fetch it. His heart beat wildly as he crossed the floor and a slight giddiness from the stale air of the room – for he had been too tired on the previous night to remember to open the window – assailed him. When he picked up the tin of cigarettes he caught sight of the money.

There certainly was an immense amount there. He had not realized previously what a lot it looked. A pile of silver, in the early morning chill, felt frosty against his fingers and sent a little thrill up his arm.

Well that dough would have to be planted before very many more hours were over.

He fumbled with the tin and drew out a cigarette. There were only two others left. That meant he would have to be going out soon. A fellow could not lie in kip all day without some fags to keep him company. He struck a match and held it to his cigarette with trembling fingers.

His reflection in the mirror looked pretty ghastly. A stubble of yellowish hair covered his upper lip and his chin. His face was grimy and his eyes red-rimmed. His hair was tousled. There was a general puffed, frowsty look about his cheeks.

He blew the smoke out of his nostrils. He had held it down in his chest as long as he could.

What was the time likely to be?

Having neither watch nor clock, he could not tell. The grey, filtered, rain-washed light that percolated through the window told him nothing. No one was outside in the street below, not even a coalman with his melancholy dirge. It was too late in the year for there to be a 'Wallsy'.

One thing was certain, though. It was not between noon and two. During that couple of hours, the streets in this, as in every other proletarian neighbourhood, were full of school-children with their shrill, piercing voices and their interminable arguments. It was, he decided, either eleven in the morning or three in the afternoon, and whichever time it might be, clearly the best course was to go back to bed and finish off this fag instead of standing there barefoot and wearing only a shirt.

He jumped back into bed and pulled the covers up over his shoulders. From time to time he had to put a forearm out into the cold so that he could take his cigarette from between his lips. Otherwise he kept himself as warm as he could.

He reviewed the coming day.

Soon he would get up, get up properly, that was, and shave and dress. Then he would write a letter, send the money away, have some grub and go along to see Maisie. Poor kid, she must be feeling ever so excited now. Oh hell, yes, and that Curly had screwed her place. She would be full of that when he saw her. He would have to do his best not to laugh. Funny how those people who tried to catch steamers always got caught themselves in the end.

It was poetic justice or whatever they called it.

The cigarette end was burning his lips. He took it out of his mouth and threw it into the fireplace.

Why did they call it poetic justice for God's sake? It was bad enough to have to contend with ordinary justice. Someone had told him that Lord Darling wrote poetry. Perhaps that was what it meant. It was kinda funny that justice and punishment had come to mean the same thing. If everybody got justice then, and you heard speakers in the Park demanding it, everybody would get punished. Well, it was possible that everybody deserved it. He could remember a fellow saying to him back in stir that when people said that Justice was blind, they really meant that it shut one eye. Oh, it was all too complicated.

He fell off again into the heavy, dreamless, day-time sleep. When he was re-awakened it was by the sound of children's voices in the streets outside. It was after twelve o'clock. They were coming back from school. He roused himself.

If he lay like that, he could lie for always. Come on.

With the air of a man embarking on a difficult task with a set purpose he jumped out of bed and splashed some cold water into the wash-basin. He plunged his face into the water and tried to open his eyes while they were still submerged. He came up, spluttering and shaking like a dog. That was better. There was nothing like cold water to make a fellow feel good.

He soaped his neck, ears and arms, and rinsed off the soap. Now for a shave.

He looked at the razor and the lather brush with disgust. It was too much bother to heat the water for a shave, and it was hell with cold water. Hell grew no more tolerable with standing and looking at it.

He lathered his face and went over to the dressing-table so that he could look in the mirror while he scraped away. It was not a pleasant process and, by the time he had his face clean of bristles, he was very glad to cool it by plunging again into the wash-basin.

He dried himself vigorously with a pleasantly rough towel and, putting on his trousers, socks and shoes, pulled his suitcase from under his bed. There was a cheap packet of notepaper and some envelopes inside it. He took them out and, sitting down at the dressing-table, began to write in pencil. The envelope he could address in ink at the post office.

He licked the pencil with his tongue before writing. This action he took as much in order to induce thought as to increase the legibility of his letter. When he had written the address, the date and 'Dear George', he paused for further reflection. There was still another cigarette in the packet.

He lighted up. Ideas began now to flow a little more freely. He wrote rapidly in his board-school hand.

'Dear George – You will be surprised to get this letter not hearing from me since I came from that place,' he began. (For some reason he always opened his letters with the phrase, 'you will be surprised'.) 'As a matter of fact I have not been out long as you know. That is why I have not written. I am writing now to tell you that I have done a little bit of business and my customer paid cash so I did not have to hang about waiting for payment for my goods. I am sending some of the cash for you to look after for me like you do. I am sending you a hundred and five pounds in a registered letter you can keep the fiver but please look after the hundred pounds for me I know you will not let me down. Send me the money as I ask for it when I write to you you will see the address of the place I want you to send it to at the head of the letter when I write. As a matter of fact I am changing my address soon. I don't mind telling you that I am going to live with a girl. She wants me to marry her but between you and me I won't.

'Send me the money as I ask for it. This is a nice little bit I am sending you this time so look after it good I know you will play straight with me and not let me down. If I touch lucky I shall be sending you along some more soon look after it good. I don't want to have to come down your way George and give you a bashing but I know I wont have to as you wont let me down.

'Well George that is all I hope that things are breaking good with you as they are with me. I hope you and yours are quite well.

'Good-bye Your pal
'Jim Kennedy.'

He put the letter into the envelope, leaving the flap unsealed.

He picked up comb and hairbrushes and did his hair. Stooping down, he polished his shoes. Finally he slipped on his coat, picked up his hat and went out. It was always a great relief to him to get dressed and to have that ordeal over and done with for another twenty-four hours.

In the street he thought for a moment.

What had he to do?

Cigarettes had to be got. Yes, but that could wait. So could breakfast. No, the first thing to be done was to get rid of this letter. Where was the nearest post office? There was one in Victoria Street nearly opposite the top of Vauxhall Bridge Road. To reach that he would have to pass Victoria Station. There were always bogies about in the station approach. It would be silly to run the risk of being thieved with this brief in his pocket. Ah, there was another post office in Churton Street. That was the place to make for.

He made off in the direction of Churton Street. He looked about to see whether there was a public clock anywhere so that he might accurately know the time. There was none in sight. It was a hell of a district this Pimlico. It was a pity that he had ever come to live in it, although he had been so eager at first to go there. As a district it was depressing. The houses, for one thing, had been built for far wealthier people than were living in them. It was the coming of the railway, he supposed, that had prevented it from being like Belgravia only a few yards away. And then the people who lived in Pimlico were a funny lot. Failures of some sort nearly all were. Genteel people reduced to letting lodgings as a means of livelihood, 'students' of every race and colour, middle-class apers of the wealthy who found that by living in a cheap, central district they had more money to live in the style which they tried to imitate from the *Tatler*, and a fair sprinkling of prostitutes and crooks to give a seasoning to the mixed dish: that was the make-up of Pimlico's humanity.

He had reached Warwick Street. There, at last, was a clock. If the clock was right, then the time was a quarter past twelve.

The market stalls in Warwick Street, which at night added a vivid gaiety to the street scene, looked by day merely squalid. The ground around them was littered with bits of paper and cabbage leaves. Pale, harassed-looking women, for the most part with string-bags hanging from their arms, stared either at the stalls or into the windows of the cut-price shops; spinning their money out as best they could, they would be buying cheap tinned salmon, condensed milk, hard soaplike Canadian cheese, and salt-encrusted, badly cured Empire bacon. Those who scorned margarine would purchase imitation imported butter at tenpence a pound. On Saturdays they could get cheap scraps of dusty meat from the stalls. Few, if any, ate real food.

At the corner, a man stood selling the midday editions of the evening papers. He held two bills. One read:

ALL THE RUNNERS
AND SELECTIONS

The other read:

YARD SEARCH IN
MIDNIGHT ROOF DRAMA

The Gilt Kid crossed over. It seemed to him that his heart must have stopped beating. He had been trying to drive the idea of the previous night out of his head by thinking of Pimlico and the social condition of its inhabitants. The sight of these two bills brought it all back to him with a shock.

He held out two pennies and took in return a copy of either paper. These he tucked under his arm. He did not feel like opening them just yet. Some inherited taboo made him desire to put off the evil moment. Yet, as he walked through into Churton Street, he could not but be conscious of the papers under his arm.

So the Yard was on the job, eh? Well, that was only to be expected. The Squeak must have gone in pretty damn soon, though, for the papers to have got the story already. Of course the slops had been turning up at the block of flats just as he was making his getaway. Yes, and coming along in a jam jar too. That made them look like Sweenies.

Yes, he was forced to admit, whichever way he looked at it things did not look too pleasant.

'Yard Search,' it had said. Oh, blimey, that looked as if they might have a clue or a description.

Fear touched his heart with its icy finger.

He was at the post office. Going inside, he picked up a pen, dipped it in the gratuitous ink and addressed the letter. He stepped over to the frigid-faced girls behind their wire-netting barrier, changed the silver for a money order and put in notes making up the hundred guineas and registered the letter. While the proceedings were going on he looked around him.

There was not much chance of screwing this place. There was plenty of dough in post offices, of course, but the only way to get at it was by sticking the place up. Stick-ups weren't no good in England. In the first place there was always the risk of the cat: in the second a crook doing a stick-up always took the chance of being recognized: finally stick-ups were no good because people did not let themselves be stuck-up. They weren't scared of the gun for they knew it would not be used. If a few post office people got rubbed out, then they would put up their hands quick enough. That fellow who did the Glasgow bank knew his onions.

THE PAPERS

When the Gilt Kid had handed the letter over to the girl, then he felt a little more relieved and able to face the world. At last a certain amount of incriminating evidence was out of his possession.

He walked up Denbigh Street into Wilton Road. There were plenty of cafés in Wilton Road and he would be able to get his breakfast. It was a strange thing that he always seemed to be having his meals at unusual times of the day. Never since he had been out of stir had he managed to get in three square meals a day at their proper times. Well, it was a change from the monotony of the nick anyhow. When a man first came out he felt fine, eating when he liked and what he liked, getting up when he wanted to get up and going to bed when he was bored with being out of bed, but he soon got used to liberty, just as he soon got used to restraint. It was the regular life in prison though that did a fellow good, they said. That was what made a prisoner put on weight. He did not have a lot to eat, but he had the same amount and at the same times every day, he had the same number of hours' sleep and the same minimum of fresh air and exercise.

His inconsequent thoughts ran on. He was trying not to worry about what might be in the papers. It would be quite bad enough when he had read them.

He paused outside a café reading what was painted in white upon a brown board on the pavement.

STOP HERE FOR A SQUARE MEAL
THE WELCOME CAFE NOTED FOR OUR VARIETY OF
DISHES AT POPULAR PRICES

That sounded all right.

He went in and sat down. For a wonder the café was not kept by Italians. The English proprietor lounged across in his shirt sleeves.

'Good morning, sir. Nice day,' he said. 'What can I get for you?'

He handed a card to the Gilt Kid who, having glanced at it, ordered two pork sausages, two rashers, two slices of bread and butter and a cup of tea. That would do for a start.

While he waited for his meal to be prepared he opened one of the midday papers. It was quite fresh and had a smell of ink about it. He flipped over the pages, avoiding the racing information and the woman's page. At last his eye was caught by a headline.

MIDNIGHT ROOF DRAMA

That was it.

'Let's have a large Gold Flake, please.'

He had felt in his pockets without remembering that he had finished all his cigarettes. A man could not concentrate on what he read without something to smoke.

The cigarettes were brought to him. He lighted up and then, blowing out a cloud of smoke, read the paragraph.

It was quite short and, after giving a brief description of the fight on the roof, published a short interview with the survivor. Mr Percy Whale was, apparently, his name. He was a tenant of a flat in the block.

'In an interview,' it read, 'with our reporter, Mr Whale described the episode dramatically. "It was obvious," he said, "that they were desperate characters. Despite my every effort the man got away. I put up a stern battle, but his method of fighting was so dirty that I stood no chance. Such criminals are a menace to the public. Unfortunately owing to the darkness of the roof and the hurried conditions of the whole affair I was not able to give the police a description of my assailant. I can say no more than that he was tall, thickset and exceptionally powerful."'

The paragraph concluded with the words: 'Scotland Yard are examining every possibility. There is every hope of an immediate arrest.'

The Gilt Kid put the paper on the chair beside him and laid his cigarette on the edge of the table. He blew out his breath noisily.

It was not so bad, he thought. Things might be a lot worse. In the first place this Percy Whale, who, incidentally, seemed to be a bit of a bloody liar, talking that way about a 'stern battle', had been unable to give any description to the bogies. Furthermore, there had been as yet no mention of the word 'murder'.

Of course, that meant nothing. Probably the paper was not entitled to use the word until either an inquest had pronounced a verdict to that effect or until someone had actually a murder rap against him.

That last bit – 'there is every hope of an immediate arrest' – was just plain nonsense. The Yard always came across with that or something like that in order to cheer themselves up and give everybody the wire that they were on the job.

They had both been killed then, Scaley and the queer fellow – Ginger, that's right – Ginger who had been a porter at the flats.

The Gilt Kid picked up his cigarette and puffed away.

Well, he had asked Scaley about the porter and the damned idiot had not found out.

His order was brought to him, he threw the cigarette butt on to the floor and put his foot on it. Picking up the knife he set about the sausages and bacon. The other paper, and what news if any that it might contain, could wait until after breakfast.

When he had finished eating, he lit a fresh cigarette and, stirring his tea, picked up the other paper. This carried the story in two parallel quarter columns on an inside page. He folded the paper so that the part which he wished to read was visible and propped it up against the sauce bottle.

A man in a bowler hat came in and sat down opposite him. He ordered stewed steak, carrots, boiled potatoes and a cup of tea.

The Gilt Kid glanced at him involuntarily, but uninterestedly, and sipping his own tea read the account.

The headings were more startling in this paper.

HAMMERSMITH BURGLAR HURTLES TO DEATH

And underneath:

CONFEDERATE ESCAPES AFTER DESPERATE ROOF
BATTLE — PORTER KILLED AND WOULD-BE CAPTOR
INJURED BY VIOLENT FUGITIVES

The story it told was much the same as had been in the other paper. The only difference was that the language was a trifle more lurid. Percy Whale gave a similar interview and a few more details about the gallant way in which he had tackled the desperadoes. There was a picture of him, too, the bastard. Scotland Yard was, as ever, on the job, but had not yet got any clues to work on.

So that was that.

No doubt the later editions would have a fuller story of what had happened. He would have to buy another paper, to see what it had to say, but, up to the present, there looked like being little or no danger. Whale had not been able to give a description and even if they took the liar up to the

Yard and let him look through the pictures in the Rogues' Gallery, it was unlikely that he would have been able to pick out the Gilt Kid. If he did, it would be nothing more than a very shaky identification which Jimmy Nunn's alibi would be quite capable of counteracting.

He laid the paper with its fellow on the chair. He was not going to be quite dopey and keep cuttings like some batchy bastards did. That was a dead tumble.

It was a pity that he was not quite certain about the legal position. He ran his mind over such other similar cases as he could remember. One came back into his mind with a shock.

Browne and Kennedy.

Oh hell, they had topped the pair of them. It looked like a couple of blokes were always responsible for each other. It could hardly be called murder, though, just falling sort of accidentally off the roof. It was not really accidental death either. Probably it was manslaughter. If it were manslaughter, it was quite bad enough. Nobody liked to have a manslaughter rap pinned on him.

He tried to consider what charges would be made against him if they did him. One was certain: 'breaking, entering and feloniously carrying away' however much it was – two hundred and fifty-nine nicker – from the offices. There was no burglary rap because the offices had not been inhabited and no breaking of any sort had taken place at the flats. There would be 'using personal violence on Percy Whale to resist lawful apprehension', unless they made it a bit worse and called it 'grievous bodily harm'. And, maybe, they would add manslaughter of poor old Ginger on top of it all.

Not so good.

He lighted a new cigarette from the stump of his old one and continued his reflections. The man opposite had, by now, his stewed steak which he was eating with a noisy relish.

If they brought all those charges, the Gilt Kid came to the conclusion, he was hooked for about ten-stretch in stir and probably eighteen strokes of the cat as well. Scaley was the lucky one, getting creased that way. Taking it all in all, if the worst did happen, Scaley would have received by far the lighter of the two sentences. Well, if a guy went on the crook and things broke bad and fell he had to take what was coming to him. The fellow was right who said 'he who takes what isn't his'n, when he's cotched he goes to prison'. There was no possible argument about that.

He pushed his hat to the back of his head with an unconscious gesture of perplexity.

He did not quite know what to do or think. Perhaps they might be after him. That chance could not be ruled out. If they were, he would be claimed by the first bogy who recognized him: if they were not, it was possible that he might reign for quite a long time yet.

Maisie.

He had to go and see Maisie.

It was a damned good bet that Maisie would be in a bad temper. Curly would have cleaned her gaff out on the previous night: that would make any girl get wild; it would make Maisie more than wild. She reckoned herself to be a real wide kiddy and to have her flat screwed just like any steamer would give her the needle badly. Yes, she certainly would say a few words about that.

On top of that she was expecting the Gilt Kid to come round with a marriage licence in his pocket. Since he was going to show up with precisely oxo of that sort, she would not be cheered up any at the sight of him. Of course, he could flash a few oncers before her eyes if he wanted to gee her up. And she, thinking that one or two of them might be coming her way, ought to feel a bit glad. Still, she was expecting to hear the old wedding bells chiming, and there were going to be none this trip. He would have to do something about Maisie. Although she was half-doolally she was apt to get her rag out pretty quick. Old Bedbug, apparently,

used to keep her quiet by bringing her flowers and chocolates, but who the hell had ever heard of a screwsman rolling
up to his mort's ken with a bunch of violets. Sounded silly,
nancy. The jane'd be bound to think he had done his nut.

No, he would have to think of something better than that.

Sammy Morris.

Sure, yes. Sammy Morris was the boy. The Gilt Kid had
done hundreds of pounds worth of business with him,
flogging crooked stuff. Now was the chance to do a bit more
– buying something from the astard-ba this time. Yeh, that
was a bet. Buy her a knocked-off fur-smother or a nice little
groin for a fiver, and kid the cow that it had set him back a
score of quids or a pony. A screwsman wanted to flash his
dough around a bit. It showed that he was big-hearted, and
what was a better way than by dolling up his jane?

Yes. That certainly turned the trick.

He got up and paid the bill.

Outside the café he caught a taxi. Giving the driver an address just off Tottenham Court Road, he leant back on the cushions and lighted a fresh cigarette.

The thought of what he had read in the papers returned to his mind, but he thrust it away with an indignant effort. Maisie. He would try to think about her.

He forced his mind into that train of ideas. Yes, she certainly was a great girl, looked a smasher and did not act the mug to half the extent she used to. Anyone taking a quick look at her might think she was on the up-and-up. She would give that impression, too, to anyone who heard her talk and saw her act.

Though, so help me – and at the thought he clenched his fists – she would have to give up that rye mort touch. Personally he was not going to stand for that caper. A fellow on the knock-off could not have her come that acid. Why she would probably want him to give up the crooked lark altogether and get a job or some damn thing of that sort. Nice he would look punching a bloody time-clock every morning and saying 'Yes sir'. God damn it, a bloke might just as good be inside. And what in the name of God she was going to say if she were to hear they might be after him for murder . . .

Murder. Hell. What did he want to bring this thing up for?

She would have to learn to play straight with him, too. Keep her mouth shut when necessary, pick up steamers whose gaffs he could go and screw; why, he even could take her round drumming with him. There wasn't no better fanny in the world than to lumber a crooked tart along with you if a fellow went drumming. Everyone knew that.

And if he caught her coming any capers with another bloke, why he'd do her in straightaway and no argument about it. Do her in. That would be another murder.

There he went again. Could he never keep the word out of his mind?

He looked out of the taxi window. They were now nearing St Giles's Circus. In a minute they would be in Tottenham Court Road. Well that was OK. It was just as well he was in a taxi. Nobody would be able to stop him if they were after him over that Hammersmith turnout. Yes, it might be just as well to keep under cover for a little, until perhaps the linen-drapers gave him the office that the chase had not been taken up.

The taxi stopped. The Gilt Kid sprang out. Paying the driver, he knocked on the door. From an upstairs window a face he could see was eyeing him cautiously.

Good old Sammy. Trust him never to take no chances.

Footsteps were coming along the passage. A dingy woman opened the door and stood there drying her red hands on her apron. Her expression was partly furtive, partly brazen. It was clear that no bogy coming round on the snoop was likely to get much change out of her.

The Gilt Kid smiled and raised his hat. Such an act of politeness would, he knew, give her something to chew on.

'Mr Sam Morris in?'

'Dunno.'

Her eyes suddenly grew blank; her face was a flabby whiteness.

'That's all right, missus. You don't want to worry about me. Just tell him Ken's here. The Gilt Kid.'

Her eyes narrowed and then, closing the door, she went down the passage. The Gilt Kid could hear her shouting voice echoing hollowly in the narrow hallway.

When she reopened the door her manner was a little more friendly.

'That's all right, mister,' she said. 'You can go up. Can't be too careful you know. Not in this life. You know your way.'

'Sure, second floor.'

He crossed the hall and ran up the staircase two steps at a time. The air in the house was fetid and a faint aroma of cabbage clung to the walls. He rapped on the door of Sammy Morris's workshop.

'Come right on in.'

With difficulty he turned the slippery door-handle and stepped into the room. Sammy Morris left the pair of trousers which he was pressing and came forward.

'Well, Ken,' he said, 'how you was? They let you out?'

'No. I'm down on the Moor doing a lagging. How's the luck?'

'Shocking, shocking. Couldn't be worse.' For all that Sammy Morris had been born in England he still found a trace of difficulty over the letter 'double u'. 'Tell you what, you couldn't have come at no worse time.'

He made a deprecatory gesture and then moved backwards across the room so that at last he was resting against the window sill. All the time his eyes never left the face of the Gilt Kid who, advancing and sitting down on the edge of an ironing-board, still kept his hat on his head and his hands in his trousers pockets.

For a couple of seconds there was a silence which the Jew eventually broke.

'How many times must I tell you don't come here? How do I know they don't put a tail on you? If you got anything, get on the blower. Phone me. Tell me to come to your place. I tell you it's safer that way. They don't tail you to my place, I don't come no tumble, see?'

'Yes, that's all right, Sammy, but . . .'

Sammy Morris held up his left hand.

'That's all right, my boy,' he said magnanimously. 'Just remember, though. I don't want to go to no prison. Now what you bring me this time? Stones, a bit of red?'

The Gilt Kid shook his head.

'What then? Snout?'

The Gilt Kid shook his head again. Sammy Morris began to make wildly angry passes with his hands.

'Don't go telling me you bring me a skin. Furs ain't worth nothing now I tell you.'

'Use your nut, Sammy. If I brought a skin I would have a parcel. I'm not a bloody contortionist.'

'Well, what you bring me then?'

'Nothing.'

'Nothing? What the hell you mean, nothing?'

'Just plain nothing, Sammy.'

'Then what you come here wasting my time for? Listen, Ken. You're a good boy. I like you. Me and you done a nice little bit of business together, but if you come to borrow money, I tell you, I ain't got none.'

'No, I ain't come to borrow money.'

'Then what you come for?'

Sammy made a despairing pass over his curly hair. He knew that nobody, least of all Ken, was likely to pay him a friendly call.

'Just to do a little bit of business.'

'You come to do business and you don't bring nothing to sell. Funny kind of business. What kind of business you call that? Go away. Don't come here wasting my time.'

He took a couple of indignant steps towards the Gilt Kid.

'I came to buy.'

'Buy?' Sammy was frankly incredulous as he checked his stride. 'You come here, talking about buy. What d'you mean about this buy?'

'Why, just buy. Purchase, if you like the word better.' The Gilt Kid laughed tolerantly. 'That's all right, Sammy, boy.

Don't go crackers. I've had my little joke and now I'll come clean. Listen.'

He crossed his swinging legs and lighted a cigarette. Sammy went back to the window sill.

'I got a girl,' the Gilt Kid began. 'She thinks I'm gonna marry her, but she's damn wrong. She thinks I'm going along to her place today with the wedding licence in my sky. I'll be there, all right, but there ain't going to be no wedding licence. Get it?'

'Sure. But just where do I come in?'

'Oh you come in all right. I'm just getting to that. I want to buy her a present to sort of cheer her up. I thought I'd buy something from you on the cheap and put in the old gee that it had set me back a hell of a lot.'

'Ah.' Sammy rubbed his palms. 'That was a good idea. Now, I got the very thing for her. How about a nice fur coat. One of the nicest coats you ever see. Say, you give that coat to your girl, you give it to any girl, I don't care what girl, just give it to a girl and she'll love you. Wait a bit, I'll fetch it.'

He made as if to move. The Gilt Kid spoke.

'Just a minute, Sammy. How much?'

'Twenty pound?'

'A score of quids? Never in your natural. What the hell kind of a girl do you think she is? Just you leave that coat where it is. Some place where the moths won't get at it. I'm not buying it.'

'Let me show you the coat, though. I tell you what, Ken. I be a fool to let you have that coat for twenty pound. I'm robbing myself. I'm only doing it because I like you, because we done a lot of business in the past. I tell you what I'll do. I'll give you the coat for fifteen.'

'Sit down, Sammy. You're not selling me that coat for fifteen, nor for ten neither.'

'Ten?' There was a shriek of horror in his voice.

'Yes, I said ten. Now, what I meant to spend was a couple of nicker. You got a nice little groin?'

'A ring. Yes, Ken. I got the very thing. How would you like a nice ring with a beautiful single diamond?'

'Fine. Only don't try to work off none of your jargoons on me.'

'Jargoon nothing. Don't you know a diamond from a white sapphire?'

'Sure I do, but not when they've been baked in the oven. Now, just fetch that groin and bring it back quick before you have the time to pull any of your fancy tricks on me.'

'I wouldn't pull no tricks on you, Ken,' Sammy reproached as he went off into the adjoining room to fetch the ring. He came back with it in his hand. It threw off a white flash of fire. The Gilt Kid, who had moved over to the window, could scarcely repress a gasp. If it looked as good as that on Sammy's grimy palm, it must have been a real winner when it was on its proper blue velvet stand.

'How much?' he asked.

'I'll give it to you for a tenner.'

'A tenner,' echoed the Gilt Kid, taking it into his own hand. 'Well, Sammy, all I can say is I might be a burglar, but you're a bigger robber than I ever thought of being. Ten nicker for a little stone like that. Here, take it back.'

He handed it back brusquely.

'The stone mayn't be big, but it's perfect. The cutting, too, look at the cutting.'

Sammy thrust it on him again.

'I don't want to look at the cutting. Not if it's going to cost me ten pounds. I tell you what I'll do, I'll give you three for it?'

'Three pounds you offer? Say, Ken. What religion are you?'

'C of E I suppose. Why?'

'You want to come to the Synagogue along with us. You're beating me at my own game. Three pounds? What's the matter with you, mad?'

'No, I'm all there. Got anything a bit cheaper? If you haven't, I'll go some other place.'

'Listen, Ken. I tell you what I'll do. I don't know why I'm doing it. I must be crazy, but I'll let you have this ring for eight pound.'

'No, take it away. I don't want it.'

'Come on Ken. Give me seven and a half and we'll call it a bargain.'

'You heard what I said. Three. Look here.' He took a sudden step forward. 'I'll be a sportsman, Sammy. I'll offer you four.'

'Did you say sportsman?'

'Sure. Why?'

'I thought you did. Making sport of me, hey? Listen Ken. I won't be hard on you. I'll make a deal. Give me seven nicker and the ring's yours.'

'Seven nicker? I said four. Sorry, Sammy. Outsiders are running too good today. The bet's off.'

'Seven nicker.' Sammy bounced it up and down on his palm. 'I tell you what Ken. This groin, if you buy it at eight nicker it's a bargain: you've done real good. If you give me what I ask, seven, why, you're committing robbery with violence. Seven quid's the price. I won't go a ha'penny lower. I like you, Ken, but I can't go robbing myself. Get that. Give me seven.'

'Sorry Sammy. The bet's off, I told you.'

'As you like.'

Sammy shrugged his shoulders and slid the ring into his trousers pocket.

'Well Ken, I'm glad to have seen you. Drop in any time you're around, but just now, well I'm a bit busy you see.'

'OK Sammy, you win. I know when rock bottom's

reached. Give me the damn groin, you robbing bleeder. Here's seven nicker.'

Sammy handed over the ring.

'That's a whole lot of money you got there, Ken,' he said when he saw the strength of the Gilt Kid's roll.

'It certainly is. I'm well-fixed just now.'

'Well-fixed? That's good.'

He took the notes and then, as if motivated by a sudden idea, stepped up quite close to the Gilt Kid.

'Yes,' he said slowly, 'that's a whole lot of money, ain't it? Say Ken, you haven't been to see me before, not since you came out of the queer place, did you? Ha. H'm.'

'So what?'

'Just this. I hope you ain't been doing no business with anyone else.'

The Gilt Kid laughed. These Yiddisher Kids were mustard. They hated like hell to think that there was any dough that hadn't come their way.

'What would I go and see anyone else for in the name of God? You've always been straight with me, Sammy. At least I've never caught you doing any carving.'

'So that's all right then. I'll just have to read the papers and see if there's been any nice little ready money jobs been pulled.'

The Gilt Kid thought fast, trying hard not to lose any colour. Sammy was getting just a little too warm for his liking. Before long he would be putting on the black.

'You're the hell of a fellow, Sammy. You must be about the biggest bloody crook in the Smoke.'

'Say. What gave you that idea?'

'You've the crookedest mind of any fellow I've met up to yet and that's certainly saying something. You seem to think that a bloke can't have any dough unless he's been screwing.'

'Well, don't try to tell me you won it as a crossword prize.

You may be a bargainer, Ken, but you can't gee me up all that.'

'Who said I was geeing? This is the dough that I had saved up and carefully planted before I got nicked. If you like to think me a liar – well, you're open to. It makes no difference to me.'

'All right, Ken. I believe you. Thousands wouldn't. Only don't let me hear you've been doing business with anybody else, that's all.'

'Yeh? On the lines, well you're innocent this time but don't do it again.' He extended his hand. 'So long, Sammy. Thanks for the groin. I'll look in again as soon as I've anything for you.'

'That's right, Ken. Drop in any time you're passing. But, if you've been doing anything you shouldn't, well, just get me on the blower. That's the best way. Good-bye.'

''Bye Sammy.'

With the ring in his upper left waistcoat pocket the Gilt Kid's next preoccupation was concerned with the time. It must be getting along. He didn't want Maisie to think that he was standing her up. She would be wild enough as it was, even with the ring and all. In Tottenham Court Road he caught sight of a clock. It was a quarter past two.

Why the hell, he wondered, don't I buy a watch? I'm always having to find out the time from public clocks. Knock one off. That'd be a bit simpler. Hell of a stupid thing it was to go buying things. Next buckshee kettle that comes my way I'll just stick to it. That's all.

At St Giles's Circus he intended to hop a bus and get straight up to Maisie's. The sooner he got the interview with her over the better he would feel. That was clear. He crossed crowded Oxford Street, dodging under the noses of the omnibuses. His eyes, sharpened and wary to city sights as those of a gamekeeper are to the woodland, noticed a couple of detectives standing near the mouth of the Tottenham Court Road Underground Station. One of them was he who had pulled him up in Shaftesbury Avenue the preceding night. They were, he knew, on the lookout for pickpockets, but even that consoling thought did not check his heart from missing a beat.

Even if they did not nick him for the Hammersmith job, he reasoned, they might pinch him for being on the whizz. He could imagine them giving their evidence in the court.

'Kept the prisoner under observation for twenty minutes, your worship. He attempted to board two eastbound buses, jostling the passengers unnecessarily, and then crossed to the south side of Oxford Street where he attempted to board three westbound buses. When arrested, the diamond ring listed as Exhibit A was found on the prisoner's person . . .'

Bastards. All bogies were bastards and he was a bloody fool not to have taken a taxi.

Before reaching the kerb, he tried to sheer off to the right, jumping to avoid a delivery boy on a green tricycle. As his feet touched the pavement, his eyes noted that he had been spotted. His heart began to hammer and the only too well-known dryness of his throat made itself felt. He had to thrust his clenched hands into his trousers pockets to prevent them trembling.

He turned smartly to his right and walked off along the south side of Oxford Street. If he broke into a run he would make a tumble of it for sure. The bogies would know something was a bit funny somewhere. He would grab the first taxi he saw. There was no use trying to dodge into a big store and hide himself. They would be bound to cover all exits. Meanwhile his feet were like fourteen-pound shots.

In Soho Street there was a café taxi-drivers used. With luck he would get a taxi there and take it on the lam out of the goddamn place.

A woman, not so traffic-wise as she might have been, got in his way. He took a pace to his right to avoid her. She took one to her left. He swerved to the left, she dodged to the right. He could sense the advancing detectives behind him. Thoughts tumulted in his mind.

Bloody fool to have panicked. Trying to run. Made a dead tumble out of it. A regular humpty dumpty. And God damn this tart. No more dodging. Push straight past the bitch.

He tried to do so. The soft female body recoiled beneath his weight. She fell to the ground. He stumbled over her. The pavement hit hard against his knees. Damn. He was soiling his suit, and just when he had to go and see Maisie. He scrambled to his feet. A hand fell on his shoulder. He tried to shake himself clear. A grip fell on his arm. Wildly whistles shrilled.

A blind rage seized him. He knew not, and cared not, whether his assailants were civilians or police. Whoever they might be, they were certainly going to discover that the Gilt Kid was a rough handful. He struck out hard with his clenched fists at a white moon of a face that he saw. Primitive satisfaction was his portion when he saw red blood start against the face's white blur. He shook off a restraining hand that girdled his arm. Once more he struck out. This time his fist touched no flesh. A burning pain came to his head. He swayed for three seconds while the mist in front of his eyes changed from red to black. Something had hit him in the face. He fell to the ground . . .

When he came to he was lying on his back on the pavement. His head hurt like hell. The pain came over him in gusts every time he breathed. Something hot and sticky was running down his forehead. Gradually his eyes regained the power of focusing. The two detectives were standing over him. One of them had had his mouth knocked all crooked. There was some satisfaction in that. Three uniformed policemen were pushing back the gaping crowd.

He laid a hand flat on the pavement beside him and tried to push himself to his feet. A detective caught him roughly by the shoulders: a second snapped handcuffs on his wrists. It was a good enough pinch.

The Gilt Kid raised his manacled arms. His intention had been to wipe off some of the sweat and blood from his forehead, but a rough hand brusquely jerked his arms down again. He was too tired to resist. He felt deathly cold and wanted to vomit. Wearily he listened to the detective's voice.

'James Kennedy, I am a police officer and I am going to arrest you as a suspected person loitering with intent to commit a felony and for violently resisting arrest. I warn you that anything you say may be written down and used as evidence at any subsequent proceedings against you.'

'OK,' he said, 'I'm nicked. Lead the way.'

Pushed by the two detectives, he was trundled into a taxi-cab. The London crowd, eager to see a barney, disappointed to see it end, moved off to their ordinary afternoon tasks. His hat remained on the pavement, a single, mute reminder of the fracas.

In the taxi-cab the three at first kept silence.

The Gilt Kid it was who spoke first.

'Where you taking me?' he asked. 'Marlborough Street?'

'You'll know soon enough.'

'Too bloody soon, I expect. What you nick me for? Sus?'

'You heard.'

'Well, I don't give a damn for a sus. I ain't got a light on me incriminating and I'm not under the Act. So it'll be a carpet, if that.'

There was no answer from either. He tried again.

'Give us a smoke.'

'No.'

'Come on, be a sport.'

'No.'

'There's some fags in my sky. Come on.'

'Wait till you get to the station.'

'Yes, and have you take the bastards off me.'

He began to struggle again. Both the detectives drew truncheons.

'Want another dose of this, eh?'

'Oh, so *that's* what hit me.'

He subsided and then glanced up at the detective on his right.

'Christ, I didn't half catch you one in the mouth. Must hurt a bit, eh china?'

Both captors preserved a grim silence. The taxi-cab drew up.

Both detectives laid restraining hands on him until the cab-driver had opened the door of the vehicle. Then, each of them seizing one of his arms, they led him up the steps into the station.

As the Gilt Kid stepped inside the Charge Room with his wrists secured by steel and with a human bloodhound holding each arm, his heart sank. The very atmosphere of the Charge Room was enough to make a man sick. All government institutions were the same. Police stations, the army, prisons. And his head was aching like hell. All the false forced vivacity of the taxi-ride had deserted him. He was down to bedrock again. He was just a tired, wounded, rather scared human being in the grip of a tremendous force against which he had no chance of fighting.

He stood there by the desk, dully and unresisting, while the charge was read over to him. The picture of a magistrate's court came before him. He could hear the words: 'When charged he made no reply.'

The desk sergeant looked up at him.

'Been in the wars a bit, haven't you, son?'

'Been very violent,' countered a detective.

'All right. Turn out his pockets. Let's see what he's got.'

A handkerchief from his breast pocket, a packet of cigarettes, a box of matches, silver from his trousers pockets. They wrenched open his jacket and felt inside.

'Hallo. What's this?'

The detective had drawn out a bundle of notes.

'Well-fixed, ain't you? Where did you get these from?'

'Find out. That's what you're paid to do.'

'Where did you get these from?'

'Didn't you hear me say, "find out"?'

'Where did you get these from?'

'Find out.'

'Where did you get these from?'

'Find out. There's no need to ask me again. I won't get out of breath before you do.'

The detective laid the notes on the desk beside the silver and cigarettes. The desk sergeant looked admonitorily at the prisoner. He spoke, waggling his pen.

'You're being very foolish, son. If you don't give an account of that money, none of it will be returned to you for the purpose of your defence and for your use whilst on remand. It will be retained until its source has been ascertained.' He paused and then, seeing no answer on the Gilt Kid's wooden face, went on more sternly: 'Continue the search.'

From one of the Gilt Kid's waistcoat pockets the searchers drew a small screw of tissue paper. On seeing it the Gilt Kid gave a start which made the officer holding him tighten his grasp. The desk sergeant unfolded the paper. There was a diamond ring inside.

'Ho, ho, ho. And what is the meaning of this pretty thing?'

'It's a ring, can't you see, dopey?' The Gilt Kid was determined to give as much trouble as possible.

'Sure it's a ring. And how do you happen to have a diamond ring in your pocket?'

The desk sergeant held it glittering in his palm. The Gilt Kid gave no answer.

'Sulky, eh? Won't give an answer when spoken to, eh? Well, we've got a way of dealing with people of that sort. Now, let me see, my lad,' he glanced down at the charge sheet. 'Let me see. What address did you give?'

'No fixed place of abode.'

'"No fixed place of abode". Now, it's a very funny thing that a man with no fixed place of abode should have a diamond ring and a lot of pound notes. Very funny. And that he should violently resist arrest. It seems to me that a magistrate would remand a man of that sort for inquiries.

Has he got anything else on him? No. Well, put him in a cell for a bit. That should cool his aching head.'

Still being held by the arms, the Gilt Kid was propelled along the passage to his cell. His handcuffs were not removed. The door of the cell clanged to. He sat down on the wooden seat and stared dejectedly at the floor. Imprisonment, solitary confinement, porridge, sewing mail-bags, calling screws 'sir', all that bloody caper was going to start again, was it? Hell.

He tried to rest his aching head in his hands, but his handcuffs prevented him getting any ease. He got up, moved to the door and shouted out.

'Anything else in this nick?'

His voice echoed along the empty cell-corridor. The echoes died away. For a moment there was silence. Then an authoritative voice yelled back at him.

'Pipe down. Stop making that noise.'

Not knowing whether it was the cell's constable or another prisoner being funny he shouted again. This time there was no reply to his shout.

He spat into the open latrine and then sat down on the bench again.

Wish the bastards'd let me have a smoke. They usually leave you your fags. It's only common humanity. First time I've had them taken off me at the police station. Take them off you at the stir, though. First time they've ever left the darbies on me when I've been in the cell. They must think me a desperate character or something. I'd give them desperate if they'd let me get at them again. I bet they're wondering where the hell I got that groin from, too. Well, let 'em wonder. Perhaps, though, it'd be a bit better if I could account for it. Tell them I bought it for my girl. That's true enough anyway. Then they'll be bound to ask where did I get it? What then? I can't exactly come the copper on Sammy. That would be hardly the thing. Oh hell.

The automatic flushing of the closet startled him for a second and then he relapsed into his thoughts again.

They can't hold me on that groin. 'Being in possession of stolen property.' Well, what of it? It has to be proved that I knew it to be stolen. I know. I bought it off a man in a pub, last night. Bit thin that. Perhaps a jury might swallow it. Particularly if I get a good mouthpiece. Yep. That'll have to do. They don't seem to have weighed me up about that Hammersmith turnout yet. Maybe they won't. God knows. There won't be any bloody numbers taken of those notes, so they can trace 'em up till they're blue in the face. I should worry. Poor Maisie though. Unfortunate bloody kid. She'll be wondering what the hell's up. Breaks with old Bedbug, finds her gaff screwed, and then I don't bloody well show up. She must be saying a few words. Kind of a Jonah she is though. Every time I'm going to see her I get claimed for some damn thing or another.

He tensed his body as he heard footsteps and voices outside the cell.

'This the bloke?'

'Yes.'

Someone was lifting the shutter of his peephole. An eye was peering in.

'This is him right enough. Well, he ain't managed to blow from here anyway.'

A key rattled in the lock, the door swung open. One of the detectives and three uniformed constables tramped into the cell. The Gilt Kid looked up at them. As a point of honour he tried to keep his face expressionless, but the entry of anyone into his cell was a welcome event to break the monotony.

The detective hovered in the background. The three constables, burly in their blue and silver, advanced on him. One of them smiled savagely.

'So this is the bloke who cut up rough, eh? Well, we like

rough handfuls, don't we boys? The rougher they are the rougher we are. Stand up.'

The Gilt Kid did not move. His heart was thumping. Anyhow he could try to put up a brave front.

'Sulky, eh? Won't speak when he's spoken to? I'll settle that. Get up you bastard.'

The policeman caught the connecting link of the Gilt Kid's handcuffs and yanked him to his feet. He dodged, bounded forward between the uniformed men at the detective and, raising his hands above his head, dashed the heavy steel into the startled officer's face. Before he fell to a sledgehammer blow behind on the back of his neck he had the joy of seeing blood spurt all over his victim's face.

CROSS-EXAMINATION

When he came to he was lying on the cell floor. He seemed to be one ache. No longer was he conscious of a headache or of sore ribs. It was impossible to distinguish one area of pain from another. Cautiously he put out his tongue and ran it over his cracked and swollen lips. Then he moved his head. A spasm that was quite unbearable stabbed him behind the eyes. He lay still for two full minutes, not daring to move. Then, he gathered his courage together and tried to find out just how bad he was.

There was one thing for which to be thankful. They had taken off those damned bracelets. He fumbled at his face. It was, he found out, all cut and swollen. His hair was all matted with something sticky. Blood probably. Exerting himself he clambered up into a sitting position. The effort cost him every ounce of energy which he possessed. The walls spun round before his eyes. Nausea welled up inside him. He remained sitting on the floor for another two minutes, and then, pushing himself up on to his feet, he managed to totter to the bench.

Things were a little clearer to him now. Although he was badly knocked about and bruised it hardly seemed that anything was broken. He seemed to be able to move his limbs all right. His clothes were all fouled, his collar had burst open and his shirt was spattered with blood. That would make a nice impression on the magistrate when he came up in court the next day. Previously he had always managed to extract a consoling pride out of the newspapers saying, 'The prisoner, who presented a smart appearance in the dock . . .'

Keys were rattling in the lock once again. Abject fear

made lead of his heart. He would have shouted had his tongue not been glued to the roof of his dry mouth. Another bashing would make him go mad. He would not be able to stand it.

The door opened. Two plainclothes men walked in. The Gilt Kid tried to drive the look of pleading from his aching eyes. It was hardly the thing to show them what he felt. He watched them as they stood by the open cell door. One of them he had never before seen. It would have been quite easy to have dashed between them and to have made his escape out into the cell corridor. All the fight had, however, gone out of him.

'Hallo, Kennedy,' said the unknown one, 'my God, they've been knocking you about. Damn shame if you ask me. Come along now, Kid, we're going to take your fingerprints.'

This assumed air of kindness did not deceive the Gilt Kid.

'What do you want to take my dabs for?' he asked wearily. 'God knows you've got them already.'

'Don't worry about *why* we're going to take them. Come along now like a good Kid.'

He got up and walked out of the cell with them, one behind, one in front. At the end of the corridor was a small bowl fixed into the wall with a brass faucet above it. In front of this the Gilt Kid paused.

'Let's have a bit of a rinse here first?' he asked.

'Sure, go ahead.'

He cooled his aching head in the cold water, removing the dirt and blood. The flesh of his face was puffy and tender beneath his fingers. When he stood up again one of the detectives handed him a coarse canvas towel.

'Thanks.'

He dried his face and hands and, stepping almost briskly after the refreshing wash, followed his captors into a small office.

On a table lay the inkpad and the sheet of paper necessary for complying with the regulations with regard to taking fingerprints. The Gilt Kid allowed the unknown detective, who was apparently the senior of the two, to take his fingerprints. He offered neither resistance nor comment. When the officer had finished he turned to his prisoner.

'Sit down a minute, Ken,' he said kindly.

The Gilt Kid, taking a chair, sat down at the table, the two detectives sitting opposite. The senior spoke.

'Bit of a bastard being locked up without a smoke, wasn't it?' he asked, taking out of his pocket a large packet of cigarettes.

The Gilt Kid's eyes lighted up, but his reply and demeanour were still sullen.

'You ought to know.'

The detective put a cigarette in his own mouth and laid another tantalizingly on the table.

'They used to call you the Gilt Kid, didn't they? Did they put a "u" in it or not?'

The Gilt Kid preserved his stubborn look and made no answer.

'Like a fag?' his interlocutor asked, puffing out a cloud of smoke.

'You know damn well I would.'

'Well that's easy. Just answer a few questions, and sign the statement my colleague here will prepare for you. Then you'll get all the smokes you want.'

'Listen. I'm charged with loitering with intent to commit a felony; though how the hell a man can be loitering when he's running like butter on a hot spoon I'm damned if I know. If you think I'm going to make a steamer of myself and let you hang about half a dozen more charges on me, you're mistaken. See?'

'Who said I was going to hang any more charges on you? Now be a good kid, Ken. Take it easy. Here's a smoke for you.'

He pushed the cigarette across the table to the Gilt Kid and held out his own so that the latter could light up. The first two puffs were heaven to the Gilt Kid. Then he steeled his mind.

If they thought they'd get him by smarming they got another coming. The thing was to calm down, take any favours they might have to give, but answer nothing.

'OK,' he said. 'What do you want to know?'

'That's a good boy.' The questioner leant forward, his hands loosely clasped in front of him on the table, but his eyes firmly fixed on the Gilt Kid's face. 'Well, where did you get the dough?'

'What dough?'

'The dough you had on you when the other officers arrested you. The thirty-two pound four and tenpence you had.'

'Oh that.' There was contempt in his voice as who should say 'Call *that* dough?'

'Yes, that.'

'That's my own money.'

'Your own money, eh? Earned it perhaps, or did your rich old uncle die last week in Camberwell?'

'Don't be funny. I done time for that dough. Come to think of it I earned it if you call making brushes earning money. That's the dough from the job I got nicked for.'

'Is that so? Well, why wasn't a restitution order made at your trial?'

'For the simple reason I had the money planted.'

'Where?'

'Think I'm going to drag a straight boy into this, have a lot of bogies going round his house and all that? Not likely. You go and do the poor kid for receiving.'

'Right. Now I come to think of it. How did you fall last time, somebody shop you?'

'No. Caught on the job.'

'Caught on the job, eh? Well, well, miracles happen. You get caught on a job and yet you have money which you stole from that job. All I can say is the officers who arrested you didn't give you much of a rub-down. Still. Let that pass for a minute. We'll list it as money stolen prior to your arrest. That's all. Now. Let's see. Where were you arrested?'

'Oxford Street.' The Gilt Kid had smoked his cigarette so low that he was burning his fingers.

'Yes. You were running, weren't you?'

'Yes.'

'Why?'

'Because I saw a couple of bogies.'

'And do you always run when you see CID officers?'

'No.'

'Well, why did you this time?'

'Because I thought they might nick me.'

'Why might they arrest you?'

'Because . . . Oh hell, never heard of a fellow with cons against him being nicked for suspect?'

'Right. You ran from the CID officers because you thought they might arrest you for having acted in a suspicious manner. Now then. That ring. What do you know about that?'

'About what?'

'About that ring which was in your possession on your arrest.'

'Nothing much. It is all right, isn't it?'

'What do you mean "is it all right"?'

'I mean is it a good one? They didn't catch me for a mug?'

'It's a valuable diamond ring. How did it come into your possession?'

'I bought it.'

'Where? From whom?'

'I don't know.'

'What do you mean, "I don't know"?'

'I can't remember the fellow's name. Point of fact I never knew it. I was talking to a bloke in a pub last night and he showed me the ring. Said it belonged to his missus. Wanted a tenner. Said he was down on his luck.'

'What pub?'

The Gilt Kid thought hard for a minute. Inspiration came to him. They'd remember him in the gaff he and Curly were in. 'Place in Shaftesbury Avenue. I don't remember the name. I could take you there, though. They'll remember me.'

'Yes, and have you escape. Well, let that pass, too, for a minute. You bought the ring from a man you don't know in a pub whose name you can't remember. Now, why did you buy it? Hoping to turn it over quickly to someone and make a packet out of the deal?'

'No. It wasn't that. I bought it for my girl.'

'Yes? And where does she live?'

The Gilt Kid hesitated. There ought to be no harm in giving Maisie's address. She knew nothing about him that could let him in for it. Yes, that was it. He gave her address.

'Where?' asked his interlocutor.

The Gilt Kid repeated the address. The detective leant across the table. His hands were no longer loosely clenched. They were gripping each other till the knuckles showed white. A triumphant glitter was in his eyes.

'And would it surprise you to hear,' he asked, 'that a burglary took place there last night?'

'What? Somebody been screwing Maisie's gaff!' exclaimed the Gilt Kid with well-feigned surprise and indignation. 'Bloody nerve I call it.'

'Yes,' went on the CID man, 'a burglary took place there last night and this ring in question answers to a description of one of the stolen articles.'

'What!'

The Gilt Kid had very nearly leapt from his chair. His

face was ashen. This was a turnout. Damn good thing that he'd not been round to Maisie with the ring or, by Christ, there'd have been a moan. He calmed down suddenly. A comforting thought had come to him.

'That's OK,' he said. 'Bit strange, ain't it, to buy for your girl a piece of stuff that's been knocked off from her. You can't hang that job on me, though.'

'Can't I? Why not?'

'Because I got an alibi. I can account for my movements up till round about midnight last night.'

'Up till round about midnight. H'm. That's funny.'

'What's funny? What's eating you now?'

'Just this. I was wondering how you happened to know that the burglary took place before midnight.'

'Oh, I just thought that. Later on I was at home in kip, and of course living in a furnished room I've got no proof I was there.'

'Where did you say you were living? In a furnished bedroom?'

'Sure. Why?'

'I thought you told the desk sergeant when you were charged that you had no fixed place of abode.'

There was a silence. The Gilt Kid saw that his tongue was getting himself into difficulties.

'Well?' The detective's voice rose in a happy note.

'Well what?'

'Now listen, Ken. You reckon you're a real wide boy. Well, you are. I grant you that. You've got guts, too. The fight you put up shows that. But, kid, the cards are stacked against you. You can't win. Better come clean, let's have the real yarn now. Why, your statement's enough to convict you. Read it over to him.'

The silent scribe laid down his pen, picked up the sheet of paper on which he had been writing and, clearing his throat, began to read.

'The money found in my possession on my arrest was stolen. It is the proceeds of a theft made before I went to prison. A friend was looking after it for me. Standing in Oxford Street I saw two plainclothes police officers. I ran away from them because I thought they might arrest me for having acted in a suspicious manner. I bought the ring from a man I do not know. It was in a public house in Shaftesbury Avenue. I cannot recall the name of the house. My movements up till midnight last night can be accounted for. I do not know at what time the burglary took place. I cannot account for my movements after midnight . . .'

'See. That's what you told us while you thought you were being wide. Let's have the truth now. Which was it? Did you do your girl's place while she was out, or did you do it with her connivance so that she might draw the insurance money? I know it was one of the two.'

'I tell you I know nothing about the bloody job.'

'You don't, eh? Well, we've got enough to ask for a remand while we check up on you.'

'That statement's not worth a light. I won't sign it.'

The detective laughed sarcastically.

'Oh, you're not going to sign your statement. Well, answer me this. How many times have you been arrested?'

'This makes the fourth.'

'What do they say when they arrest you?'

'"I am a police officer and I warn you that anything you say may be taken down and used as evidence at your trial."'

'See? "Anything you say"– come on. Use your nut, Ken boy. Give us the yarn and everything will be all right. I'll tell the judge you have many redeeming qualities and that you tried to get work but your record went against you. You'll have plenty of smokes here at the station and I'll see that you have some of your money returned so that you'll be OK in Brixton and be able to have a dock brief when you go for trial. How about it?'

'Nothing doing. You're not going to hang a bum rap on me.'

'All right. Have it your own way.' The detective sighed. 'Lock him up again and see he doesn't get another smoke.'

The cell door had been slammed to behind the Gilt Kid
once more. He lay full length on the bench with his inter-
locked fingers supporting his head. He looked distastefully
at the dirty white tiles of his cell wall. These police station
cells were a disgrace to a reputedly civilized country. It would
be a pleasure to get into a proper cell at Brixton. There was
that hair-raising, heart-searing ride in the Black Maria to be
undergone though; and then Wandsworth. How long was he
likely to get? Put it at a carpet for the sus, and then for this
breaking-and-entering lark at least eighteen months for a
man with two cons. Unless the judge was damned kind-
hearted it looked like being twenty-one months. Damned
unlikely that there would be any of the concurrent touch
about it. Yes, at the very best it was good-bye for twenty-one
moon. It was going to make four convictions for him. Four
cons sounded the hell of a lot. He would be uncommon
lucky if the judge didn't put him under the Prevention of
Crimes Act for seven years. And when a bloke was on the
flypaper, well he just stayed on. Twelve months for suspect
every time a bogy so much as looked at him.

Oh God, he was done for now. Talk about wasted bleeding youth.

Well they'd find him a rough enough handful in the nick.
What the hell did it matter if he did all his time on bread
and water. There was going to be damnall to come out to.
It was no good dodging the issue.

He gingerly touched his aching head.

The dirty sons of bitches were probably thinking: 'That'll
teach the bastard to cut up rough.'

He loosened his tie, got off the bench and spat in the latrine.

Damn the slops. He would give them something to think about. They were going to be rough, eh?

Well come on Kid, make an excuse, get one into the cell and bash daylight out of him and if there was half a chance cut and run for it. There was no hope of a successful break, but it'd give them some trouble. OK. Here goes.

He rang the bell and stood close up against the door. It was a pity he had no stool or anything to bash him with when he came.

For about a couple of minutes he waited there, his mouth dry, his heart hammering. At last he heard the cell constable's footsteps echoing hollowly down the corridor. He clenched his teeth and his fists. His nostrils were wide open and the maxillary muscles bulged out of his cheeks. That red mist danced in front of his eyes again.

The constable's footsteps halted. Now for it.

The muscles were rippling down his tensed arm.

An eye peered through the spy-hole of the cell.

'What do you want now ringing the bell 's if I had nothing to do but wait on you?'

'Just come in here a minute. I got something to show you.'

'Yes, your fist I suppose. Think I was born yesterday? Look here, if you go ringing like that when you haven't got no cause to you're for it, see?'

'Oh I'm for it am I?' Rage shook the Gilt Kid at the failure of his plan. 'Well, get a load of this. I'm for it maybe, but not half so much as you're going to be when I come up before the court tomorrow. What the hell d'you mean by keeping me in the cell all this time without any food or anything to read? I'm an unconvicted prisoner I am. Not even had a glimpse of a magistrate yet. You look like being for the high jump, mate, if you don't watch your step. And another thing. These bruises are going to look pretty tomorrow. I won't half tell the tale tomorrow and I can handle my old tongue, too.'

'I'll say you can. Too bleeding much. That mouth of yours is going to get you into serious trouble. I ain't got all afternoon to stand here listening to you making speeches even if I wanted to. Got any money?'

'You know damn well the bogies claimed the lot.'

'Well, you'll only get the issue tea.'

'Hurry up with it then and see there's plenty of sugar in it. Now beat it.'

Satisfied with his conversational, if not with his physical, exchange, the Gilt Kid sat down again.

The minutes dragged. It was getting very boring. He would try to bum a paper when the screw came back. A smoke would go down well.

He searched his pockets in the hope of finding a cigarette butt which the search had overlooked. He found one in his waistcoat about three-quarters of an inch long. There would have been no sense in making a fool of himself by asking the screw for a light for such a short one, so he broke it up and chewed it.

The nicotine tasted good. He could stand a whole lot of that.

After having chewed reflectively for a couple of minutes, he spat a brown stream of tobacco juice on to the floor; his mind began to work more clearly again. If a man could not get a smoke, there was nothing like a chew to get his old nut in order.

If they had anything on him over that Hammersmith turnout, he was done. Finished. They could be pursuing those inquiries while he was in Brixton on remand over the other job. He looked done over the other. Fancy Curly flogging Maisie's groin to Sammy. That was a queer mix up. Well, he could hardly come the copper and have Curly put away, because then they would prosecute him for receiving and that was as bad if not worse. And if he shopped Sammy he was done. No buyer would ever look at him again, besides all the West End Yids from the billiard hall would beat him up. Anyhow, it was a dirty trick grassing his pals. No, he would have to take the rap. That's all. The danger was getting a murder charge. To hell with that.

He got up and paced up and down the cell.

There was one thing though. They ought to find it impossible to hold him on both. A fellow wasn't likely to be screwing in Maida Vale and Hammersmith at the same time, not unless he was a contortionist, and had a flying carpet. There was an ordinary carpet on the suspect charge.

He laughed at his weak pun.

That was an idea though. Plead guilty to the Maida Vale turnout, let them sentence him on that and he was as clear as a bell at Hammersmith. Sure.

He sprang to the bell and rang it again.

Its echoes died away. No footsteps came. He went on walking up and down. The more he revolved the idea in his mind, the more it pleased him. If the bogy helped him, he might get away with a stretch for the lot. By behaving himself he would be out in ten months, and there was that hundred nicker which he had planted. Sure enough, things might be a whole lot worse. He would have to have an understanding with the bogy before he came it. It ought to be pretty easy to come to terms, for he would let them have an open-and-shut case. If they would not have his terms, he wouldn't let them have his statement. That was simple. Stood to reason.

The cells constable was coming down the passage. He stood outside the door shouting.

'What the hell's the matter with you ringing your bell? What do you think you are, a blasted fire engine or something? God help you when they get you in stir; if you behave this way, they'll half-murder you. I'm not kidding.'

'All right, all right, all right, don't get your rag out.'

'Get me rag out? You've got your nerve talking that way. Here's your tea. Take it and look sharp. I don't want any funny business.'

He began to unlock the door.

'That detective still here?' The Gilt Kid was shouting above the sound of the rattling key.

'What detective?' The door swung open. The cells constable had a mug of tea and two slices of bread in his hands.

'The bloke who was running the rule over me just now.'

'Yes. 'Spect so. Why?'

'Do us a favour and fetch him along.'

'What, d'you want to tell him a bedtime story too? Take my advice, kid. Drink your tea and shut up. Don't get argy-bargying with him, or he'll make it very nasty for you at your trial. I tell you that mouth of yours is going to land you in a whole pack of trouble before you're through.'

'Fetch him along, mate. I want to make a statement.'

'If you're up to one of your tricks . . .'

'All right, have it your own way, but it'll sound pretty bad in court when I say I wanted to make a statement, but you wouldn't let me. Think that out, mate. They'll probably give you the belt from this job and send you out on beat and traffic control again. Think of the dough you'll lose not being able to fiddle with the prisoners' grub.'

'Well, if you really want to make a statement . . .'

'Haven't I been telling you that, dopey?'

'But if you're up to one of your games . . .' He hurled the last protasis over his shoulder as he walked down the corridor once more.

The Gilt Kid sat down and wolfed his tea. There was no sugar in it and the bread had been spread with margarine, but it went down well. What was more, he was putting them to plenty of trouble, running up and down to his cell; that was the way to treat all screws and slops, just as though they were servants; and it helped to break up the monotony of being confined, which was a great thing.

A key was in his lock. He drank down the last mouthful of tea as the two detectives came in. Now was the time to box a bit clever.

'Well, Ken,' the senior detective was saying. 'I hear you're going to talk.'

'Sure,' he said pleasantly. 'I been thinking it out. The way I weigh it up's this. You boys have got it on me. You can put it in hard for me or you can make it easy. If I don't help you, you won't help me. That's right, ain't it?'

'You've got it figured out right, Ken boy. That's the way to talk sense.'

The Gilt Kid held up a hand.

'But before I make any statement I'm coming to terms with you. You do what I want, I'll do what you want.'

'What do you want?'

'Just this. I'm prepared to make a statement implicating myself on that Maida Vale job. I'll make the statement and plead guilty. In return I want you to drop the charge of me being a sus, to let me have three nicker back for my use in Brixton, to give me a cigarette right now and a packet of twenty later on, to make it easy when I'm in court and to see to it that I don't come under the Act.'

'Well, I can promise you all that except the last. Here's a fag for you now.' He held out a cigarette. 'But whether or not you come under the Act will be a matter for the Director of Public Prosecutions.'

'That's easy. Don't send him the papers of my case.'

'I got to do my duty as a police officer.'

'OK. I'll do mine too. Do your duty and you don't get no statement.'

The detective pulled at his pendulous lower lip.

'Right, Ken. You win. I'll get you away with about a stretch or fifteen moon.'

'Good boy. Give us a light.'

The detective held out a match. Having lighted the cigarette the Gilt Kid inhaled luxuriously.

'Now take me up to that room, I'll talk.'

THE STATEMENT

The Gilt Kid sat back from the table, puffing at his cigarette. 'Read it over to me,' he said, 'before I sign it. What kind of a mug do you take me for? There might be enough in that brief to get me done for rape, arson, incest and high treason for all I know.'

'All right,' said the detective wearily. 'Have it your own way.' He cleared his throat, then read:

'My name is William Kennedy. Having been duly cautioned by the officers who have arrested me, and realizing my legal position, I am voluntarily and under no compulsion making the following statement. On the 17th inst., on an invitation by the occupier, I went to the flat occupied by Miss Maisie Gill. While waiting for the door to be opened, I realized what an opportunity was presented for a safe and easy burglary. This I determined to carry out. Leaving the flat in the evening, I returned again at 10pm, knowing that Miss Gill would be out. I entered by means of the roof. The property listed as stolen was all taken by me. The absence of fingerprints is due to the fact that I wore gloves. I left the flat at about twenty to eleven, having stolen everything of value. I do not know whether anyone saw me enter or leave. I worked on my own. In Trafalgar Square, by arrangement I met a man whom I know as Chinky-eyed Len, to whom I disposed of all the stolen property with the exception of the diamond ring which was found in my possession on my arrest. I do not know the present whereabouts of Chinky-eyed Len or his real name. He is frequently to be met in the bars and cafés of the West End. I had met him in the interval between my two visits to Miss Gill's flat, and, telling him that I was going to do a burglary, arranged to meet him later. There was no collusion between Miss Gill and myself, nor between Mr Bedborough and myself. I have no cause for any complaint in my treatment by the police.'

'All right, pal. I'll sign that. Give us the pen.'

Taking the pen from the detective, the Gilt Kid repressed a smile. Chinky-eyed Len was a hot one. That ought to make the bogies go tearing all over the West End looking for him.

He laid down the pen.

'S'pose there's no chance of my getting the magistrate to deal with this? I'm going to plead guilty, so perhaps he won't send me for trial.'

'You've got just two chances of that, son.'

'Yes, I get you. A dog's chance and no chance at all. Well, I'll soon be in Wandsworth saying "Roll on cocoa".'

'Too true you will. You'd better be getting some kip in now. Don't worry, I'll see you get off easy. You'll have to take a ride in the Black Maria tomorrow.'

'What the hell? Why can't you do me here?'

'Job was done on another manor. You've got to be up at their court.'

'Well, there's a bastard for you. Why, Gaw blimey all bloody hurray, I thought I was going to dodge that ride in the Black Maria.'

'Sorry, can't be did. C'm on now. Don't want to stay up all night chewing the fat, do you?'

WAITING

The Gilt Kid was happy, next morning, when, his ride in the Black Maria over, he hung about in the male prisoners' waiting-room at the police court. Anyone felt happy when he got out of the Black Maria.

He looked disgustedly at his fellow prisoners. There were four of them, all bums. They were just the sort of people who got the boys a bad name and started people chucking off hot air about the 'lower criminal classes'. One was up for begging, one for obstruction with a coster's barrow, the third for hawking without a licence, and the fourth for bashing his old lady. Not one of them a decent screwsman could chat with.

He ran his hand over his chin. Too bad they had not allowed him to grab a shave. Made a fellow look awful having a black eye and no shave. Gave people the wrong idea.

The arrested beggar came up to him. He spoke with his professional whine.

'Been having a bit of a battle, aincher mate?'

'Yes. Me and a few flatties had a bit of an argument.'

'What they done you for, mate? Copper bashing?'

'Turn it in. They done me for screwing.'

'You a screwsman then, mate?'

'No, I'm a choirboy. Why don't you come right out with it and ask me if I've a fag instead of sparring about with these damfool questions?'

'Could you spare one, mate? I ain't had a blow since I was knocked off.'

'And then it was only kerbstone twist, I suppose. Here, cop this.'

He handed round his cigarettes to his fellow prisoners.

'What d'you expect, mate?' asked the coster, lighting up.

'First they'll give me a laydown at Brixton while they run the rule over me and then remand me to the Old Bailey. That's about all, I reckon.'

'Got any cons?'

'Two.'

'Blimey, just wait till the judge gets hold of you. He'll make you say "Roll on cocoa" a few times.'

'No, I'll get chucked at the Old Bailey. I got dough. I'll get hold of a mouthpiece who'll tell the tale proper and make the jury shed tears of blood. Stone me, I shouldn't wonder if the old mug don't give me a oncer out of the poor box.'

The Gilt Kid had hardly finished his improbable conjecture before a voice interrupted him.

'Who the hell'd give you a oncer out of the poor box. Why when they hear the Gilt Kid's coming they'll nail the cowson down in case you nick it.'

The Gilt Kid wheeled round. Behind him was a short, red-haired man with a wide grin on his face.

'Kingy!' he exclaimed.

'That's right. George King, just surrendered to his bail on a charge of being a suspected person loitering in the neighbourhood of Baker Street Tube Station with the intention of picking pockets.'

'Didn't know you was in a whizz mob, Kingy.'

'No more I ain't, mate. It was the bogy's idea. "Ginger King," he said, "I'm going to nick you for a dip." And nicks me he done. Up I comes last week, and, being a married man without none of my furniture up the spout, they gives me a week's bail.'

'Going to get away with it?'

'Not a hope, mate. Not a bleeding earthly. What good's my word against his? "Answer me that, George King," that's what the old boy'll say. "Although there is a shadow of doubt in your case, I cannot allow you to benefit by it. The public must be protected. You will go to prison for three months and be kept at such hard labour as you are capable of." That's what I'm expecting.'

'That's right, mate. They got you where they want you.'

'Not half. The beauty of it's this. Same bloke nicked me as a sus a couple of weeks back and I got chucked.'

'Beat 'em to it? How'd you manage that?'

'Simple. I got nicked along with another bloke, name of Cooky Richardson. Know him?'

The Gilt Kid shook his head.

'One of the Kilburn boys he is. Gets round Marble Arch.'

'No. I don't know him.'

'Well, Cooky's under the Act, see. And being as how he's liable to get a stretch for that, the old boy says to him: "Being a person amenable to the Prevention of Crimes Act and being, therefore, on this charge liable to a term of twelve months imprisonment with hard labour, you have the right to elect for going for trial by jury." Cooky being wide and knowing there's a thin chance he'll creep, says he'll go for trial.

'I can't go for trial, so I have to stand down, see, while his case was being done, so I can't say exactly what happened. But, later on, I gets put in the dock.

'"George King," says the magistrate, "you are charged with being a suspected person." Then he turns to the bogy.

'"Is there any further evidence to be offered against the prisoner," he asks, "than there was against the man Richardson?"

'That starts me thinking. He's said "the man Richardson". Now if he'd have fullied Cooky, he'd have said "the prisoner Richardson". So I stands there in the dock feeling fairly hopeful.

'The old boy looks at me again.

'"George King," he says, "you're in a fortunate position."

'I looks kind of comic like at the dock and even he can't help smiling a bit, but then he pulls himself up and goes on.

'"Your companion Richardson being an habitual criminal elected to go to the London Sessions. The case against him, although strong enough to make me convict him, was too weak for the purpose of a jury. Since I cannot send one man to prison and discharge another on the same evidence, I have no option but to dismiss your case. You owe your release entirely to the fact that you and your companion are both habitual criminals." That's how I get chucked.'

'Blimey, that's queer. And it's the same bloke's knocked you off again?'

'Yes, mate, it's the very same identical bloke.'

'Strike a light! He won't half wop it in for you.'

'You telling me? I've as good as bought my ticket for a trip to Wandsworth. They been knocking you about a bit, mate, ain't they? That isn't half a yock you got there!'

Ginger King, having volubly and at great length told the tale of his own woes, was, at last, ready to listen to the Gilt Kid's. The coster had been dealt with, and the beggar left to go before the magistrate just as the Gilt Kid answered.

'Yes, there was a bit of a coring match when they claimed me. Picked me up as a sus and then hung a screwing rap on me.'

'Going to get away?'

'They'll fully me to the Old Bailey, I reckon.'

'Seen any of the boys?'

'One or two. Let's see. Curly, yes, I seen him and Dean Street Dan, and Sc —' The Gilt Kid stopped himself just in time. The best bet was not to mention he had met Scaley. 'I've not been out a fortnight yet,' he finished lamely.

'Claimed you again pretty soon then. Heard about Scaley?'

The Gilt Kid held himself in.

'No, what's up?'

'Gaw, blimey, the morning papers is full of him.'

'Well, use your nut. I've been in the nick all night. Where'd I get a look at the linen-draper? What's happened, then?'

''Tisn't half a turnout. Looks like Scaley and another bloke went down to Hammersmith to do a job. They gets into a fight with the watchman. Both Scaley and the watchman gets creased.'

'What? Done in?'

'Hardly think so. Falls off the roof from about eight storeys. Killed stone dead, they was.'

'That's kind of tough on Scaley. Who's the other bloke?'

'Dunno. He got away clean. He'll have to use his nut to stay away, too, because the papers reckon they'll do him for murder.'

'Got a description of him, have they?'

'Well, it was dark, see. Powerfully built, and well-dressed, that's about all they've got to go by, yet. But they'll sweat blood to get him. You know what the slops is like when there's a chance of doing a screwsman for murder.'

'Uh-huh. P'raps he's a wide boy, though,' retorted the Gilt Kid, his chest swelling with pride at the description of him which had been issued. 'He might of got himself a good alibi and they won't be able to touch him.'

'If he's lucky.' King's voice showed his disbelief.

'William Kennedy! William Kennedy! How many more times have I got to call you? Anybody'd think you don't want to be tried.'

The cells constable was yelling at the door.

'Good luck,' called King as the Gilt Kid walked out.

'Thanks, mate, and I need it,' he answered over his shoulder.

IN COURT

The Gilt Kid stepped up into the dock. While the clerk of the court was reading over the charges he looked around. This was the first time that he had ever been up here. All police courts looked much the same and had the same smell: dusty with law books, musty with unwashed flesh.

There was the usual crowd of loafers at the back of the court. Among them he picked out Bedbug and Maisie. She was dressed kind of snappy but looked tired. Bedbug looked as if he felt a mug. He must be wishing he was some place else. The Gilt Kid smiled and waved at Maisie, but she frowned back at him.

Saucy mare, he thought. Can't even be civil to a bloke when he's in trouble.

He made a grimace at her, expressing his disgust and then turned to his front again. The clerk of the court was saying: 'William Kennedy, are you guilty or not guilty?'

'Guilty, your worship,' answered the Gilt Kid and then thought, that's funny. He had been convicted twice and acquitted once before, but this was the first time that he had ever pleaded guilty.

The magistrate put his fingertips together and rested his head against the padded back of his high chair. His face was tired and without expression. He had too often seen the sordidness of life to be impressed by its tragedy. It was only a sense of duty – a quality which he rated very highly – that made him listen with any care to the wearisome cases that came before him.

The detective entered the witness-box and took the oath, holding the testament negligently in his hand and not bothering to look at the printed words on the card. The magistrate turned a pair of uninterested eyes upon him. The clerk began to write hurriedly with a scratchy pen.

'The facts of this case, your worship,' said the detective, 'are quite simple. The prisoner pleads guilty and has made this statement.'

The words came out with effortless ease. He was used to giving evidence. He handed the document to the clerk, who in turn handed it to the magistrate. This last, put on a pair of rimless pince-nez and, pursing his thin lips, looked dispassionately at the statement. At length, he laid it down on the table and looked severely at the detective.

'Too frequently,' he said in a high-pitched, precise voice, 'in cases in which the police prosecute, the prisoner is convicted solely on a statement made by himself. This is a practice which I deplore. Unless there is some corroborative evidence I shall make it my business to discharge the prisoner, since I have no means of knowing how this statement has been obtained, nor what physical or mental pressure was exerted, what threats or promises held out, in order to induce the prisoner to plead guilty.'

Hope beat wildly in the Gilt Kid's heart. Perhaps he was going to beat this rap and still use it as an alibi against the other. That sounded almost too good to be true.

'I propose,' answered the unruffled detective, 'to call the following witnesses: Miss Gill, the occupier of the burgled flat, a gentleman named Mr Francis Bedborough and two police officers. In addition there is a diamond ring which I shall put in as an exhibit. It is part of the stolen property and was found in the prisoner's possession on his arrest.'

'Very well then. Now, these witnesses. Are this lady and gentleman in court?'

'Yes, your worship.'

The magistrate removed his pince-nez. It was a gesture of annoyance. He waved them in his right hand as he spoke.

'That is irregular, most irregular. A police officer of your experience should have known better than to have allowed it. Let them wait outside until they are called. Prisoner, you may sit down.'

The Gilt Kid sat down wearily.

I've never known, he thought, a case which didn't start without a barney like this. The old boy's in a bad temper, too. What is it going to mean? Is he going to be on my side or has he just got his rag out with everybody?

He heard Maisie and Bedbug leave the court. The clerk, released temporarily from his interminable writing, was scratching his nose with his pen.

'Now then, officer,' the magistrate's cool, high voice continued. 'I suppose you're going to waste my time, making me listen to all this evidence and then you will ask for a remand so as to get the case prepared. Let me see that statement again.'

The clerk handed it up to him. The magistrate read it through once more. In spite of his pince-nez, which he once more put on, he held the paper at arm's length.

Snotty old swine, thought the Gilt Kid. Suppose he thinks it stinks or something, or maybe he don't want to come into close contact with anything coming from a crook.

The magistrate handed the statement back to the clerk of the court. His movements were so slow that the Gilt Kid began to feel bored.

It was a bit of a loser, feeling bored before the trial had started. There were sure to be at least two separate days of it here and another at the Old Bailey. He was likely to snuff it before they got the damned thing over. He had to find something to interest himself in, so he looked hard at the magistrate, weighing up his face.

His forehead was high and his eyes rheumy and bloodshot; his nose was pinched and slightly hooked; his lips were thin and precise; he had not shaved very well that morning

– that must be why he was in a bad temper – and there was a cluster of short white bristles on the point of his chin.

Funny, thought the Gilt Kid, how you could weigh a bloke up by his map. Now, he would say about the old boy that he was kind of bitter, because he had missed coming out on top. He had started off as a mouthpiece, and thought he was going to be one of the Big Shots in that lark, but he was out in his guess and it kind of got him to think that he was only a police-court magistrate who wasn't even allowed to sentence a bloke when there was anything like a big charge against him. That was why he took it out of the bogies.

He felt kind of sorry for him. It must be fierce sitting up there every day, listening to stories about fellows who had a lot more guts, and had seen a lot more life, than ever he had or would. What was the old boy saying now?

'The evidence which you propose to put before the court bears out this statement?'

'Yes, your worship.'

'And as the witnesses are available, the case needs no further preparation?'

'No, your worship.'

'And there are no further charges made against the prisoner which you wish to investigate?'

'To the best of my belief, no, your worship.'

Well, that's handy to know, said the Gilt Kid to himself.

'Very well,' said the magistrate, 'unless the prisoner himself wishes it, I shall not grant a remand. It is intolerable that unconvicted men, whether or not they have pleaded guilty, should be kept in prison awaiting the pleasure of a parcel of policemen.'

Blimey, thought the Gilt Kid. He *is* wild. Let's hope he's not the same way with me. The gaoler, touching his arm, made him stand up. The clerk of the court was addressing him.

'William Kennedy,' he boomed, 'do you want a remand?'

'No thanks.'

He sat down again.

The court droned on.

The detectives gave their evidence. Maisie was called, gave her evidence to the effect that the property had been hers, and identified both the prisoner and the ring.

'Do you wish to ask this witness any questions?'

'Not yet your worship.'

Bedbug gave evidence. Yes, the flat had been burgled, he had himself telephoned the police.

The magistrate suddenly barked:

'William Kennedy. Stand up!'

The Gilt Kid rose to his feet.

'William Kennedy. The evidence before me is clear. On your own admission you have committed the very serious crime of housebreaking. It is indeed fortunate for you that you have not been guilty of any violence. These crimes of housebreaking and flatbreaking are far too common. You must go for trial. You are committed to the next Sessions of the County of London held at the Sessions House, Newington Causeway. There is no need for me to tell you that you should not apply for bail. In any case I will not grant it.

'Next case.'

The Gilt Kid lounged against the dock rail. Behind him, he knew, were sitting Maisie and Bedbug. His mouthpiece had done a good job of work for the dock brief and chewed them up properly. They had looked a couple of fools. Were their faces red?

The chairman of the Sessions turned to the detective.

'What is known about the prisoner Kennedy?'

The detective glanced at a slip of paper.

'Quite a lot, my lord, I regret to say. In 1930 he was convicted of housebreaking in this court and put on probation for twelve months. In 1932, he was tried at the Sussex Assizes for burglariously breaking and entering, but was acquitted. In March 1934 at the Old Bailey he was convicted of housebreaking and sentenced to nine months' hard labour. He is 25 years of age, and has, apparently, done no work since 1932 . . .'

He paused for breath.

The bastard, thought the Gilt Kid. He's mixing it for me after me coming it the way I did and all.

'On the other hand, my lord, there are certain redeeming qualities. Never has he been convicted of any form of violence and on this occasion he vouchsafed a certain amount of help to the police. Unfortunately the receiver of the stolen goods has not yet been arrested, but the prisoner has furnished us with his name and a full description . . .'

Trying to make out I shopped a guy, the dirty son of a bitch.

'I have held several conversations with the prisoner and I am convinced of his penitence. I believe that if you let him off lightly this time, my lord, there is every chance that he will turn into a good citizen.'

The detective stood down.

'William Kennedy. You have been convicted of house-breaking. Have you anything to say before the court passes sentence on you?'

'Yes, please. You have read no doubt of the blokes who say "Crime don't pay". They're right. Crime don't have to pay. It's the other guys who do the paying.'

The chairman frowned.

'William Kennedy. Breaking, entering and feloniously stealing is a crime that young men of your age commit light-heartedly. It is apparent from your flippant attitude that you do not realize the gravity of your position. You have already been twice convicted of felonies and have thus rendered yourself liable, by the strict letter of the English law, to be sent to penal servitude for life.'

Blimey, the old cowson's going to make me do it from now on.

'As the officer in charge of your case has pointed out, however, you have never yet been found guilty of violence, and that is a point in your favour. The officer, indeed, has displayed a sympathetic attitude towards you which is most commendable. It is clear that the English police, in addition to being the most efficient, are the fairest in the world . . .'

That's a hot one. Pity he can't come to the point. I'm sick of all this messing about. Wish he'd put me out of my agony and let me know how many shaves and haircuts I'm going to draw.

'The surprise to me is that the Director of Public Prosecutions has not taken a hand in this case. I would willingly make you a person amenable to the Prevention of Crimes Act, as a little supervision over your conduct might protect the public.'

There's a lot you'd be surprised at if only you knew.

'I notice from your record that you have already had the benefit of being put on probation for a year, and I notice also that for thirty-one months there is no mention of any suspicion against your character. That is another point which I am disposed to credit in your favour.

'You have heard the officer say that he considered a lenient sentence would possibly turn you into a reasonable member of society instead of a pariah who would rather steal than work. Personally I am inclined to disagree with this. Short prison sentences are of little use. In my opinion your case merits a long period of careful supervision. I would consider sending you to penal servitude for five years . . .'

Christ almighty!

'Which would shock you out of your light-hearted attitude towards other people's possessions and might conceivably scare your confederates from their nefarious pursuits. On the other hand . . .'

Hurrah, something better is coming now.

'Supervision need not necessarily be exercised inside prison walls. You have once been put on probation. I propose to experiment with doing the same thing again. You will be bound over to come up for trial when called upon for an indefinite period, during which time you will be placed in the care of the Probation Officer. If you break your probation or come up before me on any charge whatsoever, I will deal with you as severely as I possibly can. In the meantime you can leave the dock as a free man and remain one as long as you wish . . .'

Gawd blimey! Who'd have thought it!

POSTSCRIPT

When London Books expressed interest in republishing *The Gilt Kid*, nobody seemed to know who owned the rights to the novel. Thanks to Steve Holland, a helpful researcher whom I contacted via the internet, I was put in touch with James Curtis's only child – Nicolette Edwards. She subsequently agreed to answer my e-mailed questions about her mysterious father.

Paul Willetts
March 2007

Paul Willetts: What was your reaction when you heard that London Books wanted to reprint one of your father's novels?
Nicolette Edwards: My reaction was a mixture of surprise and delight. Funnily enough, I'd recently written to his literary agents, partly to ensure that they had my current address, and also to enquire whether there was any interest in his books. My letter was prompted by an approach from a journalist who had read *The Gilt Kid* and loved it.

Do you feel the presence of your father's personality very strongly through his writing?
I do feel there is an element of my father's personality in all his books, but it's difficult to define because he was such a complex character. Here is a brief description which may help. He was extremely good looking, charismatic, enthusiastic and impulsive. His manners were old fashioned – exceptionally polite at all times. He could be very bad

tempered and didn't suffer fools, but he had a great sense of fair play. He appeared to exude confidence, but was really quite self-effacing.

There isn't much information available about your father. Would you mind telling me something about his background?

There's a lot to tell . . . He was born Geoffrey Basil Maiden in Sturry, Kent on 4 July 1907, the youngest of five children. His parents, Joseph and Bertha Maiden, built and ran an hotel in Delhi, India, where they lived for ten years or so. His mother came back to Britain for his birth and stayed for eighteen months, at which point she took Geoffrey to Delhi to join the family. He had two brothers and two sisters and, as far as I can tell, they were a happy family, living a very comfortable life. The children were eventually sent back to Britain to boarding-school. In 1912 the hotel was sold and the family relocated to Hertfordshire, where they acquired the Aldenham Lodge Hotel. Later, my grandfather bought the Foley Arms Hotel in Great Malvern. He ran that until the late 1930s.

Prior to that my father had followed his two brothers to King's School, Canterbury, as a boarder. His thirst for knowledge was somewhat satisfied there, and he was a brilliant scholar. I know he particularly enjoyed studying the classics and history. I don't think he went on to further education, but I know that he spent a year in France, during which he lived with a local family. He learned to speak French and several other languages fluently and, in later life, was employed as a translator. He spent some time working for Reuters, but I don't know in what capacity.

On the back cover of the Penguin edition of *The Gilt Kid*, your father claims that he was 'quite ashamed of his own patronymic', so he wrote under the pseudonym

'James Curtis'. Why do you think he was so ashamed of his antecedents?

As I've already mentioned, his real surname was Maiden – not a very masculine name. No doubt he was teased mercilessly at school. I don't think he was ashamed of his family, just the name. When he was an adult, though, he did become alienated from them, but that was more because of his bohemian lifestyle.

Did you ever meet your grandparents?

I don't remember them. My grandmother, who was used to being looked after by staff in hotels, died in 1941. Soon afterwards my grandfather remarried – much to all his children's disgust. His remarriage caused a rift, mainly due to the fear of disinheritance. He died in 1947. According to my mother he was a very strict father who commanded fear and respect.

How did your parents get together?

My parents met in a bookshop in Chelsea. The shop was run by my mother's sister and her husband. They all lived a rather bohemian life, socialising with artists, writers and poets. My parents had a whirlwind courtship and, I believe, my mother was pregnant at the time of their marriage in 1936. Sadly, the baby – a boy named Patrick – was stillborn.

I gather that your parents separated when you were a child. What was the cause of the separation, and was the breakdown of their marriage acrimonious?

My parents were separated by the Second World War. At first my father served in France. When he received a telegram informing him of my birth, he requested that I should be called 'Nicolette Josephine'. He was later posted to Burma and rose to the rank of major. I believe that his army career ended in disgrace, but have no evidence to support this. Knowing him, he probably assaulted a senior officer!

The enforced separation, due to military service, had an adverse effect on the marriage. He was, in any case, a difficult man to live with. Although I was never aware of any acrimony, there was no further contact between him and my mother once they'd split up. Following their separation, he didn't give us any financial support.

Did you see much of your father after the marriage ended?

Not for four or five years, not until I decided to make contact via his youngest sister Naomi's London address. I was a teenager and felt some confusion about my situation. Encouraged by a friend who couldn't understand why I didn't see my dad, I wrote to him. This must have come as a terrible shock to my father. He nevertheless arranged a meeting with this shy, gauche girl, who hadn't had the advantage of private education. It was an awkward occasion, the awkwardness alleviated by the beautiful manners that had been instilled in him.

Despite the fact that he grilled me about my knowledge of the classics and took me on daunting cultural tours of London, I persevered with him. I was always sent home with a secondhand copy of a classic book from a shop on Tottenham Court Road. These included *John Halifax, Gentleman*. I was then expected to critically appraise the book when writing my thank you letter. This I found difficult. From that period onwards, he always sent me a Christmas card and also wrote to me on my birthday.

Do you remember your father talking about his writing? If so, who were his literary heroes?

He didn't talk about his writing. I think he was embarrassed about the fact that he was no longer successful. Apart from Oscar Wilde, Homer and Shakespeare, I don't know much about his literary heroes. I think he preferred the novels and the poetry of a bygone era to those of his contemporaries.

After his initial commercial success as a writer, your father's reputation faded. How did he support himself during those years of relative literary obscurity?

His reputation declined partly due to the interruption of the war, his unmarried state, as well as his lifestyle of drinking, smoking and gambling. He seemed to lose motivation, though he still spent a great deal of time doing research at libraries. He was extremely close to his sister, Naomi. She was single, lived in Chelsea and worked as a private secretary. She offered both emotional and financial support. They seemed to understand each other because they were both quite lonely. He always said he was unemployable, which I believe to be true. He did, however, work as a night porter in some of the big hotels, including Brown's and the Dorchester. This enabled him to have quiet periods in which he could read and carry out his research.

Between the publication of his last novel in 1956 and his death, did he produce a lot of unpublished writing, or did he simply give up?

As far as I know, he was always researching new material in the hope of inspiration, and I don't think he ever gave up, because he had such a thirst for knowledge and a nervous energy that prevented him from relaxing. He was completely unmaterialistic and saw possessions as unnecessary.

A strong sense of outrage at social injustice runs through your father's books. I'm curious to know whether, in later life, that sense of outrage turned to despair. I'd also be interested to know whether his political beliefs led him into a more active involvement in politics.

The sense of outrage was always with him to some extent. He developed an obsessive interest in the IRA. I don't know when it started. As a young person, living outside London, I found it very embarrassing and somewhat scary. He lived in North London during his latter years. By that time most of his friends were Irish. He would spend his days frequenting Irish pubs and was very generous to his pals. Our worlds could hardly have been further apart. His support of the IRA didn't help our relationship, though I was amused by his requests in letters to me and my children to say 'Up the IRA!' These passionately held beliefs probably got him into trouble, particularly after his sister Naomi died. They certainly alienated him from the rest of his family who had no contact with him.

When did your father die?
He'd developed late-onset diabetes, which irritated him because he didn't want to follow a special diet. Living alone in a small bedsit, I suspect he didn't eat sensibly. In 1977 I received a phone call from the coroner's office to inform me of his death. My contact details had been in his diary. Apparently he'd gone to the local chemist, complaining of feeling unwell. He had collapsed there and then suffered a fatal heart attack in the ambulance on the way to hospital.

When he reached his seventieth birthday, he told me that he'd had his threescore years and ten, so any extra would be a bonus. He died only a matter of weeks afterwards. He left a will requesting burial with a full Latin Mass. Due to his interest in all things Irish, he had converted to Roman Catholicism back in the 1950s.

What's your last memory of him?
It dates back to about 1966, when he visited us at our flat in Kent. He always brought a bottle of wine and some Irish soda bread. My two children were two and four, so they

have no recollection of him. He tried to befriend them, but really didn't know how to relate to children. He was a great tease and had a good sense of humour, so I enjoyed the visits, though they were a bit of a strain at times.

Shortly after that we moved to the Midlands. Despite being invited, he wouldn't visit us. Although we kept up our correspondence, we didn't meet again. When I cleared out his meagre flat, rented from the council, it contained minimal furniture and stacks of books, all from libraries, all non-fiction, mainly about Irish history. There were none of his own books.

He was buried in St Pancras Cemetery. My husband and I were the only mourners. I phoned his sister Ruth to let her know that he'd died. She hadn't seen him for years. She thanked me for telling her but said she wouldn't go to the funeral. She went on to say that Geoffrey was the brightest and most gifted of her siblings and had every opportunity to succeed in all areas of his life. She added that his personality meant he couldn't cope with success and seemed intent on destroying everything good that happened to him.

London Classics

NIGHT AND THE CITY

GERALD KERSH

Harry Fabian is a cockney wide boy who will do anything for
a pound note; a storyteller who craves recognition, his endless
lies hiding a deeper, inner weakness. He is also a ponce, and
one who is walking on the edge. It is only a matter of time
before he topples over the side.

Set in 1930s London, against a fluorescent West End backdrop,
Night And The City brings the Soho of legend to life, the streets
a tangle of drinking dens and night-clubs, author Gerald Kersh's
characters flamboyant creations who add a cosmopolitan edge to
the book's journey into the darker shades of human nature.

Twice filmed, *Night And The City* remains a 'lowlife' classic,
and comes with an introduction by John King, author of
The Football Factory and *Human Punk*.

London Books
£11.99 hardback
ISBN 978-0-9551851-3-7
www.london-books.co.uk

LONDON CLASSICS

A START IN LIFE

ALAN SILLITOE

Alan Sillitoe's first novel, *Saturday Night And Sunday Morning*, was published in 1958, *The Loneliness Of The Long-Distance Runner* arriving the following year. Both were hits and led to high-profile films, which is turn cemented his reputation. Tagged an 'Angry Young Man' by the media, Sillitoe's ability to record and interpret the lives of ordinary people was nothing short of revolutionary. He has been prolific ever since and remains one of England's greatest contemporary authors.

A Start In Life tells the story of Michael Cullen, who abandons his pregnant girlfriend and heads 'to the lollipop-metropolis of London in the 1960s'. Cullen is, in theory, leaving his problems behind, but he is 'the Devil on two sticks' and becomes involved in a smuggling ring with Moggerhanger, a man who believes 'that you must get anything you want no matter at what cost to others'. Cullen is an optimist, with an eye for the ladies, but his new swinging lifestyle is soon under threat.

Includes a new introduction by Alan Sillitoe

London Books
£11.99 hardback
ISBN 978-0-9551851-1-3
www.london-books.co.uk

NORTH SOHO 999
A True Story Of Gangs And Gun-Crime In 1940s London

PAUL WILLETTS

Just before 2:30pm on 29 April 1947, three masked gunmen entered a shop in Soho. Little did they realise that they were about to take part in the climax to the unprecedented crime wave afflicting post-war Britain. *North Soho 999* is a vivid, non-fiction police procedural, focusing on what would become one of the twentieth-century's biggest and most ingenious murder investigations – an investigation which later inspired *The Blue Lamp*, starring Dirk Bogarde.

'A brilliant snapshot of '40s London, peopled by crooks, coppers and creeps. Willetts slices through time with the skill of a razor-flashing wide boy. Essential reading' – John King

Dewi Lewis Publishing
£9.99 paperback
ISBN 978-1-904587-45-3
www.dewilewispublishing.com

LONDON BOOKS RECOMMENDS

THE GORSE TRILOGY
The West Pier / Mr Stimpson And Mr Gorse / Unknown Assailant

PATRICK HAMILTON

In Ernest Ralph Gorse, Patrick Hamilton creates one of
fiction's most captivating anti-heroes, whose heartlessness and
lack of scruples are matched only by the inventiveness and
panache with which he swindles his victims. With great deftness
and precision Hamilton exposes how his dupes' own naivety,
snobbery or greed make them perfect targets. These three
novels are shot through with the brooding menace and sense
of bleak inevitability so characteristic of the author. There is
also vivid satire and caustic humour. Gorse is thought to be
based on the real-life Neville Heath, hanged in 1946.

'The entertainment value of this brilliantly told story
could hardly be higher' – LP Hartley

Black Spring Press
£9.95 paperback original
ISBN 978-0-948238-34-5
www.blackspringpress.co.uk

LONDON BOOKS

FLYING THE FLAG FOR
FREE-THINKING LITERATURE

www.london-books.co.uk

PLEASE VISIT OUR WEBSITE FOR

- Current and forthcoming books
- Author and title profiles
- Regular column by contemporary writers
- A lively, interactive message board
- Events and news
- Secure on-line bookshop
- Recommendations and links
- An alternative view of London literature